AWARDS AND ACCOLADES FOR THE
CRITICALLY ACCLAIMED AND BESTSELLING
PASSPORT TO PERIL MYSTERY SERIES

Say No Moor

"The eleventh book in the Passport to Peril Mystery series is solid proof that this series just keeps getting better and better."

—*R. T. Book Reviews*

From Bad to Wurst

"Despite the chaos that continually surrounds Emily and her irrepressible explorers, she remains a constant beacon of intelligence, practicality, and amiability. The humor is always spot-on and will surprise readers with its deft wit, originality, and satire."

—Cynthia Chow, KingsRiverLife.com

Fleur de Lies

"Don't miss the ninth trip in this always entertaining series."

—*Library Journal*

Bonnie of Evidence

"A delightfully deadly eighth Passport to Peril mystery."

—*Publishers Weekly*

Dutch Me Deadly

"*Dutch Me Deadly*, the latest adventure of [Hunter's] endearing heroine and zany Iowan seniors, offers nonstop humor and an engaging plot woven so well into its setting that it could take place only in Holland. Despite the danger, I want to travel with Emily!"

—Carrie Bebris, award-winning author of the Mr. & Mrs. Darcy Mystery series

"The cast of characters is highly entertaining and the murder mystery mixed with good humor!"

—*Suspense Magazine*

"A bit of humor, a bit of travel information, and a bit of mystery add up to some pleasant light reading."

—*Kirkus Reviews*

Norway to Hide

"*Norway to Hide* is a fast-paced, page-turning, highly entertaining mystery. Long live the Passport to Peril series!"

—OnceUponARomance.net

G'Day to Die

"The easygoing pace [of *G'Day to Die*] leads to a satisfying heroine-in-peril twist ending that should please those in search of a good cozy."

—*Publishers Weekly*

Pasta Imperfect

"Murder, mayhem, and marinara make for a delightfully funny combination [in *Pasta Imperfect*]…Emily stumbles upon clues, jumps to hilarious conclusions at each turn, and eventually solves the mystery in a showdown with the killer that is as clever as it is funny."

—*Futures Mystery Anthology* Magazine

Top o' the Mournin'

"No sophomore jinx here. [*Top o' the Mournin'*] is very funny and full of suspense."

—*Romantic Times BOOKclub* Magazine

Alpine for You

"I found myself laughing out loud [while reading *Alpine for You*]…"

—*Deadly Pleasures* Mystery Magazine

**OTHER BOOKS IN THE PASSPORT TO PERIL SERIES
BY MADDY HUNTER:**

Say No Moor (#11)

From Bad to Wurst (#10)

Fleur de Lies (#9)

Bonnie of Evidence (#8)

Dutch Me Deadly (#7)

**EARLIER TITLES IN THE PASSPORT TO PERIL SERIES
ARE AVAILABLE ON KINDLE AND NOOK:**

Norway to Hide (#6)

G'Day to Die (#5)

Hula Done It? (#4)

Pasta Imperfect (#3)

Top o' the Mournin' (#2)

Alpine for You (#1)

Catch Me If Yukon

A PASSPORT TO PERIL MYSTERY

maddy
HUNTER

WITHDRAWN

MIDNIGHT INK
WOODBURY, MINNESOTA

FIRST EDITION
First Printing, 2019

Cover design by Kevin R. Brown
Cover illustration by Anne Wertheim

Midnight Ink, an imprint of Llewellyn Worldwide Ltd.

Library of Congress Cataloging-in-Publication Data
Names: Hunter, Maddy, author.
Title: Catch me if Yukon : a passport to Peril mystery / Maddy Hunter.
Description: First Edition. | Woodbury, Minnesota : Midnight Ink, [2019] |
  Series: A passport to Peril mystery ; #12.
Identifiers: LCCN 2018029963 (print) | LCCN 2018031956 (ebook) | ISBN
  9780738755588 (ebook) | ISBN 9780738753973 (alk. paper)
Subjects: LCSH: Tour guides (Persons)—Fiction. | GSAFD: Mystery fiction.
Classification: LCC PS3608.U5944 (ebook) | LCC PS3608.U5944 C38 2018 (print)
  | DDC 813/.6—dc23
LC record available at https://lccn.loc.gov/2018029963

Midnight Ink
Llewellyn Worldwide Ltd.
2143 Wooddale Drive
Woodbury, MN 55125-2989
www.midnightinkbooks.com

Printed in the United States of America

To the scores of fans who crowded
onto the tour bus with the Iowa
gang as they travelled the globe.
Thank you.

ACKNOWLEDGMENTS

I'd like to extend a special thank you to Orphie Shellum for allowing me to hijack her siblings' names for the characters who appear in this latest installment of the Passport series. Her sisters have such unique names, I wish I could have used them all.

Thank you to the Converse family for inviting us to participate in their Alaskan adventure with them. There are no finer traveling companions.

Thank you to my editors Amy Glaser and Becky Zins, who are simply stellar at what they do.

Thank you to Christina Boys of CEB Editorial Services who, back in 2001, gave a group of Iowa seniors and one hapless tour escort a chance to travel the world. Couldn't have done it without you. You're the best.

Lastly, thank you to Brian, who has been my constant, dependable, and tireless companion on this other adventure called life. I love you more!

ONE

"THAR SHE BLOWS!" SHOUTED Dick Teig in an effort to channel the spirit of Melville's infamous Captain Ahab.

Gliding through the waves in slow motion, plagued by flocks of screeching gulls, the humpback spewed a column of spray into the air to the excited oohs and aahs of the hundred-plus guests aboard the whale watching tour boat *Kenai Adventurer*.

"Oh, wow," enthused Dick, a roly-poly retiree whose head was the size of an orbiting planet. He stood mesmerized at the starboard rail where the rest of us were shoehorned together, gawking into the water below, angling our cell phones left and right to avoid shooting video of each other's heads.

"This footage is going straight to YouTube," hooted Dick Stolee, who, as the group's tallest member, enjoyed the luxury of having the best unobstructed view. "You wanna bet this baby's going viral. The likes are gonna pile up faster than pancakes at a church breakfast."

"Didn't no one tell you?" my grandmother asked from farther down the rail. "We're not doin' YouTube no more. We found a new website what links to real global news agencies with real bylines, so we're sendin' our stuff there instead."

"We decided that for folks who've been doing this as long as we have, it was time to leave the ranks of YouTube behind and graduate to a more professional platform," explained Nana's longtime love interest, George Farkas.

Nana nodded. "It's our best chance to join the big leagues before we die."

"How come nobody told *me*?" complained Dick Stolee as the whale arched its back and, with a muted *whoooosh*, sluiced downward into the ocean's depths, its fluked tail rising out of the water in an aquatic salute that made it appear more like a member of a synchronized swim team than a mammal whose massive bulk tipped the scales at a modest forty tons.

"We took a vote on it," ninety-something-year-old Osmond Chelsvig recalled. "At the gluten-free luncheon at the senior center last week. Weren't you there?" Osmond had been a member of my hometown's election board for longer than most people had been alive.

"He was in the little boys' room," droned Dick's wife, Grace. "His doctor just upped the dosage of his water pill."

"I can't see a doggone thing," bellyached Bernice Zwerg in her ex-smoker's rasp from somewhere behind us. "Time for you rail hogs to stop being so selfish. Get out of the way. I can't see through you. I left my x-ray vision back on the bus."

I cranked my head around to find her standing behind Dick Stolee, where the only thing she had a breathtaking view of was the back of his jacket. Shuffling backward, I grasped her arm and dragged her through the horde of onlookers to position her in front of me. "How's that?"

She peered over the rail. "Where's Moby Dick?"

"Submerged."

"So how long do I have to stand here before he flashes us again?"

"Don't know. I don't think whales run on timers."

I'm Emily Andrew-Miceli. With my former Swiss police inspector husband, Etienne, I own and operate Destinations Travel out of Windsor City, Iowa, a town of about 19,000 with new housing developments popping up all over the place. We cater to a subset of tech-savvy seniors who've marked "world travel" as the first item on their bucket lists, and we're proud to have a stable of twelve regulars from Windsor City who keep the agency in the black—eight fairly normal adults, one chronic complainer, two Dicks, and my eighth-grade-educated, computer-whiz, lottery-winning, martial-arts-trained grandmother, Marion Sippel, fondly referred to as Nana.

Filling up the remaining seats on our twelve-day Alaskan odyssey are seven Windsor City locals who are the founding members of a "Norwegian only" book club that boasts the jaw-dropping distinction of having been in existence for over forty years. Their reading list isn't limited to Norwegian books, but club hopefuls have to verify their authentic Norwegian ancestry to join. Three of our regular guests—Lucille Rasmussen, Helen Teig, and Grace Stolee—have belonged to the group for a couple of decades, so it was their recommendation that convinced the other club members to sign up for our tour.

Luckily, the girls must have forgotten to mention the unfortunate number of deaths we'd experienced on our previous excursions. Memory loss among the senior set does have its benefits.

Our boat was hovering close to the rock-ribbed shore of Aialik Bay in the Kenai Fjords National Park, a long inlet flanked by a spine of jagged mountains, towering evergreens that seemed to sprout up from the bedrock, and distant peaks frosted with powder-white snow. The sky was cobalt blue, without a trace of clouds. The sun was so blindingly bright that I needed to squint behind my sunglasses to avoid burning my retinas from the reflections off the water, which made picture-taking a challenge since I couldn't see what was on my display screen. I could be taking breathtaking close-ups of Dick Teig's thumb for all I knew.

"Humpbacks can swim up to twenty-five miles an hour if they get the urge," our captain announced in a subdued voice over the loudspeaker. I guess he didn't want to startle the eighty-thousand-pound behemoth that was lurking somewhere beneath our boat. "But most of the time they keep it between eight and ten, which is what I commonly refer to as cruising speed."

"I wonder how fast Moby Dick was swimming when he bit off Captain Ahab's leg?" pondered Helen Teig, whose carefully penciled-on eyebrows could be obliterated by one inadvertent swipe of her hand.

Bernice choked on a guffaw as she glanced at Helen. "You do realize Moby Dick wasn't real, right?"

"Moby Dick wasn't a humpback," offered Tilly Hovick in her former professor's voice. "He was a sperm whale. So you really can't compare."

"I wonder what kind of whale swallowed Geppetto?" asked Margi Swanson as she squirted out a stream of hand sanitizer to create a small germ-free zone on the rail.

"Probably the same kind that swallowed Jonah," theorized Lucille Rasmussen. "The kind that spits you back out."

"Sounds like some kind of involuntary gag reflex to me," mused Helen.

Bernice shook her head. "Morons."

The captain's voice broke out over the loudspeaker again. "Looks like a pod is making its way toward us. And a big one is coming up with his mouth open like a giant fishnet. Six or seven humpbacks. Starboard quarter." Then, in an obvious tease, "All of you can swim, right?"

"Are we on the correct side?" asked Alice Tjarks as she visored her hands over her eyes to scan the water.

"We're on the right side," George spoke up.

"But what if the right side is the wrong side?" panicked Dick Stolee.

"Then we'll miss everything," fretted Dick Teig. "C'mon, guys. Other side of the boat!"

"But this *is* the right side," I objected as they stampeded across the deck to the opposite side, deserting their plum positions at the rail.

One of the advantages of living in a landlocked state is that residents aren't forced to learn unnecessary terms like *starboard* and *port.*

I switched my phone to video and aimed it in the general direction of the humpbacks as they glided together in their own version of a maritime flash mob, geysering water through their blowholes before slithering downward in their languid, balletic dives.

"Hey, Emily, did you hear about the whale watching boat that sank in calm seas off the coast of Juneau last year?" asked book clubber Thor Thorsen as he bulldozed into the space relinquished by the gang. His camera whirred frenetically as he squeezed off a number of shots using a telephoto lens that was as long as my arm. "All the passengers got rescued, but the boat apparently went down like a rock. Don't know if they ever figured out what caused it to sink, but it makes you wonder if these tour boat companies sometimes underestimate the marine life around here."

My stomach bubbled disagreeably at his comment. Like I needed to hear that.

Thor Thorsen was an impressive physical specimen. Tall and broad-shouldered, he had permanently ruddy cheeks and blond hair that was only slightly threaded with gray. His face was more intriguing than it was handsome—his wide-spaced eyes and flattened features making him look as if he had never recovered from an untimely collision with a closed door. He owned a luxury car dealership in town, but he'd recently turned the managerial duties over to his son so he could devote more time to retirement travel and his newfound hobbies, which appeared to be wildlife photography and promoting heartburn.

"Humpbacks aren't usually known for their destructive tendencies," countered Grover Kristiansen as he slid closer to me, his voice both tentative and monotone. A small-boned man attired in fatigue-green polar fleece and a wide-brimmed hat with a chin cord, he looked more like an aging Boy Scout than a former salesman for a small business. "In fact, near Monterey, California, a group of whale watchers witnessed a pair of humpbacks trying to rescue a baby gray whale from a pod of orcas, and gray whales don't even belong to the same genus."

"Is that right?" Thor muttered with disinterest as he squeezed off a dozen more shots.

"There's also documentation that humpbacks have rescued Antarctic seals that were under attack from orcas," Grover continued with rising enthusiasm, "and seals aren't even the same species! Scientists think the whales display a higher order of thinking and feeling, just like the great apes, elephants, and humans. And that's because humpbacks have specialized spindle cells in their brains that—"

"Yeah, yeah," Thor cut him off. "You can keep talking, but I've stopped listening. Tell you anything?"

Grover stiffened at the slight but refused to be cowed. "It verifies that you have a very short attention span. You should work on that, Thor. Maybe it'll help you recommend an actual novel to the book club rather than selected articles from *Reader's Digest*."

"Two more pods headed our way on the port side," announced the captain. "This is kind of unprecedented, so we're going to idle right here for a while longer so you can soak it up."

"This guy better know what he's doing," grumbled Thor as he quickly abandoned the rail to charge across the deck, followed by Grover, who chased behind him like a puppy. It was then that I noticed the woman standing beside the deck's orange life buoy station, eyes wide, a terrified expression on her little moon face.

"Mom?" I was apparently trying to suppress the fact that my parents were accompanying us on this tour, but with good reason. Mom's overprotective attitude in dealing with Nana was so over the top that I usually wore myself out running interference between them, which negatively affected my duties to the other guests—not the most efficient business model.

Mom waved stiffly as I walked the few steps to join her.

"Are you sure you want to stand this far back, Mom? You can't see anything."

"Of course I can see things, Em." She bobbed her head toward the shoreline. "Trees. Rocks. Water. The backs of passengers' heads."

"Have you seen the whales?"

"Oh, I imagine everyone on the boat has seen the whales."

I narrowed my eyes. "You haven't gotten close enough to the rail to see them, have you?"

"No, but don't concern yourself with me. I'm having a wonderful time."

In the daily routine of life, Mom will usually choose martyrdom over simple fixes. I used to think her preference had something to do with her being Catholic and reading *The Giant Book of Saints* one too many times as a child. But I've come to realize that it's probably a genetic defect that originated with Nana's Scottish Mac-Cool forebears, who always went out of their way to sacrifice their lives to avenge whatever minor slight had ruffled their kilts that day.

She switched her attention to the life buoy ring beside her. "I know you're not familiar with maritime devices, Emily, but would you have any idea how a person would go about detaching this thing if the boat started to sink?"

"The boat isn't going to sink, Mom. The tour company wouldn't still be in business if the whales went rogue and destroyed their boats on a regular basis."

"Of course not." She studied the orange ring with an analytical eye. "It's probably too small to fit around your grandmother anyway." She glanced left and right before lowering her voice to a whisper. "I don't know what she's been eating lately, but if she doesn't stop, all her elastic waistbands are going to need extenders. So"—she resumed her normal volume—"a life jacket would be much better. At least they're adjustable. Maybe the crew can spare a couple."

In addition to being obsessively preoccupied with Nana, Mom was obsessively preoccupied with order. Her idea of nirvana was to be hired as a member of a FEMA team that was tasked with re-alphabetizing the canned goods and magazine sections of grocery stores after major earthquakes, or—even better—very large book repositories, like the Library of Congress.

"I honestly don't think you need to take any extra precautions today, Mom. We're on a roll." I swept my hand skyward. "Glorious weather. Calm seas. Trust me, there's no way we're going to sink." Given my rather lengthy track record of being wrong about almost everything, I hated to speak in absolutes, but this time I knew I was right.

I hoped.

I checked my watch. "They should be serving lunch pretty soon, Mom. You wanna head down to the galley and find a seat before it gets too crowded?"

She trailed her fingers over the life preserver slowly, affectionately, as if it were a tiny ball of fur named Cottontail. "Will you promise that if something happens to me, you'll stop by the house to visit your father at least twice a week so he can practice talking to another human being? I'm afraid he might forget how otherwise. And watch your grandmother's diet. She has a nasty habit of bingeing on maraschino cherries."

"Mom, you're on vacation. This is supposed to be fun. So stop with the Grim Reaper references, will you? You're not facing imminent death."

"Of course I'm not." She flashed a perky smile. "Really, Emily, I can hardly contain myself. I'm absolutely having the time of my life. I don't think I've had this much fun since I color-coded your father's sock drawer."

Which must have been a real knee-slapper considering the only socks Dad owned were black.

Leaving Mom to stand guard over the ship's most accessible life-saving apparatus, I went in search of Etienne to enlist his assistance in helping me round up the group for lunch. The advertised meal consisted of turkey wraps, chips, and fresh fruit, but for an additional twenty bucks, we could order a platter of Alaskan king crab legs, complete with stainless steel lobster cracker, moist towelettes, and bandages.

Unfortunately, my guys are spectacularly bad when it comes to wrestling with seafood that looks like the creature from the *Predator* movies. Removing husks from ears of sweet corn? Yes. Dissecting the legs of spiny crustaceans? Not so much.

Fear of shellfish is another of the consequences of being landlocked.

Not seeing Etienne at the port rail among the impenetrable wall of whale watchers, I poked my head inside the nearby observation cabin with its indoor seating and huge viewing windows to find the room deserted. That left only the main deck galley and bow to search.

Circling around the rows of passenger chairs that were bolted down mid-deck, I noticed Thor Thorsen's wife, Florence, sitting by herself, bundled up in a hoodie and tinkering with her cell phone. As physically unremarkable as Thor was impressive, she reminded me of everyone's favorite pair of slippers—plain, devoid of decoration, and a bit frayed around the edges, but blessed with the ability to soothe the sorest of feet. She was schlepping a jumble of camera lens cases that were skewed across the width of her chest. She was so entangled in straps and nylon webbing that I hoped she didn't get snagged on some out-of-the-way hook and accidentally strangle herself.

She waved when she saw me. "Are you looking for Etienne?"

"Have you seen him?"

"You bet. Goldie was starting to feel a little queasy, so he and Margi escorted her down to the galley a few minutes ago. This is her first time on the ocean, and if she felt as bad as she looked, I bet it'll be her last. I would've taken her myself, but I didn't want to leave Thor high and dry without his equipment."

Florence was always looking to help someone. She'd received numerous citations from practically every organization in Windsor City for her leadership and outstanding community service. She had founded her own chapter of the Daughters of Norway, which many of my regulars belonged to. Word around town was that Thor often took advantage of her generous spirit, but if today was any example, she seemed perfectly content sitting by herself, lugging all his photographic equipment while he enjoyed the sights.

I eyed the straps and cases hugging her body. "Is that stuff heavy?"

"Heavy, no. Cumbersome, yes."

I was tempted to ask why big, broad-shouldered Thor couldn't carry his own camera equipment, but I figured that was none of my business. "Have you seen the whales yet?"

She shook her head. "Doesn't look like anyone at the rail is too keen on giving up their spot, so I'll wait and see Thor's photos when we get back home. It'll be just like being there."

Yeah, why go through the hassle of paying a lot of money to see something firsthand when you could wait until it was over and see it vicariously from the comfort of your own sofa?

She waved her cell phone at me, her face a question mark. "I know the boat is equipped with satellite internet, but do you think it's working? I mean, I sent a couple of text messages to Lorraine Iversen back home and I thought they went through, but I haven't heard back from her yet, which is really unusual because she's as compulsive as I am about answering texts immediately."

"She's probably juggling a million medical issues at the moment, so I wouldn't worry too much. She got a lot dumped on her plate in the last few days." Lorraine's mother had broken her hip the day before our flight, so she'd had to cancel her reservation, leaving her husband, Ennis, to make the trip without her. "Give her time. Hospitals aren't known for having the best cell service. Too much concrete and steel."

"You're probably right. But still." She frowned at her phone. "It's just so unlike her. I mean, she's my best friend. I'd like to know what's happening so I can give her a little emotional support."

"Talk to Ennis. He might have an update that'll help ease your mind."

She nodded. "Sure. I…I just can't shake the feeling that something terrible—" Leaving the thought unfinished, she turned her cell phone off and stuffed it into the pocket of her hoodie. "Shutting the thing off might help, right? Sometimes I think it'd be better for everyone's peace of mind if the cell phone went the way of the dinosaur."

Closing her eyes, she inhaled a deep breath, then let it out slowly, as if she were in the cool-down stage of an exercise program. "There." She opened her eyes and forced a smile. "I feel better already."

But she didn't look better.

She looked as if she were carrying the weight of the world on her narrow shoulders…and the strain was about to crush her.

TWO

"OF COURSE THERE'S A cure for seasickness." Margi Swanson sat opposite Goldie Kristiansen in one of the galley's long booths, tapping into the decades of medical expertise she'd gleaned as a nurse at the Winsdor City Clinic. "Get off the boat."

Goldie groaned as she propped her elbows on the table and braced her forehead against the heels of her palms. She was a living legend at our community playhouse, having appeared in stage productions for decades, so she had the theatrical chops to turn any situation into a dramatic affair. "That's it?"

Margi scratched her head. "Uhh…I think it helps to be outside in the fresh air…as long as you don't block Thor's view and get yelled at. And looking at the horizon is supposed to be better than staring at something right in front of you." She shrugged. "Truth is, we don't get much call at the clinic for treating seasickness. It's one of the perks of being landlocked."

"Would you like me to escort you back up to the observation deck so you can test out the 'staring at the horizon' theory, Mrs.

Kristiansen?" Etienne sat beside her, his voice calm, his French/ German/Italian accent soothing, his presence reassuring. He'd already given her a motion sickness pill, but at this point I wasn't sure it would do much good.

"Give me a minute, would you?" Sliding her elbows off the table, she eased her spine against the seat back and sat motionless, as if she were performing an invisible body scan. "I might be feeling a smidge better."

"Terrific!" I enthused.

"But just in case it's a false alarm, would one of you find Grover for me? I should probably draw a map showing him where all my secret hiding places are." She heaved a long-suffering sigh. "I have cash stashed all over the house. It's my personal crusade against his edict that no amount of money should ever be allowed to simply sit around not earning interest. He advocates saving money rather than spending it."

Goldie was in her early sixties and still a real looker. Red hair cut in a stylish bob. Glowing complexion. Lipstick that always matched her nail polish. Curvaceous figure that she dressed in the latest fashion trends. Chunky costume jewelry that hung from her ears, bedecked her fingers and wrists, and sat prettily at her throat. Her features were finely shaped and perfectly proportioned, giving her the kind of countenance that, years ago, might have attracted a New York model agency or Hollywood talent scout if she'd been living anywhere other than a small town in the middle of Iowa. I'd heard rumors that her good looks were a result of a nose job, facial nips and tucks, and spectacularly expensive mineral foundation, but I preferred to believe her comeliness was simply a result of great genetics.

"Okay," she wheezed, giving her head a determined bob. "I'm ready to go outside again." Hesitating, she pressed a bejeweled hand to her cheek and winced. "How bad do I look?"

"Bernice looks worse," Margi said helpfully. "And she's not even seasick."

"Thank you for that—I think," deadpanned Goldie. She regarded Etienne with doe eyes. "All right, handsome, it's you and me. Are we ready to give this cockamamie theory a trial run?"

"Just in case my theory collapses," said Margi as she slapped something onto the table and shoved it toward Goldie. "Air sickness bag. I sneaked a few off the plane with me. And don't forget this." She glided a mini bottle of sanitizer at her. "You might need that afterward. It's the new summer scent that was specifically created to celebrate Iowa's farm economy. *Pork Sorbet*."

As Etienne and Goldie made their way toward the exit, the loudspeaker crackled with the captain's excited whoop. "Breach!"

I fired a look out the viewing window just in time to see forty tons of whale flesh catapulting itself into the air right off the rail. Fins flapping, tail flopping, it smacked back into the surf in a kind of modified backflip, landing with a resounding *SPLAAAT* that rained torrents of foamy spray over the deck and onto the windows.

"Whoa!" cried Margi. "What do you bet a few folks just got soaked?"

I stared at the seawater dripping down the windowpane. "I'm afraid you might be right." I just hoped one of them wasn't Bernice.

. . . .

It wasn't.

It was Mom.

She bustled into the galley for lunch with her salt-and-pepper hair plastered to her head and her jacket sporting wet patches that were bigger than the continents on a map of the world. Spying me at the end of a table that had just filled up with seven of our tour guests, she paused on her way by.

"I have no idea where your father is, so I've decided to eat without him."

"Woman power," applauded one of my tablemates, fisting her hand in the air.

"Did you want to dry off before you eat, Mom? There's a hot-air hand dryer in the ladies' room. You could stand in front of it for a few minutes."

"Already did that." She tucked a strand of sopping hair behind her ear. "I'm not really that wet now."

I looked her up and down. "You're drenched."

"I can hardly notice." She leaned in toward me, giddy with relief. "Aren't we lucky we survived the dangerous part of the trip? All that's left is the glacier, and it probably hasn't moved in a thousand years, so...no threat there."

"Unless we get rammed by one of them icebergs," taunted my grandmother.

Mom shot a look her way. "What?"

"Iceberg," I jumped in, holding up my turkey wrap and pointing to the filling. "Lettuce. It's unusually crisp. You'll love it."

"Oh. Well, enjoy your lunch, everyone. And, Mother"—she fixed Nana with a piercing look—"meet me on the upper deck when you finish. I've arranged a surprise for you."

Nana gave a little suck on her uppers as Mom hurried away. "I don't know what that mother of yours has got cooked up, Emily,

17

but I don't want no part of it. Dang. I might have to spend the rest of the trip holed up in the potty."

"That could be difficult," said Tilly. "It's only a one-seater. There'll be a line."

"What if it's a *good* surprise?" asked George.

Nana gawked at him. "Margaret don't do good surprises. She's only got two kinds: dumb and dumber."

"I suppose you're right." He bobbed his head. "Maybe there's another restroom aboard with more than one seat."

George Farkas had been sweet on Nana ever since she'd crossed the border from Minnesota to Iowa after Grampa Sippel died. The attraction was mutual, despite the many obstacles they faced. She was Catholic; he was Lutheran. She was a lottery-winning multi-millionaire; he was middle-class. She was related to my mother; he wasn't.

"Not to direct the conversation away from family dynamics," interjected Ennis Iversen, "but did any of you know that Alaska has its own version of the Bermuda Triangle?"

Ennis, a professor of folklore and mythology at a small liberal arts college north of Windsor City, could best be described as a rumpled soul in dire need of pants that weren't baggy and shirts that needed pressing. With graying hair that he wore in a ponytail at his nape and an earlobe pierced with a gold stud, he looked more like a rabid fan of the Grateful Dead than a hardcore academic. His intelligence seemed at odds with his appearance, yet he appeared neither impressed by the former nor bothered by the latter. He was a born storyteller, blessed with a naturally deep basso that others could acquire by indulging in years of heavy drinking and chain-smoking or by answering to the name James Earl Jones.

"Alaska has a Bermuda Triangle?" I repeated. "For real?"

"The area forms a kind of obtuse triangle from Juneau in the south"—he drew an imaginary line on the table—"to Barrow in the north, to Anchorage in the center of the state. And just like the Bermuda Triangle, the region is steeped in mystery. Planes vanish without a trace. Hikers go missing. Tourists and longtime residents disappear, never to be seen again."

"Where's the Yukon?" Nana asked abruptly as she studied his invisible map.

"It's off the map, Mrs. Sippel. In Canada."

"No kiddin'?"

"It forms Alaska's eastern border."

"So you mean we're not gonna be seein' them fellas what dress like Sergeant Preston in them red jackets and funny pants?"

"Not unless our bus driver gets us hopelessly lost."

"Oh." She pushed out her bottom lip. "That's disappointin'."

"If I may," Tilly piped up. "Alaska is over twice the size of Texas, and it remains sparsely developed because of hostile terrain, dense forests, raging rivers, and impassable mountain ranges." In her capacity as a professor of anthropology, she'd traveled the world, schmoozed with witch doctors, published dozens of monographs on tribal culture, and probably forgotten more stuff than the rest of us had learned in the first place. "I'm more likely to believe that terrain plays a more significant role in disappearances than any hypothetical Bermuda Triangle theory."

"I'm not going to deny the adverse nature of Alaska's terrain," Ennis conceded, "but neither can I ignore a host of other glaring facts. Alaska has the smallest population of all fifty states, but it ranks number one among number of disappearances. For every one thousand people, four go missing, which is twice the national average. So you might ask, what's happening in Alaska that causes so many people to disappear?"

"I'm sure we've read many of the same articles," Tilly rebutted. "Many people move to Alaska with the express *purpose* of disappearing. Runaways. Women trying to escape abusive spouses. Men hoping to escape the law. People abandoning underwater mortgages and ditching dead-end jobs to start over again."

"Agreed." Ennis nodded. "But not everyone who pulls up roots in the lower forty-eight wants to disappear, yet they vanish anyway. Why is that?"

"Sinkholes?" offered Nana.

"Alien abduction?" tossed out Orphie Arnesen.

Orphie Arnesen and her husband, Al, owned a modest split-level house in a tree-lined, middle-class neighborhood in Windsor City. But it was no secret that Orphie entertained thoughts of moving into an antebellum McMansion one day, where she could gloat over her stunning Greek pillars, her acres of weedless lawn, and her meteoric rise in social status, with all its ensuing celebrity. She wasn't unhappy with her present lot in life; she simply imagined things would be better if the lot were bigger.

She was touring Alaska without Al because she'd managed to convince him that if he left Windsor City for more than a day, the entire political structure of the town would collapse in his absence. Orphie was nothing if not convinced of her husband's prospects for greatness.

"The FBI is called in to handle alien abduction cases, aren't they?" Orphie continued. "Did you know that my Al actually has to work with the FBI sometimes? City council presidents are often called upon to perform far meatier tasks than gaveling sessions to order."

"Like what?" taunted Bernice. "Calling in the pizza orders for those stupid meetings of his?" She let out a derisive snort. "Listen to the bunch of you. Sinkholes. Alien abductions. *Pfffft*. I'll tell you why folks are disappearing." She looked up and down the table, her eyes narrowing to slits. "Government takeover. They're sending in the IRS to kidnap people and whisk 'em off to black ops sites in other countries."

"For making math errors on their taxes?" questioned Tilly. "That's absurd."

George scratched his jaw. "Maybe with postal rates as high as they are, it's cheaper to fly a fella to a foreign prison than mail him an amended tax return form."

"Plane fare's probably cheaper than them fancy birthday cards what they're sellin' now," huffed Nana. "I never seen prices so high. And then you gotta fork out extra postage to mail the thing."

Despite her millions, Nana continued to practice a low-key spending style that included coupon-cutting, weekly visits to the Dollar Store, and two-buck Tuesdays at the theater...with free popcorn.

"Half-wits," scoffed Bernice. "Do you ever think to turn on cable news to find out what's actually happening in the world?"

We all watched cable news. We simply avoided the channels that Bernice watched.

"Revisiting my original question as to why people in Alaska disappear," Ennis broke in, "there are facts and there are theories. On the fact side, there's an Anchorage baker who's serving 461 years in prison for the serial murders of as many as forty-nine women in the early '80s."

"Four hundred sixty-one years?" parroted Orphie. "Where are they getting their life expectancy tables from? The Old Testament?"

"I believe the justice system realizes the prisoner won't live that long," clarified Ennis. "They just want to ensure that he's never released. He buried his victims in isolated spots near Anchorage and its environs, and to this day the authorities have no idea if they found every victim. The final tally could actually be much higher than forty-nine. And this was just one man. Think how many other bodies could still be out there, killed by men who were never caught."

As we stared at him, spellbound, he opened his bag of chips and popped one into his mouth. "The Pacific Northwest boasts a lion's share of known serial killers. I doubt Tilly will give me any flak about that. But why the cluster in this part of the country? Is it the weather? The isolation? A misguided belief that if someone lives off the grid, he can basically get away with murder without anyone ever finding out? Or is there a different reason entirely? Something more primal. More terrifying. Something that—"

"Do you have any stories that revolve around something *other* than serial killers?" I said in a rush of words as the expressions at our table drifted from attentive to alarmed.

He snapped his mouth shut and smiled self-consciously. "Sorry. I've been known to hop onto my soapbox with no encouragement whatsoever. So...why don't we move along to the theories part of my narrative? I suspect Tilly can back me up here as well."

Tilly angled her eyebrows at a stern angle. "We'll see."

"Alaska is so big," Ennis continued, "with so many impenetrable forests, it's not beyond the realm of possibility to speculate that there could be creatures, or beings, living in the densest, most isolated areas who never reached the top rung of the evolutionary ladder."

"Oh. My. God." Delpha Spillum burst into laughter. "Are you talking about Bigfoot?"

Ennis nodded. "Bigfoot. Sasquatch. The Yukon Howler. Thunderfoot. Bushman. The Woodsman. The creature goes by a half-dozen names, but the mythology doesn't change. Some of Alaska's indigenous tribes have even incorporated mention of the creature into their religious culture, from as far back as five hundred years. Prospectors. Homesteaders. Miners. They all swear they've witnessed the same thing: a creature covered in brown fur, from seven to ten feet tall in an upright stance, who weighs anywhere from four- to twelve-hundred pounds and leaves a footprint twenty- to twenty-four inches long and ten inches wide. If such a creature truly exists and proves to be hostile to the outside world, I think you'll find the explanation for why so many people vanish without a trace in our forty-ninth state."

"This is *so* bogus!" crowed Delpha. "Why are you passing along such foolishness, Ennis? The legend of Bigfoot is bunk. Hokum. Balderdash. Hogwash. *Twaddle.*"

Delpha Spillum was the recently retired editor of the *Windsor City Register*, so her brain was home to an impressive stockpile of synonyms.

"You've been reading too many folklore articles that aren't peer-reviewed," she accused. "Imagine the blowback I would've received if I'd written an article in the *Register* about the veracity of

Bigfoot sightings. I would've been run out of town on a rail, and rightly so. But here you are, a well-respected academic, filling everyone's head with all this Sasquatch nonsense. You should be ashamed of yourself."

Ennis flashed her an almost intimate smile, disguised as a boyish grin. "Why don't you tell me how you *really* feel, Del?"

Delpha Spillum had devoted her life to the *Windsor City Register*. A family-run enterprise started by her grandfather, she'd inherited ownership from her father and for forty years had treated the paper as if it were her husband, children, lover, and adored pet. With the shift in culture from print to cyber news, however, the *Register* lost significant readership and advertising dollars, so, ceding to pressure, she'd sold the business and watched it morph from a daily newspaper to a digital venture, with a print edition appearing only once a week.

Being a product of strong, psychologically stable Norwegian stock, Delpha didn't whine about the cannibalization of the family business. Instead, she bought a slew of yoga pants, leggings, speed tights, and jeggings and redirected her energy into a fitness program that included running, spinning, weight training, yoga, and Ironman competitions. At sixty-something, she was buff to the extreme and turned more than one head when she paraded around in her athletic outfits, which she wore as both street and traveling clothes. From what I could tell, her one obvious nod to her former life was her cell phone case, which was a laminated sheet of bold black-and-white newsprint. Custom ordered, no doubt, and infinitely more adult than my own Cinderella case, which had been a gift from Nana.

These weekly runs of hers to the Dollar Store were killing me.

"C'mon, Del," Ennis scolded, "don't be so quick to thumb your nose at the legends. People claim to have witnessed giant apelike creatures with furry pelts just about everywhere on the planet. I suspect Tilly might even back me up on this."

Tilly gave her head a reluctant nod. "Ennis is right." She began ticking off names on her fingers. "The Abominable Snowman, or Yeti, in the Himalayas. Almasty in the Caucasus Mountains of Russia. Yowie in Australia. Wendigo in Canada. Yeren in China. And they all seem to share the same physical characteristics—that of a Cyclopean hominid who's both hirsute and bipedal."

"What'd she say?" asked George.

"I think she said they ride bicycles," offered Nana.

"Translated into laymen's terms," Ennis jumped in, "Tilly is talking about an extraordinarily tall man who's covered in hair and stands on two feet."

"I married someone who fit that description," Bernice said on a wistful note.

"Was your husband exceptionally tall?" I asked.

"Five foot two."

Orphie frowned. "That's not tall."

"It was back then."

"You guys can believe what you want to believe," concluded Delpha, "but without concrete scientific evidence, this whole legend thing doesn't fly. My question is, if there have been so many sightings, how come not one of the witnesses has been able to snatch even a hair from the creature's pelt to test its mitochondrial DNA?"

"Actually, a geneticist from Oxford University *did* perform DNA tests," said Tilly. "Most of the sample hairs were shown to have either horse, bear, or cow DNA. But one sample proved to be a hybrid—combining the genetic markers of a polar bear and something else. But he wasn't able to prove with any scientific authority what the 'something else' was."

"Polar bear?" croaked George. "These fellas traipsed all the way to the Arctic?"

"This is where the mystery becomes even more intriguing," said Tilly. "The sample was taken from a creature in the Himalayas that was assumed to be a Yeti."

"Of course," needled Delpha. "I see photographs of polar bears scampering over ice floes on Mount Everest all the time, don't you?"

"Well, would you lookit that?" Nana's jaw dropped as she peered across the room. "Florence and Thor's done eatin' already. I bet he was hurryin' her up so's he could run back up to the observation deck and stake out the best spot to see the glacier."

We followed her gaze to watch Thor storm full speed ahead toward the exit while Florence chased behind him, weighed down by a full complement of his photographic equipment.

Ennis gave his head a disgusted shake. "Remember the month we read that bestseller about the guy who treated his wife like Leona Helmsley treated her employees?"

"I can't think of the title, but I remember Thor ranted *forever* about how much he hated it," Orphie confided. "Probably hit too close to home."

"But he failed to see *any* similarities between himself and the main protagonist," added Delpha. "Here we thought a few light bulbs might go on over his head after he read about the tragic but fitting end of a fictional character whose personality mirrored his own, but he simply panned the book. He called it a seamy melo-drama with no basis in reality." She laughed. "The irony of it all. A man who is utterly devoid of self-awareness despises a book's protagonist for displaying the same obnoxious traits that are the hallmarks of the man's own personality. Priceless."

"Some might call that self-loathing," suggested Ennis.

Orphie heaved a sigh as she directed a pathetic look at me. "We don't like Thor much."

"Then why did you invite him to join your book club?"

"Because we *really* like Florence," Delpha answered for her. "Everyone loves Florence. But Thor wouldn't allow her to join our book club unless he joined too, so we ended up with both of them."

"The wheat along with the chaff," lamented Orphie. "If you watch closely, you'll notice he rarely lets her out of his sight."

"He's probably afraid she'll run away if he's not there to watch her every move," said Ennis.

"And then the poor baby might have to carry his own stinking camera equipment," bristled Delpha.

"Out of curiosity," I asked as I watched Florence struggle to readjust the multitude of straps hanging from her neck, "what kind of tragic end did the protagonist in your book meet?"

"It was brilliant," cooed Orphie. "He and his wife take a back-country hiking trip in the wilds of Montana. His idea, not hers. She comes back. He's never seen again. Her story? Her husband was attacked by a grizzly and dragged off to God knows where. She claims she barely escaped with her own life, and naturally, the police can't prove otherwise because the two of them were so far off the grid, no one was around to witness anything."

Delpha nodded. "But in the very last paragraph, the wife is back home, trailing a nostalgic finger over the stuff in his office, and she suddenly removes a nine-by-twelve of him from its frame and rips it into a million pieces. And she does it in such a slow, satisfying manner that you *know* he wasn't mauled by any grizzly. She killed him herself."

"He was such a pompous snot," spat Orphie.

I stared after the Thorsens as they exited the galley. "What did Florence think of the book?"

"She loved it," said Ennis. "She read it twice to see if she'd missed any clues about how the wife might have knocked him off."

"For those of you still in the galley," the captain announced, "you might want to finish up your meal and head topside because we're approaching the Aialik Glacier."

Mayhem ensued as passengers clambered out of their booths to head for the exits. Ennis and I popped out of our seats to allow our table companions to vacate our booth, then quickly stepped aside to avoid being trampled.

Iowans shun the practice of being fashionably late, but my guys take it up a notch from there. With them, everything has to be a footrace to the finish, complete with tangled limbs, flying elbows, and bragging rights. In their eyes, punctuality isn't a virtue; it's a competitive sport.

"I'm anxious to see the glacier," Ennis said, laughing, "but I'm apparently not as hell-bent as the rest of them."

"Have you heard from your wife yet?" I asked as we motored into view of a broad expanse of snow nestled between two mountainous slopes. "Florence mentioned that she'd texted Lorraine several times but hadn't received a response, so she's worried that something catastrophic has happened."

"You mean, something more catastrophic than Lorraine's mother breaking her hip the day before our tour?" Ennis shook his head. "Lorraine said she'd call me after things quieted down on her end. She doesn't want to ruin my vacation with medical updates, which is pretty thoughtful of her, but that's the way Lorraine operates. Her mom's in good hands with Lorraine running the show, so I'm just going to chill out and wait for details. I think this is one of those cases where no news is good news."

"Would you tell that to Florence when you see her? She's twisting herself into knots over those unanswered texts."

"I'll do it first thing."

Climbing the stairs to the observation deck, we joined the scores of other passengers who were vying for plum spots at the rail where they could take selfies using the glacier as a backdrop. To the left of the ice shelf, the sloped cliffs were green with a forest of evergreens, while in the background, from the peaks of higher elevations, waterfalls cascaded downward over ironbound ledges, tumbling into valleys that looked untouched by human exploration. To the glacier's right, shoulders of unscalable rock hunched together at the water's edge, dark and forbidding, looking as if they had been thrust forward in a ruthless shove by the hulking, saw-toothed summits that crowded together behind them.

"The Aialik's a mile wide," the captain informed us as we motored closer, "and if you think the snowpack looks like it's tinted blue, you're not seeing things. It is. The ice is so dense, it absorbs every color *except* blue, so that's the only color visible to the naked eye."

"Do you know where your grandmother is, Emily?" Mom came up behind me trussed in an orange life vest that hugged her chest like overinflated bumpers.

"She—" I eyed the other life vest that was dangling from her arm. "Is that the surprise?"

"You bet. I talked some nice young crewman into fetching a couple." She held it up, scrutinizing the length of the straps. "One size is supposed to fit all, but I'm more than a little skeptical that it'll fit around your grandmother." She swiveled her head, searching. "Is she still in the galley?"

"She's—" I swirled my hand in the air in the general direction of nowhere. "Actually, I don't know where she is."

"Probably waiting in line for the potty. I'll just pop down to meet her."

"No!"

"What's with the life jackets?" asked Dick Teig as he circled around us. "Are we having a lifeboat drill or something?"

"It's Mom's surprise," I quipped. "For Nana."

He looked suspicious as he headed toward Dick Stolee. "Emily's mother's wearing a life jacket."

"Why?"

Dick Teig shrugged. "You suppose they're gonna surprise us with a lifeboat drill?"

"That'd be some surprise," snorted Dick Stolee. "Maybe you haven't noticed. There *aren't* any lifeboats."

"Mom," I said as I grabbed her arm and navigated her toward the stern, "how about I take your picture in front of the pretty glacier?"

The captain's voice rang out again. "You'll note that the color of the seawater has changed, folks. It's gone from a deep marine blue to a chalky aquamarine, kinda like what you might see if you stirred a little flour into a bottle of window cleaner."

"S'cuse me. S'cuse me," I said politely as I squeezed Mom into a place near the rail.

"The change to chalky turquoise occurs when particles from the glacier's meltwater enter the bay," the captain continued. "We call it glacial milk. And this is the time of year when ice usually breaks away from the main flow and forms iceb—*whoa!* Do you hear that?"

The air suddenly filled with a deep, menacing rumble, like distant thunder...or cannon fire. Powder sloughed off from the glacial wall in a snowy waterfall, and then a towering pinnacle cracked like river ice and broke away from the cliff face, crashing into the surf with an earsplitting roar that sent spray in every direction and an ominous wave rolling in our direction.

"Jesus, Mary, and Joseph," cried Mom.

"Stay calm," I soothed. "The captain knows what he's do—"

"Stay calm? You're talking to a woman who saw *Titanic* fourteen times in surround sound, Emily. I know exactly what's going to happen next. Iceberg dead ahead!" she cried. "Run for your lives! Save yourselves while there's still time!" Which caused an immediate panic among the passengers who *weren't* wearing life vests.

They stampeded blindly to left and right, spinning in circles, bumping into each other, their cries of alarm piercing the air as the wave crashed into our hull.

"Man the lifeboats!"

"What lifeboats?"

"Where's the life jackets?"

The boat plunged into a trough, pitching and bobbing like a cork before rising onto a swell. The deck lurched. The boat creaked.

"We're not in danger!" bellowed the captain. "Stop the commotion. We're not in the North Atlantic, and you're not on the *Titanic*."

His assurance was comforting, but since Mom had gone down with the ship fourteen times in surround sound, I doubted she believed him.

The good news was, at least she hadn't seen it in 3-D.

THREE

NOT ONLY DID THE newly calved iceberg *not* tear a gash in the *Kenai's* hull, it floated away so innocuously that a group of kayakers enjoyed their own adventure by paddling around the smaller chunks of drift ice in the extensive debris field. We remained at the site long enough to satisfy everyone's burning desire to include the glacier in their headshots, and then we began the journey back to Seward Harbor, stopping along the way to tuck our nose into coves where sea lions lazed on sun-warmed rocks and gulls screeched overhead.

Mom was so unnerved by the incident that she spent the rest of the trip in the galley with Dad, so she missed the islands of chiseled rock that were shaped like beehives, daggers, and porcupines; the flocks of sea birds that were perched on granite spires; the cliff-hugging, orange-billed puffins whose white chests and black wings made them look as if they were wearing tiny tuxedoes; and the endless ranges of snow-capped mountain peaks creating vistas so majestic, they looked more photoshopped than real.

Seward Harbor lay nestled in the protected cul-de-sac of Resurrection Bay, at the base of towering vertical mountains. The harbor marina was glutted with watercraft rarely seen in Iowa—tour boats, catamarans, cabin cruisers, power boats, and schooners whose naked masts resembled a jumble of giant chopsticks. Once back at the dock, we shuffled down the metal gangplank onto the pier, then made our way to the waterfront parking lot, where our coach, with its distinct aurora borealis motif, awaited us.

"Were the whales out in force?" Like a practicing diplomat, our driver greeted us outside our bus with smiles, enthusiasm, and a willing hand to assist guests up onto the first step. His name was Steele, although he didn't specify whether that was his first name or last, and he seemed to enjoy interacting with the seniors as much as he enjoyed pampering his bus. He cut quite an arresting figure in his regulation uniform and cap, looking more like an airline pilot than a bus driver, which wasn't a bad look to have, especially if the rest of the package included chiseled cheekbones, laughing eyes, and a devastating smile.

"Lots of whales," Margi Swanson replied as she climbed aboard, "but no lifeboats."

"You needed lifeboats?" asked Steele, clearly astonished.

"It was a simple misunderstanding with one of the passengers," I explained. "No harm done."

"Good thing you didn't need to abandon ship," Steele advised. "Whale watching vessels aren't equipped with lifeboats."

Dick Teig climbed onto the stepwell. "I guess *Titanic* never hit movie theaters in Alaska."

When everyone was seated, Etienne went through the bus taking a head count while I laid out the plan for the rest of the day.

"We're going to give you some free time in downtown Seward for about an hour while we wait to pick up our local guide at the Alaska SeaLife Center. Her name is Alison Pickles, and according to her credentials, she's an aficionado of all things Alaskan, so I expect she'll be able to give us the skinny on just about everything."

"What wonderful things are we supposed to do in downtown Seward for a measly hour?" demanded Bernice.

"You could shop for souvenirs," I suggested. "Or take pictures. Or grab a snack. Or—"

"Bernice has a point," Alice Tjarks spoke up. "We're wading into dangerous territory with only an hour. That hardly gives us time to get off the bus before we have to get back on again."

"I agree with Alice," said Helen Teig. "You're setting us up to be late even before we get off."

"But—"

Steele clicked on his microphone. "If any of you would like to remain on the bus, I could give you my special busman's tour of Seward, if the Micelis have no objection. It's not part of their itinerary."

Cheers. Clapping. Whistles.

I raised my hands in surrender and smiled. "Okay, okay. How can I say no to that? So, if you'd prefer not to spread your money around Seward, you can stay on the bus for an unadvertised optional tour. Once we're on the road again, it should take us about an hour and a half to reach Girdwood, which is where we'll be staying for the night at the Grand Girdwood Hotel and Resort. And as a special bonus, we'll be dining atop a mountain this evening in the resort's AAA Four Diamond restaurant with panoramic views guaranteed to take your breath away. So we still have a busy day ahead of us. Is everyone hanging in there?"

After our early morning departure from Des Moines yesterday, a three-hour time zone change, and a two and a half hour bus ride from Anchorage to our lodgings in Seward, we'd all been feeling pretty punchy last night. And the fact that daylight persisted throughout the night didn't help matters, not even with blackout drapes. Alaska wasn't Europe, but the jet lag felt the same.

"You bet!" came an anemic chorus of three voices. Everyone else had already moved on, heads bent, attention locked on their cell phones, texting or playing games, looking like airplane passengers during the flight attendant's safety measures presentation.

"All guests on board," announced Etienne as he made his way to the front of the bus. "We didn't lose anyone."

I flashed him a thumbs-up.

In the tour industry, it was the little things.

Downtown Seward was a short street of mostly one-story, flat-roofed buildings that boasted a colorful array of awnings over their storefront windows. It could probably pass for a town in the Old West if not for a few modern upgrades: angled parking spaces instead of hitching posts, two-ton pickup trucks instead of horses, multi-globe streetlights instead of kerosene lamps, a liquor store instead of a saloon, clapboard hotels instead of brothels.

A wide selection of restaurants were scattered about town, allowing tourists to sample cuisine from the far-flung parts of the world, as long as those parts were confined to places that specialized in pizza, burritos, gyros, and egg rolls. The main thoroughfare was home to a bakery, clothing store, ice cream shop, and souvenir shops that specialized in gold, silver, knives, and ulus. But a high-end department store had yet to find its way onto Seward's main street, and the construction of an IMAX theater or Whole Foods looked to be decades away.

Steele dropped me off in front of a building that resembled an old railway depot, which was a stone's throw away from the manicured green space that fronted the bay. Etienne volunteered to accompany the group on their spur-of-the-moment tour, so that left me in charge of meeting Alison. I just hoped the Iowa crowd didn't offend Steele by failing to look up from their phones long enough to see the sights he was going out of his way to show them.

I watched the bus head down the street, surprised when it pulled over to the curb to let off another passenger.

Dad.

He waved his brand-new smartphone at me, then—with a series of charade-like hand gestures—indicated that he was going to wander the grounds to take pictures.

For this trip Dad had sidelined his beloved camcorder in favor of a smaller device with fewer widgets. As skilled as he was at operating farm machinery that was big as a house, he was an abject disaster when it came to video photography, with much of his footage accidentally capturing pavement, blue jeans, footwear, and a random montage of dirt and rocks.

Two weeks ago he finally acknowledged defeat and purchased a state-of-the-art cell phone with a camera that boasted a gazillion pixels. And even though he was already operating it like a pro, I could tell he still remained confounded about his inability to master a simple lightweight camcorder. Mom had even asked me on the QT, "How come your father can operate a twelve-row cultivator, but he can't get the hang of a ten-ounce video recorder that fits in the palm of his hand?"

"Easy," I'd told her. "The camcorder isn't big enough."

"Putting your camera through its paces, are you?" I called to him.

"Yup," he called back.

I tapped my watch. "Don't lose track of time. I'd hate to have to leave you behind."

He grinned. "You bet."

Dad was so much more chatty on vacation than he was back home. Traveling with friendly people in a relaxed social setting really loosened his tongue.

Even though I wasn't scheduled to meet Alison for another hour, I headed off toward the SeaLife Center, which was a mere hundred yards away, housed in a boxy gray building with a glass front. As I neared the entrance, I noticed a pretty blond sitting on the low barrier wall that flanked the terrace, her gaze focused downward on her cell phone, thumbs flying. I suspected the woman might be Alison from her resemblance to the headshot she'd posted on her website. But what really cinched it for me was that she had a suitcase.

"Alison?" I called out as I jogged up the stairs.

Looking up from her phone, she hopped to her feet, all smiles, warmth, and confidence. "Sure am. That must make you Emily." She extended her hand in greeting. "Sorry I'm early, but it's the only available time my neighbor could drop me off."

"No, no. Don't apologize. I love that you're early. You'll fit right in." Her photo had been striking, but with her luminous complexion, shampoo-model blond hair, and fine-boned features, she was downright gorgeous in person.

"I can't tell you how happy I am to be working with you." She glanced left and right. "So where are my tour guests?"

"On a sightseeing tour of Seward and environs. They'll be back in an hour."

"Oh. So if they're touring Seward without me, is someone else giving them the spiel about the 1964 earthquake and tsunami?"

"Uhh…our bus driver might be taking care of that…or not. He didn't say." I frowned. "To be perfectly honest, I don't know what he's telling them. This was all unplanned."

"Great! I love spontaneity. No worries about my spiel. I'll fill them in on some of the more interesting aspects of Seward's history as we head north."

"Are you a native Alaskan? You didn't say on your website."

"I wish! But I'm not a sourdough, which is what true Alaskans call themselves. I'm a Californian who got bored with the golden grass, fires, mudslides, and earthquakes, so after I finished cosmetology school, I decided I needed a change of scenery. I figured Alaskans needed their hair cut and styled as often as people in the lower forty-eight, so I hopped into my little VW Bug and headed north. Pretty gutsy move for a twenty-year-old, but I haven't been disappointed by my decision, the spectacular scenery, or the twenty-odd hours of daylight we enjoy at this time of year—it's so invigorating." She smiled. "That was a dozen years ago."

"Are you still doing hair?"

"My own." She tousled her shoulder-length locks with a care-free hand, exposing a dainty, dime-sized butterfly tattoo beneath her ear. "That's about it. I learned a long time ago that the tourist trade is far more important to Alaska's economy than hair, so I made a career change. Cruise ships, bus tours—they all need local guides, not hairstylists. I'd have to work a year as a stylist to earn as much money as I do in three months as a guide. And the bonus is, I love my job. And if you'll forgive my being brazenly self-promoting, I think I'm pretty good at it."

"The reviews posted on your website were certainly convincing."

"It helps to be a people person. Guests like a tour guide who's able to connect with them on a personal level. They end up rewarding you with five-star reviews."

She checked the time on her phone before bobbing her head toward the front entrance of the SeaLife Center. "You want the dollar tour of the center before we have to leave? I have an annual pass, and I can stow my suitcase at the guest services counter. I've only toured the place a thousand times, so I know where all the highlights are."

I shrugged. "We have an hour. Why not?"

· · · · · · · · · ·

The Alaska SeaLife Center was a fascinating blend of science museum, aquarium, and petting zoo, where visitors were encouraged to fondle sea invertebrates that looked even less cuddly than a family of startled porcupines. We breezed past many of the technical displays about the salmon fishing industry and focused more on the tanks with active marine life: sea lions sluicing through Little Mermaid-like aquatic habitats, ringed seals with grampy whiskers and eyes black as marbles, red king crabs that resembled the hideously spiny creatures that hatched from the embryonic eggs in *Aliens*, moon jellyfish that floated in an illuminated tank like tiny gossamer parachutes, rose starfish that sported nearly a dozen rays and could have doubled as a ladies' brooch, and green sea urchins whose protruding spikes looked more deadly than sharpened knitting needles.

"We don't have many aquariums in Iowa," I lamented as we made our way back to the front entrance. "Landlocked states are way behind the curve about creating attractions that revolve around ocean life."

"What do you have instead?"

"A cow made of butter that's displayed at the Iowa State Fair."

"In an air-conditioned room with a backup generator, I hope."

"You bet." I laughed. "But we do have a brand-new theme park. You know how Florida has Disneyworld and Tennessee has Dollywood? Well, Iowa now has a theme park called Green Acres, where guests can enjoy a genuine farm experience in a completely artificial environment. Fun for the entire family. It's advertised as a cross between Epcot Center, Branson, and the Magic Kingdom, with interactive exhibits and attractions, an IMAX theater showing first-run movies, themed restaurants, a midway with acres of amusement rides, nightly stage performances, musical concerts, and upscale shopping. A family could spend their whole vacation there. It's the brainchild of some corporate billionaire who thinks that all Americans should have the opportunity to drive toy tractors around five hundred acres of fake farmland. In fact, we recently hired a tour escort who's there right now on her very first extended assignment. The park's only been open for two weeks, so we're expecting lots of feedback from her on whether it's a venue that more of our clientele would enjoy. And we've lucked out that it's only three hours down the road from my hometown."

The bus was already at the curb when we exited the building, parked opposite a vacant lot that was abutted by a building with enormous blue whales painted across its exposed side. After storing Alison's suitcase in the luggage bay, Steele welcomed her aboard with a handshake that lingered beyond the mere perfunctory and an almost breathless smile that hinted of a massive explosion of pheromones.

"Please tell me you didn't spill all the beans about the '64 disaster on your mini tour," she pleaded good-naturedly.

He shook his head, his eyes suddenly dreamy as well as laughing. "I pointed out the sights without filling in the historical details. They wouldn't have heard me anyway. They were too glued to their cell phones."

"Excellent. I have a feeling that you and I are going to get along famously." Giving him a saucy wink, she ran up the stairs, her voice immediately ringing out with an air of authority. "Good afternoon, everyone. I'm Alison Pickles, your local guide, and I'm here with the promise that for the next twelve days, you can expect to have the time of your lives."

There was a slight delay before the group broke out in applause, punctuated by hoots and a smattering of whistles. I guess the guys needed time to look up from their cell phones before they could react to how pretty she was.

Steele stared up at her through the open door. "Wow."

"She's a lovely person," I said, giving his arm a playful squeeze. "You'll have beautiful children." I ranged a look up and down the street. "Is my dad back—the guy you dropped off before leaving on your tour? Pioneer Seed Corn hat? Blue jeans? New cell phone?"

"My buddy Bob? Sure thing. He was waiting for us when we pulled up."

I grinned. "You're buddies already? With my dad?"

He bowed his head toward me, unable to suppress a smile. "We shared a rather intimate experience before he got on the bus. He showed me every single photo he'd taken in the last hour."

"Oh, no! I apologize for his taking up your time."

"Don't apologize. He got some great shots of Seward."

I stared at him in disbelief. "He did?"

"You wanna believe it. Interesting composition. Great angles. Art pieces in the making. He said he was going to upload them to the new website that everyone in the group was using."

"No kidding?"

"Your dad's got quite the eye. Tells me he's a grain farmer. Hate to say it, but I think he's been in the wrong profession all his life. He would have killed as a photographer." He swept his hand toward the stepwell. "I'm ready to head out if you are."

Dad a photographer? Either Steele was into primitive art or Dad had finally managed to take photos of something other than dirt and rocks.

I beamed at the thought. I guess genius sometimes needed an assist to help tease it into the open, which filled me with regret for every bad word I'd ever said about cell phones.

"So can I pick 'em or what?" I boasted to Etienne as I slid into the seat beside him.

"She's impressive," he conceded. "The real test will be how well she handles Bernice."

"My money's on Alison," I whispered as she opened the mic to begin her spiel.

"While we make our way up to Girdwood, I'll take some time to mosey down the aisle so you can introduce yourselves, but first, I'd like to fill you in on some of the basics of Alaska's history. You probably all learned in grade school that Alaska was purchased from Imperial Russia in 1867 for a mere seven million dollars. And the man who purchased it, US Secretary of State William H. Seward, became a laughingstock for allowing himself to be duped into buying a frozen wasteland that was virtually uninhabitable."

"Doesn't look like it's changed much," cackled Bernice.

Alison paused. "Excuse me, ma'am. What's your name?"

"Bernice. Why? What's it to you?"

"Because you've made a very astute observation, Bernice. Most of Alaska is still uninhabitable. In fact, after the Good Friday earthquake in 1964, Seward itself was virtually uninhabitable. Between the waterfront collapsing into Resurrection Bay, the subsequent tsunami, and the big Standard Oil fuel tanks catching fire and incinerating half the town, Seward was practically wiped off the map. As a point of reference, the road we're traveling on now? It would have been under water."

Oohs. Aahs. Murmurs of astonishment.

Etienne raised surprised eyebrows as he glanced at me, mouthing, "She can handle Bernice."

Yup. I might just have to put myself in charge of hiring all our local guides from now on.

My phone rang with a personalized chime that indicated our newly appointed escort for the Green Acres theme park tour was on the other end. "Hi," I answered in a hushed voice. "Everything okay?"

"Geez, what's wrong with your voice? Omigod—has someone died?"

"Our local guide is talking in the background. I'm being polite."

"Oh. No dead bodies yet. I guess that's good. How big are the mosquitoes?"

"I haven't seen any yet."

"You will. I hope you stocked up on repellent. So…about my next assignment."

"Next assignment? You've just begun *this* one."

My ex-husband, Jack, who'd undergone gender reassignment surgery to become a curvaceous knockout named Jackie, had recently divorced her philandering husband and had been desperate for a job. We'd offered her a travel escort position in our agency and were giving her a test run at the new theme park—five days (two of which were travel days) and four nights, with only eight guests, all of whom were widows and widowers. A small group. A minimum of days. No jet lag. No language barrier. No Bernice Zwerg. With her theater background and extroverted personality, I figured her first tour was bound to be a rousing success, which might induce us to assign her to more lengthy trips abroad.

"I know I'm just getting started, Emily, but I'd like to request a destination other than a converted Iowa cornfield. I feel as if I've been transported back to the Dust Bowl days of the early thirties. Really, my sandals are absolutely ruined. You can't even see the rhinestones."

"Why are you wearing rhinestone sandals in a cornfield?"

"Why does any woman squeeze her feet into strappy flats with a dinky toe box and no discernible arch support? Because they make my feet look small. So…can I expect to be reimbursed if I list them as a loss on my clothing allowance?"

"You don't *have* a clothing allowance, Jack." Even though the world now knew her as Jackie, we both understood that she'd always be Jack to me.

45

Silence. "You were serious? No kidding? I thought you were pulling my leg."

"So aside from your wardrobe malfunctions, how are you doing so far? Any concerns with the group?"

"These people are so sweet, Emily. The dust doesn't seem to bother them at all. They're not even wheezing. They're much more tolerant than your regulars. Less whiny. More mentally alert. Better auditory skills. They're still neurotically punctual, but I don't mind because they adore me. It's so cute. The guys follow me around like lost puppies and the ladies are all clamoring for beauty tips. I might throw a makeover party in my room tonight because if there's one thing that bonds us girls, it's our eagerness to learn how to apply expensive cosmetic products. And I brought plenty with me, so I'm happy to share."

"That's really nice of you, Jack." Despite her narcissistic tendencies, she did show occasional signs of thinking about someone other than herself.

"I know. I'm hoping it'll be worth a few brownie points on my evaluation. Oops! Gotta run—the boys just bought me a novelty snack: deep fried corn on the cob dipped in chocolate. Maybe I can scarf it down before the dust hits it. Bye for now. Oh, and I'll mark you down as an undecided on the clothing allowance thing."

"No! *No clothing allowance.*" I followed up by texting her those same words in capital letters, just in case she hadn't heard.

She replied by sending me a happy face emoji.

I love being taken so seriously by my employees.

FOUR

OUR JOURNEY TOWARD GIRDWOOD on the Seward Highway had us meandering through a national forest, around gleaming bodies of water, and alongside mountainous foothills, enjoying what Alison told us was one of the most scenic byways in America. It provided plenty of Kodak moments between Seward and Girdwood, but not one PDQ, 7-Eleven, or Kwik Trip, making it a virtual desert in the convenience store department. I'd never seen so much natural beauty unspoiled by signage for cheap gas, 64-ounce fountain drinks, or chili corn dogs.

"The area up ahead used to be a thriving little town called Portage," Alison announced as a long bay came into view. "It had a great location on the bay here, which is the Turnagain Arm branch of Cook Inlet, but the Good Friday earthquake completely obliterated it. The only reminder that it once existed are the trees we're about to pass on your right—or at least what's left of them. We call it the Ghost Forest."

Steele slowed the bus as we passed a sunken marsh choked with fractured tree trunks that were gray as ash. "This is what happens when sea water inundates a root system. It kills the entire forest, leaving what you see today—a really spooky bog of petrified spruce trees. Not a place you'd be keen to visit on Halloween." She peered out the windshield with concern. "I hope we don't lose our sunny day, but I'm seeing clouds on the horizon, and in the higher elevations, that could mean fog. Let's hope it holds off until after dinner so you can appreciate the view of Turnagain Arm from two thousand feet up." She turned back to the group, wagging a finger at them with intended good humor. "I hope you're paying close attention to what I'm telling you because there's going to be a test later."

The bus erupted in laughter and applause. Not even Bernice hurled a wisecrack.

Yup. Alison sure was a people person.

As signs appeared announcing our approach to Girdwood, Alison continued her narrative. "In the 1800s Girdwood was known as Glacier City, but that changed after an Irish immigrant landed in town. His name was James Girdwood. He had arrived in New York City when he was twenty years old, made a fortune selling Irish linen, then decided to head west. He did so much to improve the Glacier City settlement, they eventually named it after him."

I wasn't sure what improvements she was talking about because when we drove past the town's one main street, it looked as if Girdwood was an isolated backwater with a few eclectic businesses housed in ramshackle buildings. That a town this rustic could be home to a purported grand hotel seemed an impossibility...until we rounded a bend down a long forested road to discover a sweeping structure bounded by evergreens and mountains and landscaped with ponds, fountains, statuary, and a profusion of summer flowers. The multi-tiered pagoda-inspired roof ranged over an area that looked to be the length of two football fields, presiding atop an updated version of what resembled a Far Eastern palace. Sleekly designed, with dramatic architectural angles and acres of window glass, it was the proverbial diamond in the rough...and we'd be enjoying its amenities for two whole nights at a substantial discount.

Could I strike a deal or what?

As we pulled into the circular drive, Etienne took over the mic to reiterate our schedule. "You should be able to check into your rooms immediately, so after you've freshened up a bit and sneaked a peek at the amenities the hotel has to offer, head down to the lobby around six o'clock. Our dinner reservations aren't until seven, but I'd like to give you time to explore the mountaintop before you sit down to eat. There's no dress code for the restaurant, so you can be as casual as you'd like. And since it'll stay light until at least two or three in the morning, you won't have to worry about squeezing in all your picture-taking before dark, because it won't be getting dark."

"How are we supposed to get up to this mountain?" shouted out Dick Teig.

"Aerial tram. The station is located just behind the hotel. After we've gathered in the lobby, we'll all walk over together. Any other questions?"

"I have one," called Delpha Spillum. "If the inside of this place looks as good as the outside, do we have to leave?"

"Do you mean tonight?" asked Etienne. "Or ever?"

"I'm just saying that if we have access to a pool, hot tub, and sauna, I might skip tonight's festivities in favor of spending a relaxing evening pampering myself."

"Me too," said Goldie Kristiansen. "*Aerial tram* sounds like it might be worse than *whale watching boat*, and thank you very much, but I've had more than my fill of motion sickness for one day."

"Oh, come on, ladies," encouraged Alison. "The tram ride only lasts seven minutes and the views from the top are spectacular. The hotel swimming pool and sauna will still be here tomorrow, unlike your dinner reservations, which were probably made months in advance. Trust me, you'll kick yourselves tomorrow if you stay behind."

"We'll see," hedged Goldie. "I could end up kicking myself if I *do* go, so I might just decide to join Delpha."

· · · · · · · · · ·

Even though Etienne and I arrived in the lobby a half hour early, most of the gang were already there, snapping selfies against the posh backdrop of leather furniture, potted plants, intimate lighting, and expensive artwork. Flitting from the stone fireplace with its antlered moose head, to the spear-wielding Eskimo sculpture in the middle of the floor, to the Arctic habitat display above the main entrance with its stuffed polar bear and blue lighting, they were atwitter with excitement. Not, I suspected, because they were about to dine in one of Alaska's finest four diamond restaurants, but because they were finally getting a chance to break out their selfie sticks, purchased in bulk from Pills Etcetera for a fraction of the price advertised by the big-box stores.

Iowa seniors are incredibly adept at scouring the weekly shopper's guide to find really good deals on flimsy plastic items made in politically repressed countries.

Dad was sitting in one of the leather armchairs by the fireplace brandishing his cell phone while Osmond, George, and the two Dicks stood behind him, pointing fingers at whatever Dad was showing them. "Look at that." I nudged Etienne. "Dad's having a conversation with the guys. Isn't that sweet? He's really opening up."

"I'm not sure it's an actual conversation, bella."

"Why?"

"His lips aren't moving."

"I don't know what's so special about the pictures your dad took," groused Bernice as she walked toward us. "Shoot, Osmond's ten-second video of 'Bird Sitting On Large Rock' is more popular than your father's stuff." She swiped her finger over her touch screen. "Number of likes for Osmond? Sixteen. Average for all your father's uploads? Two. Look at the trash he posted." She angled her phone so I could see and began flipping through his photo gallery. "A lamppost. A garbage can. Pickup trucks. A squiggly crack in the sidewalk. Talk about derivative. He needs to get with the program. Think outside the box."

"But...but Steele was *very* complimentary when he saw Dad's photos."

"Oh, right. It takes a *huge* amount of effort to suck up to the boss. You are *so* naïve. Who has more credibility about photography? A pretty boy bus driver or the woman whose face once graced the pages of a whole host of now-defunct magazines?"

I gave her a squinty look. "Did you post content too?"

"Of course."

"How many likes do you have?" Maybe on this website, *two* likes might be considered good.

"I'll put it in perspective for you: Dick Stolee's stupid video of 'Glacier Gives Birth to Iceberg' has 148 likes. *My* video, which I've cleverly entitled 'Panicked Boat Passengers Narrowly Escape Death from Approaching Tsunami,' had over a thousand the last time I looked."

"There was no tsunami," I argued, my voice rising in tandem with my shock.

"Okay. A wave. Same thing."

"No, it's not."

"Loved the selections in your father's photo gallery," chirped Alice Tjarks as she brushed by us.

Bernice snorted. "Must have been Alice who gave him the two sympathy likes. There's a bleeding heart in every crowd. Lunkheads."

I sighed as Bernice shuffled off, my heart breaking as I watched Dad sit in contented silence while the Dicks whooped it up behind him. I looked up at Etienne. "Do you think Dad'll be crushed if his photos get panned on that website?"

"I think your father has his priorities in the right place, bella. He'll survive despite the snub." He kissed the crown of my head. "Be right back. I want to check the front desk for messages."

I thought about perusing his photo gallery myself but figured my hands were tied until someone gave me a URL more specific than "new website." Scanning the room, I spotted Nana in an alcove with George and was about to wend my way in their direction when Orphie Arneson stopped me.

"Have you heard anything about a tornado hitting Windsor City, Emily?"

My stomach went into freefall. My breath caught in my throat like an oversized hairball. "Omigod, not another one! Was anyone hurt? When did it happen?"

"I don't know if it happened or not, but Al was supposed to call me at precisely five o'clock and he didn't, so I was wondering if a tornado might have gone through and taken out all the cell towers."

I felt a little lightheaded as air rushed back into my lungs. "So you think the reason Al didn't call was due to a massive technical problem?"

"I guess having all our cell towers wiped out would be considered a technical problem, right?"

"Was he going to call you at five o'clock *his* time or *your* time?"

"I told him to call me at five o'clock every day." Her gaze floated upward as she searched her memory, looking suddenly guilty. "But I might have forgotten to specify which time zone."

"If he thought he was supposed to call you at five o'clock Iowa time, you should have received a call at two o'clock Alaska time."

Orphie shook her head. "Never happened."

"So that narrows things down, doesn't it?"

"It should. But he didn't call me at five o'clock Alaska time either."

I checked my watch. "It's closing in on nine o'clock in Iowa. Anything going on tonight in Windsor City that might be occupying his time? City council meeting, maybe?"

Her eyeballs seemed to freeze in her sockets as she stared at me, looking abashed. "Oh geesch, that's right. Council meeting tonight and there's a lot on the agenda, so…" She tucked in her lips and lifted her shoulders in an embarrassed shrug. "I'm so sorry, Emily. I'm remembering now that he said this could be an all-nighter, so he might not have a chance to call at all. He's so dedicated." She smiled proudly. "I keep encouraging him to run for Congress. Of course, the downside is we'd have to move to Washington. But the upside is he'd only have to work half as much."

As I maneuvered my way around the furniture toward Nana, I saw Alison hurry across the floor to join us, looking like a million bucks in a short flirty skirt and clingy top. "My watch stopped," she apologized as she joined the group. "Am I the last one to arrive? I was terrified I'd be late on my first night out."

"Yeah," Bernice said dryly. "You're lucky we didn't leave without you."

"We're still missing a few," Margi Swanson commented.

"Mostly the book club folks," added Tilly.

"If the book lovers keep holding us up like this, I vote to leave 'em behind," fussed Bernice. "We could be knocking back drinks in the restaurant bar already if we didn't have to stand around here waiting for those bozos to arrive."

"This is their first time traveling with us," explained Margi, "so they obviously don't have their schedules quite synchronized with ours yet."

"Speak of the devil," said Dick Teig, breaking into applause as Thor Thorsen strode toward us, charging in front of Florence as if she were an afterthought.

Whistles. Hoots. More clapping.

"'Bout time you showed up," needled Dick Stolee.

"What's your problem?" challenged Thor. "We're here, aren't we? No thanks to Florence. Blame her if you have any complaints."

Why did I get the impression that Thor was quite willing to blame Florence for just about everything?

As the guys continued to razz Thor, Delpha Spillum appeared from a side corridor off the stairs, looking out of breath and uncustomarily rattled as she loitered on the perimeter of the room, her gaze darting back and forth as if she were searching for someone. I couldn't tell from her swirly pink-and-black speed tights if she'd decided to join us for dinner or remain at the hotel, but if she was looking for someone, I suspected it might be Goldie. Could it be that the ladies had decided to make alternate plans that included neither a mountaintop nor an aerial tram?

I waved to her from across the lobby, but she'd shifted her attention to the arrival of the remaining latecomers, Goldie, Grover, and Ennis, who were making their way across the floor, egged on by cheers and more clapping.

But Delpha was neither cheering nor clapping.

Her teeth were clenched, her eyes were narrowed, and her gaze was locked on the trio, not with longtime affection and accord but with pure, unadulterated loathing.

FIVE

"Tower swing!"

Everyone grabbed for a handhold as the tram car swayed left and right on its way past one of its supporting towers.

Woos. Giggles. Stumbling. But Goldie Kristiansen didn't look as if she was about to lose her cookies, so that was a plus.

With fewer than two dozen of us in a tram that held sixty, everyone was able to claim a decent spot at one of the car's observation windows, so we were spared any complaints from Bernice about not being able to see. The gang collapsed their selfie sticks to limit the risk of knocking each other's brains out inside the tram, but they continued to snap their selfies, with large images of their own teeth and nostrils obscuring the ruggedness of the terrain below.

Dad had yet to master the art of the selfie, so with Mom oohing and aahing beside him as she pointed out mountains and trees, he shot his photos the old-fashioned way, with something other than his own face filling the frame.

"Okay, folks," announced our youthful tram attendant in his mirrored aviator glasses and shaggy hair, "I'm Cody, and we're taking off here at 250 feet above sea level and will work our way up to 2,330 feet. That'll take us seven minutes at a gnarly twelve miles an hour."

Thor stood in front of a window with his camera whirring nonstop as he aimed it back down the slope toward the hotel. Florence stood dutifully at his side, weighted down by only two camera cases this evening. I spotted Delpha at the opposite end of the car, so as our attendant continued to talk, I inched my way in her direction, fearful that if she was warring with her longtime friends, it would have a negative impact on the rest of the group. Since my escort's manual advised that a competent tour escort would try to smooth over guests' altercations before they got out of hand, I was on it.

Cody's microphone crackled. "If you look out the window to the right of the cabin, you'll see the Turnagain Arm branch of Cook Inlet. It looks like a big mudflat now, but it has one awesome high tide, second only to the Bay of Fundy. The wave on the leading edge of the incoming tide can sometimes be as high as ten feet and reach speeds of fifteen miles per hour, so if you want to hang ten in Alaska, that's the place to do it."

"I'm tickled you decided to join us tonight, Delpha," I enthused. "What changed your mind?"

"My stomach. I saw the restaurant's menu and decided it looked a lot more appetizing than deli take-out at the hotel."

"Was Goldie okay with that?"

"Sure. Why wouldn't she be?"

I shrugged. "You made an evening of luxury at the resort sound so tempting that I just wondered if she might be disappointed that you opted to follow the program."

"Nope." But her voice was tight despite her denial. "We talked it over by phone and agreed that when I get back tonight, I'll reserve time for the two of us in the sauna tomorrow, along with appointments for massages and facials. We're going to make a day of it while the rest of you do whatever it is you're planning to do."

"Dog mushing demonstration for some. Free day for others."

"I might even manage to squeeze a hike in. Did you see the brochure in the room? There's hiking trails all over this mountain. I might have to test out a couple just to walk off tonight's dinner." She leaned over to give her quadriceps a vigorous rub. "Two days without meaningful exercise. I feel like my muscles are turning to mush."

"So you and Goldie haven't…haven't had a falling out or anything?"

She gave me a bewildered look. "Goldie and I have been best friends forever—since we were in kindergarten. I can't think of anything that would cause us to have a falling out." Her bewildered look grew defensive. "Why would you even think that?"

"I—"

"I'm closer to Goldie Kristiansen than I am to my own sister, and…and I resent your suggesting that there's bad blood between us. Goldie and I are like *this*." She wrapped her middle finger around her forefinger in the iconic symbol of togetherness. "There's nothing I wouldn't do for Goldie or she for me. And it's been like that forever." She skewered me with a decidedly unfriendly glare. "No disrespect, Emily, but I'd appreciate it if you wouldn't feel so free to make insinuations about things you know nothing about. Now, if you'll excuse me."

"I'm sorry. I—"

"To your left you'll notice multiple rivers of snow in the valley," Cody continued as Delpha headed to the opposite end of the cabin. "Those are glaciers—six of them, and there's a seventh at the top of the mountain that's within walking distance of the restaurant. But if you plan on seeing it, I suggest you do it before that cloud front up ahead decides to run into us."

Had I misread the hateful look Delpha had given her friends back in the lobby? Or had I simply imagined seeing something that wasn't there? Either way, I think I just failed the tour escort competency test big-time.

As I regarded the dense evergreen forest below us without actually seeing it, Bernice shuffled up beside me. "Where's pretty boy tonight?"

I looked over my shoulder to locate Etienne. "Over there with Osmond and Alice."

She clucked in disgust. "Why do you assume I'm talking about your husband? You think just because he has piercing blue eyes, whipcord muscles, dimples like the Grand Canyon, and a sexy accent that I was talking about him? Hey, he's not the only show horse in the circus anymore. I was talking about hottie number two. The one with the soap-opera name that oozes sex."

"Steele?" I chuckled. "He sent me a text saying that although he'd love to join us this evening, he had a ton of paperwork to catch up on, so if he wanted to keep his job, he needed to devote some serious face time to his mileage charts. Driving a bus involves a lot more work than simply driving the bus."

"Beauty *and* brains. Too bad he wimped out. Oh, well." She smiled, lifting her eyebrows in anticipation. "Lots of nights ahead of us yet."

Yup. That's exactly what this tour was missing: Bernice putting moves on our bus driver. *Oh, God.*

"We had 460 inches of snow at the base of the resort this last winter," Cody announced as we neared the terminus, "and 980 inches at the top. Lucky for you tourists, most of it has melted. Tower swing!"

We grabbed for handholds again as the car swayed on its cable. I glanced toward our destination—at the building with its ranch-style design, open decking, and dark exterior siding—and was surprised to find it rather unremarkable looking. Perched on stilts that bore into the side of the mountain, it looked less like a Four Diamond restaurant and more like a Swiss mountain retreat whose occupants were professionally trained female assassins that James Bond would have to eliminate in order to save the world.

"Trams leave every ten minutes or so," Cody said as we arrived at the platform, "and they're in operation until a half hour after the restaurant closes. Watch your step as you offload." He unlatched the locks and slid the door open. "Enjoy yourselves, folks."

"This way!" instructed Alison, who'd already positioned herself at the head of the group. After leading us beyond the tram platform to an observation deck at the back of the structure, she motioned for us to form a circle around her. "If you'd like to hike to the glacier, follow the sign posts thataway." She pointed to the heavy-shouldered mountains that formed a protective bowl around us. "It's not that far away, so you can get there and back with plenty of time to spare before dinner. If you'd prefer to simply wander around the immediate area, I'll caution you to be mindful of your footing. The landscape rises *and* falls, so if you have balance issues, try to stay on the even terrain. That round building over there is the Roundhouse Museum. If you want to check out old photographs of Girdwood and read about the construction history of the facilities around you, that's the place you'll want to visit. If none of that sounds appealing, I'd recommend the restaurant bar, where you can lounge in a relaxing atmosphere while sipping your favorite libation until dinner."

"Where are *you* headed?" asked Grover, his gaze traveling up the length of Alison's long, shapely legs.

Alison stared down at her short skirt and strappy sandals. "Since I'm not exactly dressed for hiking, I think I'll head over to the museum. I never tire of seeing those old photographs. And you're all certainly welcome to join me. Oh, and before I forget, steer clear of the avalanche guns. Don't go near them. Don't touch them. Big problem if you do. Okay? So let's all plan to regroup in the restaurant at seven. Enjoy your exploration!"

"Where are we going, Thor?" asked Florence as she struggled to shift the camera bags to a more comfortable position.

"I'm going to the museum, but I think you should check out the glacier. I don't want to waste my time hoofing over there if it's a photographic bust. You can text me a picture when you get there and I'll decide what I want to do."

Florence looked puzzled. "We're not going together? But… what if you need one of your other zoom lenses in the museum?"

"I'll manage, Florence," he said sharply, adding in a more belligerent tone, "Godfrey Mighty, can't you get by on your own for even a few minutes? Quit following me around like you're my shadow, would you? Go…go do something on your own for once."

Stunned silence from the group, followed by gasps and uncomfortable stares.

Florence stood perfectly still, absorbing the shock, Thor's words hitting her like a slap to her face.

"Florence would do plenty on her own if she didn't have to spend so much time catering to your stupid whims," Delpha shot back. "You load her down like she's your personal pack mule. Look at her! Why can't you carry your own damn equipment? What are you, six?"

Thor slatted his eyes. "I don't recall asking for your opinion."

"Tough. I might have sold my newspaper, but I haven't shut down my editorial comments."

"Hey, mind your own business before I—"

"Before you what?" she challenged. "Bring it on, Thor, whatever you've got. I'm not afraid of you."

"Stop!" demanded Florence, her voice echoing through the valley like a rifle shot. "I'm sorry all of you have had to witness this little scene. You have my word it won't happen again."

And with those words, she seemed to transform before our eyes as if a switch had been flipped—shedding her timid cocoon to emerge in more formidable form, like a superhero character without the flashy costume. She suddenly seemed taller, fiercer, more cunning.

She nodded toward Delpha, her words measured. "Thank you for leaping to my defense, but I'm perfectly capable of handling any issues I might have with my husband by myself, without the need for outside interference. Not now. Not ever." She lasered a look at

Thor. "Enjoy your visit to the museum." Shrugging out of the nylon straps that crisscrossed her chest, she dumped his camera cases on the deck. "You might want to take these with you." Dusting off her hands and squaring her shoulders, she smiled with impish satisfaction. "Who's up for hiking to that glacier?"

It was as if she'd hit the reboot button after a disruption in programming. Shaking off the awkwardness of the moment, the group began to breathe normally again, followed by foot shuffling and obvious indecision. Orphie and Goldie rushed to Florence's side in a show of solidarity, but Florence shook off their attempted hugs in favor of marching down the stairs and striking out toward the glacier with both women in tow.

"I'm going with Florence," announced Tilly as she headed toward the stairs, her walking stick making little thumping sounds on the decking.

"Me too," said Nana, chasing behind her.

"Hurry up, Bob." Mom grabbed Dad's arm, dragging him toward the stairs, close on Nana's heels. "We've gotta keep up because you know she's gonna try to lose us."

"Wait," objected Osmond. "We should take a vote. Show of hands: How many people think we should see the glacier fir—"

"Oh, put a sock in it, would you?" Lucille Rasmussen bristled at him as she scurried after the girls.

They scattered in opposite directions after that, as if an invisible dividing line had been drawn. Thor snatched his equipment off the deck with a grudging gesture and followed most of the guys behind Alison, while most of the women followed Florence. Most of the women, that is, except Delpha, who stormed down the stairs in menacing silence, taking off in the direction of the ski lifts, and

Bernice, who stood sneering as she watched both groups depart. "The drama of it all," she jeered in a mocking tone. "I'll be at the bar, trying to forget that I'm holed up with these clowns for the next two weeks."

As she headed off toward the restaurant, I exchanged a frustrated look with Etienne. "How does this happen? These people were all supposed to *like* each other."

"It's the age-old battle of the sexes, bella. The ladies versus the gents. And the ladies are obviously intending to stick together."

"I suppose." My phone chimed. I checked the readout. "Jackie again."

"You'd best answer that."

"Would you like to talk to her?" I held the phone out to him.

He waved off the invitation. "I heard Alison say 'avalanche guns,' so I'm thinking I should locate them before the Dicks do, just in case. I can't see them spending an hour in a museum, no matter how good-looking Alison is."

"I'll catch up to you after I finish my call." I raised my phone to my ear. "Hi, Jack. What's up?"

"Um…does your insurance cover catastrophic medical emergencies?"

I froze like an arthritic limb. *Oh, God.* "What happened?"

"Well, I was applying a base coat of my uber-velvety sheer and luminous foundation on Mildred's scrubbed and gently polished face when things started to go wrong."

"What kind of things?"

"Her face swelled up like a helium balloon."

Oh, God. "She must have been allergic to something in the makeup. But she was still breathing, right?"

"That was the next thing that went wrong."

I needed to sit down.

"She started complaining about her throat closing up."

I hurried into the building and found a seat in the foyer area of the restaurant.

"She said she felt like she was breathing through a straw, so I thought I better call 911."

Heart racing, hands trembling, I nodded. "Definitely the right thing to do, Jack. Good call."

"And my timing was spot-on because about the time the paramedics walked through the door, she stopped breathing."

I hung my head. *Oh, God.* "So...so is Mildred—" My voice cracked. "Please don't tell me she's dead, Jack."

"No! She's not dead. She's sitting here drinking some pop."

"In the hotel?"

"At the hospital. The paramedics got her breathing again, but because of her age they decided to transport her to the hospital anyway. They don't like it when eighty-six-year-olds suffer cardiac arrest."

My heart rate slowed. My hands stopped trembling. "Thank God she's all right."

"Yup. Mildred's a sport. But they're going to keep her in the hospital overnight for observation, just as a precaution. They want to make sure her face returns to its normal size." She lowered her voice to a whisper. "Which is a good thing because between you and me, Emily, balloon-faced is not a good look for her."

"Do you want me to talk to her?"

"Not necessary. I have everything under control except for the insurance thing, which Mildred was asking about. Does her health insurance cover this or does yours, because she doesn't think her supplemental will kick in to pay for out-of-network charges."

"Well, I…give me a few minutes to call our agent, and I'll call you right back."

After being shunted to his voicemail, I left a message, then sat waiting patiently for his return call. Amid the deafening clank and grind of motors as the tram released another carload of tourists onto the platform, I accessed the file for the guests who were signed up for the Green Acres tour so I could peruse Mildred's application and medical history. No checkmark in the box for known allergies, but she was obviously allergic to something. I studied the rest of her application while the door to the restaurant opened and closed with newcomers drifting in to have a look around. I looked up occasionally to find men in sport coats and women in shimmery dresses heading toward the hostess podium, but the majority of the folks who popped in for a look-see were typical tourists dressed in jeans, shorts, sweatshirts, and baseball caps that promoted the American flag, the Chicago Cubs, and Kermit the Frog drinking what looked like a mug of beer, which was just plain wrong. Kermit wasn't old enough to drink, was he?

On the last page of Mildred's application, I noticed a checkmark in a box that suddenly took on more importance, so by the time the agent finally did call, I was practically giddy with relief. When our conversation ended, I called Jackie with the good news.

"Tell Mildred she doesn't have to worry about medical charges. She bought the catastrophic travel insurance we offered, so she's covered one hundred percent."

"Huh. So those policies aren't scams?"

"No, they're not scams! We're not offering fake insurance out of a call center in Nigeria."

"Okay, okay. I'll tell Mildred. She'll be tickled pink." She lowered her voice again. "Mildred doesn't *seem* like the litigious type, but out of curiosity, what happens if she sues me?"

"We're insured for that, but do me a favor and don't offer any more beauty makeovers, okay?"

"You got it."

The time on my phone read 6:47, which was way too late to start exploring the grounds, so instead I decided to sit and wait for everyone to arrive, which should be any moment now. I mean, by Iowa standards, the whole group was already unforgivably late.

The minutes ticked by.

6:48.

6:49.

I stared at the door, expecting it to burst open and the gang to stampede through.

6:50.

6:51.

Where were they? This wasn't like them.

Too anxious to wait any longer, I exited the restaurant and—with the roaring whirr of the tram motors ringing in my ears—hurried out to the observation deck…where I was enveloped by a thick cloud of haze that was as blinding as an Iowa blizzard. I swept my hand through the haze, hoping to see the outline of something familiar in the distance, but nothing was visible in the white-out—not the museum nor the ski lift nor the neighboring mountains.

The frontal system that had threatened all afternoon had finally descended, marooning the gang on the mountaintop, unable to see a hand in front of them.

Oh, God.

SIX

"HEL-LOOOOOOO?"

Rather than echo mellifluously through the mountains and valleys, the word thudded headlong into the fog and dropped to the deck like an anvil.

I squinted into the mist, flapping my hands in front of myself to clear a space, but the mist refused to be cleared.

I made a megaphone of my hands. "Etienne? Nana? Mom?"

Crickets.

Uff-da. How could they find their way back if they couldn't see anything? What if they went the wrong way in this soup? They could fall off the side of the mountain, one by one, like…like lemmings.

A wave of panic washed over me.

Oh my god. They could all die.

As I was about to run back into the building for help, I noticed a slight glimmer in the haze—a far-off corona of light that pierced the fog like a lighthouse beacon and seemed to be floating in my direction.

"Etienne?" I shouted again.

"Emily!" It was Etienne's voice, muffled as if by cotton batting and seeming to radiate from every direction, but his voice nonetheless.

Relief surged through me. "You're headed straight toward me, sweetie!" At least I thought he was. "Keep walking. You're almost here."

"I'm not alone."

The corona of light drew closer, and as it did, I noticed another, and another, until it seemed he was dragging a string of Christmas tree lights behind him.

"Almost there," his voice rang out. "Don't let go of your selfie sticks until I tell you."

I inched my way across the observation deck and down the stairs, then tapped the flashlight icon on my phone and aimed the beam outward.

Etienne appeared like an apparition out of the mist, one hand holding his cell phone, the other locked onto the selfie-stick of the person behind him, guiding him forward. "Keep moving," he instructed as a whole conga line of people emerged from the haze, each one clinging to the selfie stick of the person in front of and behind them like links in a chain. "Gather around Emily so we can count heads."

"Isn't this somethin'?" Nana scampered over to me in her size 5 sneakers. "The clouds just come down from the sky and swallowed us up. Too bad we can't see nuthin' like this back home."

Well, we probably could, but the closest thing Iowa had to a 2,300-foot mountain was Lars Bakke's grain elevator.

"I started out with fourteen," affirmed Etienne. "Have we lost anyone along the way?" As he began counting heads, a trill of both relief and excitement swept over the group as they acknowledged their good fortune to have escaped with their lives on the way back.

"One false step and it could have been over the edge for all of us," Alice marveled in a breathless rush. "Down the mountain, into the valley, and *splat*."

"Let's hear it for Etienne," urged Lucille. "The man who saved our bacon!"

Clapping. Cheers. Whistles.

"How would we have gotten back if Etienne hadn't found us?" asked Grace Stolee.

"We would have had to wait until the fog lifted," said Tilly.

"We couldn't have done that," argued Dick Teig. "We would've been late for dinner."

"We're already late for dinner," cried Margi. "Look at the time!"

"Fourteen," announced Etienne. "All guests accounted for."

Reverting to full panic mode, the gang swarmed up the stairs and across the deck like locusts descending on a field of corn.

"All the good seats are probably gone by now," lamented Helen Teig as they stampeded into the building amid a rumble of whines, groans, and muttering. And in a swirl of mist, they were gone.

"There's one silver lining to fog that's thick as pea soup," I quipped as I wrapped my arms around Etienne's waist. "At least there won't be any fighting over who gets the window seats at dinner tonight." I gave him a bone-crushing squeeze and held him close. "I was so worried about you."

71

"I'm sorry, bella." He pressed his lips to the crown of my head. "The conditions changed so quickly."

"I'll never understand how you found your way back in this murk."

He held up his phone. "GPS enhanced by topographical maps. I downloaded a few so-called lifesaving apps from the National Geographic Society before we left."

Which made me feel a twinge guilty about cancelling my subscription to their magazine a decade ago.

"My hunch was right about the Dicks," he continued. "They lasted less than two minutes in the museum before leaving to search out the avalanche gun, but since I'd arrived first, I was able to monitor them…until the conditions started to deteriorate. So the three of us decided to trek over to the glacier, which was rather fortuitous because the group was dithering about what course of action to take—either stay where they were until conditions improved or head back to the terminal and risk tumbling down the mountainside. So they were inching toward major gridlock."

"How come they didn't just take a vote?"

"Osmond was in the museum. They were afraid that taking a vote without him would be unethical."

"Of course they would." I tossed my head back and laughed. "Is that when you stepped in with your conga-line selfie-stick solution?"

"It seemed the only way to have them hold onto each other while using the flashlights on their phones at the same time. Since Goldie, Florence, Orphie, and your parents don't have selfie sticks, I interspersed them between the people who did, and miraculously, we made it back without any injuries and just in time for dinner."

"Genius." I rose onto my toes and placed a gentle kiss on his mouth. "You're like…like the St. Bernard rescue dog of the Grand Girdwood Resort and recreation area."

"With proficiencies in alpine rescues and crowd control"—his voice grew husky as he whispered close to my ear—"and other skills that are best demonstrated in the privacy of the bedroom." He returned my kiss then with a slowness and warmth that made the bottoms of my feet tingle.

Woo! The Swiss side of his brain might be downplaying his derring-do, but the Italian side was really turned on.

When we entered the restaurant foyer, the excitement level of the group seemed to have increased exponentially. Laughter. Chatter. Back-slapping. "You don't know what you missed," Dick Teig tittered to Osmond and George. "Get a load of this glacier."

Osmond stared at the screen. "Glacier looks an awful lot like your face."

"The glacier's behind me." Dick stabbed his finger at the screen. "But if you look real close, you can see a tiny sliver of it right here beneath my left ear. And look at this one. Alaskan fog. It's gonna become part of my exclusive photo gallery of 'Fog from Around the World.'"

I spied Alison in the center of the lobby, smiling politely, her eyes looking as if they were glazing over as Grover Kristiansen held her hostage in conversational hell, talking at her like a rapid-fire Gatling gun. Ennis and Thor were mingling with the gang nearby, but I didn't see Delpha and her pink-and-black speed tights anywhere. "Can I have your attention?" I called out over the chatter. "Is Delpha already here or are we still waiting for her to arrive?"

Heads swiveled left and right. Palms flew up. Shoulders lifted.

"Destinations Travel party," the hostess announced from the podium. "Your tables are ready."

The group pushed forward like a surging tide, eliciting a terrified gasp from the hostess. "Single file, ladies and gentlemen, please! Single file."

"Hold it!" hollered Osmond. "We need to take a vote to decide how we should line up. Show of hands: How many—"

"Random order!" declared Thor Thorsen without waiting for Osmond to finish. "Let's get this show on the road. Get in line or get left behind."

A collective gasp. Indecisive looks. But once Thor stormed to the front of the pack, everyone merged helter-skelter behind him, giving in to his strong-arm tactics without so much as a whimper. Omigod. Was this how long-held democratic practices died? When people allowed themselves to be ordered around by a bully? Intimidated by a meanie? Browbeaten by a self-appointed tyrant?

I stared wide-eyed at Nana as she scrambled into line in front of me. "Why are you letting Thor run the show like this?" I asked in a low voice, shocked that the gang seemed to have lost their collective backbone.

"We're not settin' no precedent or nuthin'," she whispered with a toss of her head in Osmond's direction. "We're just hungry."

Okay. That made me feel better. I'd fixated on the wrong part of their anatomy. The issue wasn't with their backbones. It was with their stomachs.

"Why don't you go in with the group to see them seated," encouraged Etienne. "I'll wait out here for Delpha."

I shook my head. "I'm gonna pop my head into the ladies' restroom here and by the express takeout place. If she's not in either place, I'll send her a text. With any luck we'll both join you in a few minutes."

After failing to find her in either the restaurant restroom or the one at the opposite end of the observation deck, I texted her a message: *WE'RE BEING SEATED FOR DINNER. WHERE ARE YOU?*

Her reply came after I'd waited another five minutes in the restaurant foyer: *HIKING BACK TO RESORT INSTEAD. ONLY 2 MILES.*

I couldn't say her decision surprised me. After her run-in with Thor and her dressing-down by Florence, she'd probably had her fill of adversity for the evening. But I worried that her decision was both ill-timed and dangerous. *WHAT ABOUT THE FOG? CAN YOU SEE?*

CLEARING AS I HIKE FARTHER DOWN.

Which settled my nerves a bit. *BE CAREFUL THEN,* I texted back.

OK.

I entered the dining room to find that not much had changed since the blowup on the deck. Alison entertained Ennis, Thor, and Grover at a separate table for four; Florence, Goldie, and Orphie were seated in a circular booth with Mom and Dad; and the rest of the gang occupied a long table near the stone fireplace. I informed Etienne of Delpha's decision when I took my seat beside him. "I feel terrible for her. Detaching herself like this might help her regroup after her embarrassment on the deck, but I bet she'll regret missing out on this meal. It's supposed to be awesome."

"It's already paid for, bella. So why don't we order something off the menu and deliver it to her door when we get back to the hotel? I'm sure they'll be happy to box it up for us."

Since Goldie was inconveniently located at another table, I couldn't ask her about Delpha's food preferences, so after perusing the menu myself, I sent Delpha another text: *WILL BRING MEAL BACK TO YOU. YOUR CHOICE? LAMB, SALMON, BEEF, DUCK, OR CRAB CAKES?*

After a couple of minutes, I received her reply: *CRAB. THX.*

Apparently, crustaceans are considered less repellent to Iowans if they're disguised as cake.

The meal so exceeded my expectations that I wasn't sure I'd ever be able to walk through the door of another Blimpie's to order a mere hamburger. The braised boar appetizer was exquisitely succulent. The scallop bisque left my taste buds dancing. The Alaskan paella was a mouthwatering sensation of the flavors and textures of scallops, fresh fish, shellfish, and pork. But the pièce de résistance was the pear and cranberry cobbler that arrived warm from the oven with a scoop of ice cream on top.

Our table companions were obviously less impressed with the meal than either Etienne or I because they spent most of their time poring over their recent photos, uploading them to their news website, and updating their Facebook pages. They picked at their appetizers, allowed their soup to go stone cold, and only nibbled at their entrees…because, apparently, the mere process of lifting a fork to their mouths would severely limit the amount of time they could spend fiddling with their phones.

They did manage to scarf down their desserts, however, because by the end of the meal, they probably realized they'd be returning to the resort with empty stomachs. I regarded them with disappointment as the dessert plates were cleared. "How were your meals?"

They nodded offhandedly as they continued to stare at their phones.

"You might actually have enjoyed the meal if you'd given it even half the attention you just showered on your social media sites."

Dick Teig looked up, staring at me aghast. "Sounds to me like you're inviting us to turn off our phones. Am I hearing you right?"

"Mmm...yes."

"Well, speaking for all of us, I think I can safely say that although we appreciate the invitation, we'd rather starve."

"Show of hands," said Osmond. "How many people would rather star—"

"No voting," I snapped.

"But Emily," said Margi, eyes sparkling, face beaming, "we can't turn off our phones. I feel the most incredible jolt of excitement every time my phone pings with an incoming text."

"I react that way, too," confessed Tilly. "It's as exciting as the sensation I felt after drinking an elixir prepared by my witch doctor friend in New Guinea."

Margi wrinkled her nose. "*Eww.* How much did you have to drink?"

"Very little, actually. He served it in a shrunken head, so it was probably less than a shot."

"We're addicted," declared Bernice with a glance in my direction. "Deal with it."

"I will, but I don't want to hear any complaining when you're all forced to seek medical attention for the excruciating pain of texting thumb."

"Fear mongerer," sniped Helen Teig.

"You once told us that if we didn't look up from our phones, we'd miss out on the beauty of our surroundings," accused Grace Stolee, which inspired everyone to lean back in their chairs and throw long looks at the impenetrable fog pressing against the windows.

"You really nailed that one," Bernice wisecracked.

"I haven't mastered the art of predicting the weather yet, Bernice."

"Right." She smiled smugly. "Except that by racing off to gawk at that stupid glacier, no one got to see what I saw right from the bar stool I was sitting on, before the fog set in." She flicked her finger over her display screen. "Snow-capped summits." She panned her phone to left and right so everyone could see the panorama. "Breathtaking mountainscapes." She kept flicking. "A few useless valleys."

"Dang," said Nana, gazing at her screen in awe. "Them mountain scenes are as dazzlin' as Dick's fog close-ups. Can I have a look-see?"

Bernice handed her phone over to Nana, who flipped through the photos with a discerning eye. "Who's these strangers what's in some of your pictures?"

"Distracted tourists who kept wandering into my frame. There oughta be a law that prevents people from walking around without watching where they're going. Imbeciles."

Nana touched the screen to expand the photos. "Huh."

Bernice snapped to attention. "What?"

"I think I figured out what's got these folks so distracted. They're all lookin' down at the cell phones what they're carryin'." She expanded the photo again. "They look like pretty nice ones too."

"See there?" I spoke up, capitalizing on Nana's segue. "Cell phones are to blame for ruining Bernice's photos."

"Bernice is criticizing *other* people's cell phones," Dick Teig pointed out. "Not ours."

"But when you're the ones doing the distracted walking, *you're* the other people!"

Silent stares.

"I don't get it," puzzled Margi.

"She's basically saying that Bernice hates everything," said Dick Stolee.

"I did not!"

"Show of hands," Osmond piped up. "How many people think that—"

"No voting!" I balked.

Etienne placed his hand on my forearm, his voice calm. "It's been a long evening for everyone, so if you've all finished your dessert, why don't we head toward the tram so we can catch the next car down the mountain? There's no rush, but it's already nine thirty, so—"

Napkins flew. Chairs collided. A flurry of tangled limbs and then they were gone, leaving the other two tables of guests to stare after them. "In case you hadn't guessed," Etienne motioned to the remaining tables, "they're heading for the tram."

I regarded our empty table and shook my head at the futility of my efforts. "They're hopeless."

"What is it you Americans say? When you're in a hole, stop digging?"

That might be true, but it did nothing to address my constant fear that if the gang continued to pay more attention to their phones than to where they were walking, one of them was eventually going to end up dead.

SEVEN

AFTER PICKING UP A nifty doggie bag that contained Delpha's entire meal, we boarded the gondola and rode back down the mountain in the ever-present daylight. And as Delpha had indicated, the farther we descended, the more the fog dissipated, so that by the time we arrived at the resort, the fog had completely lifted, although the sky was still overcast at the higher elevation.

"We are treating you to a late start tomorrow," Etienne announced as we flooded into the lobby. "If you close your blackout drapes, you might even get a good night's sleep. The breakfast buffet in the hotel restaurant begins at six and ends at eleven. For those of you signed up for the dog mushing excursion, plan to meet Alison here in the lobby at ten o'clock. She's on dog duty tomorrow. The rest of you will be on your own to either spend the day taking advantage of the hotel's amenities or catch the shuttle into Girdwood to explore the town. Any questions?"

I looked out over the group, wondering if Florence and Thor would be able to settle their differences overnight or if Florence would be giving him the cold shoulder for the rest of the trip. I didn't think their sudden schism would alter the seating on the bus too drastically, but if they decided they didn't want to share a room anymore, we'd be dealing with a major headache.

"No questions?" Etienne concluded. "Then we'll see you tomorrow. Sleep well, everyone."

I watched Florence continue to huddle with Goldie and Orphie while Thor bounded off toward the elevator. I supposed Florence could always bunk with Orphie without too much trouble, but I didn't want to get ahead of myself. Maybe the Thorsens would do us all a favor and sort things out themselves.

Etienne checked the time on his phone. "Do you suppose Delpha is back yet?"

"I certainly hope so. It wouldn't take her three hours to hike two miles downhill, would it? What's her room number?"

After our insistent knocks on her door went unanswered, we decided that either she was in the pool and spa area or a two-mile hike down a two-thousand-foot mountain did indeed take longer than three hours. Etienne handed me her food. "Why don't you head back to the room and relax, bella? I'll check out the pool and join you in a few minutes."

Once back in our room, I located the neat stack of hotel literature left on our dresser and pulled out the map legend for the resort. There were several trails leading down from the mountain. One meandered over what looked like treeless terrain in a series of squiggly switchbacks. Another skirted the perimeter of a dense patch of wooded terrain that offered fewer switchbacks. Yet another cut directly through the woods in what was probably a shorter but potentially more dangerous route. Unfortunately, I had no idea which one Delpha had decided to take, which made any kind of time calculation impossible.

I slanted a look out our hotel window at the great hulking mountain whose summit remained cloaked in fog. "Where are you, Delpha?" I whispered aloud, which is when it struck me that I had the capacity to find out. I mean, I could simply call her. Duh.

I picked up my phone.

I let it ring and ring and ring until I got shunted to her voice-mail.

I sent her a text: *ARE YOU NEAR THE END OF THE TRAIL? GETTING WORRIED.*

I stared at my screen, waiting for a response.

Knockknockknockknock.

I hurried to the door.

"Your father has really gone and done it this time," fussed Mom as she barged into the room, dragging Dad behind her.

"What's he done?"

Mom crossed her arms and drew her eyebrows together over her nose. Dad tucked in his lips and shrugged.

"Show Emily the picture."

After tapping the screen, he handed his phone to me.

"Trees. Very nice content, Dad. Tall, pointy trees, all clumped together. Did you take this from the tram?"

His phone pinged.

"Yup."

Mom sighed her frustration. "You have to look more closely, Emily. Do you see anything else? And no, this isn't a hidden objects game."

"Uh…"

His phone pinged again.

I expanded the photo and studied it more closely. "Well, there's a shadowy patch over in the corner here that looks like—" I squinted at the shadow, its form slowly morphing into a shape that caused my mouth to drop. "Holy crap." I ran to the desk to examine it more closely under the light. "No way can this be real. It can't be real because it looks like...like..."

"A big hairy beast," tittered Mom. "Bigfoot. Exactly. Here I was thinking we could get through a vacation without your father drawing unnecessary attention to himself, but *nooo*."

Ping. Ping. Ping.

"He decides to send his photos off to that website your grandmother recommended, and now his phone won't stop pinging."

"Who's contacting him?"

"Everyone! They're all clamoring for a piece of him. They want phone interviews. And TV interviews. And newspaper interviews. This is apparently the biggest news since...since that famous Hollywood star gave birth to an alien baby."

I pulled a face. "Which star was that?"

"I don't remember. They all look alike to me."

"The stars or the babies?"

Ping. Ping.

"If your father had kept his old camcorder, this wouldn't have happened. He'd have taken pictures of the same old pavement and blue jeans and been ignored by that website instead of being hounded by the press. The international news has already picked up the story." She made a gimme motion for Dad's phone. "Look at this headline: *It Lives!!! Iowa Grain Farmer Shoots Photo of Bigfoot*

Monster in Alaska. And how about this one: *Flesh-Eating Beast on the Loose in Alaska Forest*."

Oh geesh. If this turned into a media circus, our schedule could be completely derailed. On a brighter note, Ennis would probably be thrilled that his crackpot creature theories might not be considered so crackpot anymore.

"Why didn't you say something when you saw the thing, Dad?" I asked gently.

"'Cuz I was only taking pictures of trees." He gave me a beleaguered look. "Those fellas at the website were the ones who spotted it. Not me."

Etienne walked through the door, his steps slow, a grim expression darkening his features.

"What's wrong?" I asked, my voice cracking with sudden fear.

"There's been a mishap on the mountain. The people at the front desk are waiting for the rescue squad to arrive, so they're understandably rattled, but when I told them who I was and that I was missing a guest, they shared what they could with me. The victim is female."

Dread needled down my spine like pincers.

"And she's wearing pink-and-black speed tights."

My knees weakened and my stomach soured. "Oh my god. Delpha?"

Etienne nodded. "She's dead."

EIGHT

"JESUS, MARY, AND JOSEPH," cried Mom. "It's Bob's creature. It's gone on a killing spree!"

Etienne regarded Mom as if she had spinach growing out her ears. "What creature?"

"Bigfoot! Sasquatch! Bob got a picture of him." She stabbed her finger at the window. "On that mountain. From our gondola." She flicked through several screens before holding up Dad's phone in front of Etienne's face. "See this picture? See this shadow in the corner? It's been verified by numerous international news sources. It's Bigfoot. And it's out there lurking in those woods someplace."

Ping.

Etienne eased the phone from Mom's hand and expanded the picture, growing very quiet as he studied the image. "I can't say with any assurance what it is...other than it's fuzzy."

"Are we looking at the same picture?" Mom hovered over Etienne's arm. "That camera has, like, a million pixels. How can you say the image is fuzzy? It's clear as a bell."

"The crea—the *shadow*—is fuzzy, Margaret."

"But don't you think the fuzziness makes it look kinda cuddly?" asked Dad.

Etienne handed the phone back to Mom. "The anomaly in Bob's photo is a curiosity. It is not—I repeat, *not*—an explanation for what has happened to Delpha."

"It is as far as I'm concerned," argued Mom.

"Margaret." Etienne's tone was tempered, patient. "Until we receive feedback from the local authorities, we'd be wise not to speculate about what caused Delpha's mishap. She might have stumbled down a ravine or suffered a medical emergency, or walked into a tree while texting on her phone."

I clapped my hands over my mouth to muffle my gasp. Omigod. Hadn't I just warned them that something like this could happen? Had Delpha, despite all her athletic training and expertise, been engaged in distracted walking when she died? Had she been texting while hiking?

But if that were the case, then...

My breathing slowed as I grasped the implications.

Then I could be complicit in her death because the person she'd been texting was probably...me.

"Or," Mom reiterated, "she might have been attacked by Bigfoot. So when are we going to know what happened to her for sure? Because as long as that thing is out there, none of us are safe."

I clutched Mom's forearm. "You can't repeat your theory to *anyone*. Please, Mom. You'll cause a panic if you start spreading wild rumors. Etienne is right. You have to let the police do their work before you start presenting your own version of the facts."

She arched her brows—a sure sign that she was digging in her heels. I sidled a desperate glance around the room, searching for a way to divert her attention, but no magazines needed arranging. No black socks needed color coding. Nuts.

"I won't presume to tell you how to run your business, Emily, but don't you think your guests have a right to know about the hazards they're facing?"

"But Mom, think about our guests with high blood pressure, with heart trouble, with anxiety problems. How do you think they'll react if they hear they're being stalked by a flesh-eating creature who might be lurking a stone's throw away from the resort?"

"How do those news folks know it's flesh-eating?" asked Dad. "What if it's a gluten-averse lacto-vegetarian? I've heard that's a very popular dietary choice these days."

The expression on Mom's little moon face remained so implacable that I realized I was going to have to ratchet my argument up a notch, which meant zeroing in on the one thing that meant more to her than alphabetizing periodicals or color coding socks.

"What about Nana, Mom? You know she's getting up there in age. Do you think she's strong enough to cope with the stress of being stalked by a monster who may or may not be flesh-eating?"

In less than a heartbeat, Mom's features collapsed like a tower of Jenga blocks. "Jesus, Mary, and Joseph, Emily. Your grandmother—news like this could kill her. She's so old and frail, a threat as terrifying as this could literally jolt her heart into an arrhythmia and cause it to stop beating." She seized my forearm in a death grip. "You can't tell her. You can't breathe a word that it's obvious Delpha was killed by the fuzzball that Bob accidentally photographed. We can't tell her anything about your father's photo. It would be far too frightening for her to process. Your grandmother's very survival is at stake. Promise me, Emily."

"I promise," I said, wincing as I peeled her fingers off my arm.

"Good. Come on, Bob. We're leaving. I have to rethink our itinerary."

"What's wrong with the one we have now?" he asked as he hurried to the door behind her.

"Desperate times call for desperate measures."

Ping! Ping! Ping! went Dad's phone.

"And would you please turn off that phone of yours? Maybe if you ignore their messages, those news services will get the hint and leave you alone."

Slam!

Etienne gave me a questioning look. "Did you mean to do that? Your mother will never let your grandmother out of her sight now."

"I know." I cringed. "I think I just threw Nana under the bus. But I couldn't let Mom connect a string of mythical dots between Dad's photograph and Delpha and let her pass it off as fact. Can you imagine? Our guests would probably be so freaked out, they'd all want to go home. That's called tour suicide."

My phone chimed. I checked the name on the readout. "It's Nana." I scanned the message. "Great. Apparently, Bernice just sent a text blast to the gang with a link to the news articles about Dad's creature."

Etienne waited a beat. "And?"

"And, I quote, 'Dang. How come your father was the only one what seen Bigfoot? Can we go back up that mountain tomorrow? If we don't run into no fog, maybe I can get a selfie with him.'"

Etienne grinned. "Your mother was right to be concerned. I don't believe I've ever heard your grandmother sound quite so terrified."

I gave him the look. "This isn't funny, Etienne. And you know the real kicker? *I* might be the one who caused Delpha's death. Not freaking Bigfoot. *Me.*"

He grazed his fingers over my cheek, his eyes soft, his voice an undertone. "What are you saying?"

"You suggested it yourself. What if texting is to blame for Delpha's death? The person she was texting was probably *me*. Remember? I sent her a message asking what she'd like to order for dinner. What if she took her eyes off the trail for a split second while she was texting back and…and…" I gulped down a mouthful of air. "There's no way to whitewash it. I as good as killed her."

I blinked away tears as Etienne folded me into his arms, cradling my head against his chest. "Do you suppose you could postpone accepting all the blame for this until we have more information? If she'd been crossing a busy city street, her texting might have precipitated her death, but hiking down a mountain trail is entirely different."

"But you told Mom—"

"I *know* what I told your mother, Emily. What else could I have said to challenge the conclusion she'd jumped to? My only recourse was to pepper her with a litany of viable scenarios, none of which changed her mind, by the way." He snuggled me closer and rested his chin on the top of my head. "That didn't happen until you threw your grandmother under the bus."

"Please don't remind me. If Mom does something weird and ruins Nana's holiday, it'll haunt me for the rest of my life." I wriggled out of his embrace, yearning for some sign of reassurance. "So...you don't think I played a part in Delpha's death?"

"I don't. And I say that not as your husband, but as a former police inspector. So will you try to erase the notion from your mind? Please?"

I nodded. "I'll try. But—"

He held up his finger to put me on pause. "To that end, I'm going down to speak to the manager about the situation. Delpha is our guest as well as the hotel's, so I'm going to encourage him to include us in all phases of the investigation. We need to keep her family apprised, so it's rather essential that we're not left out of the loop." He flashed a tentative smile. "Would you mind if I leave you for a while?"

I shook my head. "I need to let everyone know what's happened to Delpha. It's not something I'm looking forward to, but it's better they learn it from me than from someone else's post on social media."

"Would you prefer we tell them together?"

"I can handle it." I heaved a discouraged sigh. "I've had lots of practice."

. . . .

I sent a text blast to everyone in the group except Mom, Dad, and Alison, asking them to come to my room as soon as possible so I could make an important announcement. I figured I'd tell Alison later in private to spare her the upheaval of what could be an extremely emotional group meeting.

They began to arrive almost immediately in groups of two, like the animals on Noah's ark, only with better language skills. And despite the lateness of the hour, they didn't seem tired. I guess relentless daylight tended to energize everyone. They made themselves at home in our room, sitting on the bed, the chairs, the window sill, and the desk, but the buzz in the room wasn't about my unexpected announcement.

It was about Dad's photo.

"I don't see the resemblance to Bigfoot," complained Margi as she stared at her display screen. "It looks like a fir tree to me."

"Then how do you explain the arms?" prodded Helen Teig.

"What arms?" asked Osmond.

"You see those appendages attached to the thing's body?" snapped Helen. "They're called arms."

Osmond squinted at the image on his phone. "They look like evergreen boughs to me."

Nana's eyes rounded to the size of bull's eyes. "You s'pose it could be one of them hybrids?"

"You mean, something that harkens back to ancient mythology?" floated Tilly. "Like the half-human, half-horse centaur? Or the half-human, half-bird harpy? Or the half-human, half-fish merman?"

"You got anything that's half man, half tree?" asked George.

"What are you people discussing?" interrupted Ennis. "What Bigfoot photo?"

In one sweeping motion they whisked their phones into the air and starting talking over each other like analysts on the ten-member panels on CNN, prompting me to let fly one of my signature whistles to quiet them.

Cringing. Hands clapping over ears. Cries of "Ow!" as phones inadvertently collided with ear cartilage.

I answered Ennis's question myself. "My dad was shooting pictures of the scenery on our way up to the restaurant, and, according to some online news bureaus, he managed to capture a photo of what appears to be…uh…Bigfoot."

"Or a random fir tree," muttered Margi.

"Are you serious?" barked Ennis. "And you didn't think to tell me?"

"I only found out myself less than a half hour ago."

"You're not in our Golden Oldies group." Bernice directed a pouty face at Ennis. "So you don't get any of my up-to-the-minute breaking news items."

"Well, could I be included in the future? Who's got this photo cued up so I can see it?" he demanded, his hand outstretched in anticipation.

George slapped his phone into Ennis's palm. "Bigfoot's down here in the corner, partially disguised as a tree."

"He is *not* disguised as a tree," protested Helen. "If you enlarge the picture, you can clearly see his enormous head and long, hairy arms."

"Dude," snorted Dick Stolee as he elbowed Dick Teig, "his head looks even bigger than yours."

"That's not possible," deadpanned Helen.

"How did a bunch of online news bureaus get hold of Bob's photo in the first place?" questioned Ennis as he studied the image.

"It's on account of the website what we found," said Nana. "He uploaded all them photos what he took, and some eagle-eyed fella musta spotted the creature in the trees."

"Creature, my foot," hooted Bernice. "It's fake news made to look like real news to create fake buzz on the Twittersphere."

"It is not," countered Helen. "You're just jealous that your photo isn't the one that's in the limelight."

Bernice skewered her with demon eyes. "My photos will get recognized, and they'll make a bigger splash than Bob's ape. And it won't be any of this cheesy amateur fake garbage."

"You don't know that Bob's photo is fake," challenged Alice. "Those news bureaus are reputable organizations. They're the ones who posted the photo of that candle in their famous montage of ordinary objects that resemble human faces."

"What candle?" asked Grace.

"The one whose wax melted into the spitting image of Mr. Potato Head."

Dick Teig snuffled with laughter. "Try not to take this too hard, Alice, but Mr. Potato Head isn't human."

"That's right. What was I thinking?" She waved her hand as if to sweep away her mistake. "It was Mr. Peanut."

"My favorite was the cornflake," chimed Nana.

"Whose face could you possibly see on a cornflake?" asked Tilly.

"It was s'posed to be Elvis, but it looked a lot more like Robert Mitchum to me."

"Does anyone have a magnifying glass?" Ennis called out. "I can't make out enough definition to draw a conclusion about Bob's photo, but I'm seeing nothing that would prevent me from speculating that this could actually be Bigfoot. And if it is, Bob's accidental photo might open the portal to one of the most monumental discoveries of the twenty-first century." He glanced around the room. "Where is Bob? Is he actually late?"

"Mom and Dad aren't joining us. I've already shared my announcement with them. So…if we're all here, I'd—"

"Delpha's not here," Goldie spoke up. "Aren't you going to wait for her?"

I exhaled a slow, controlled breath. "Delpha's the reason you're all here, and I fear there's no way I can soften the blow. She was apparently involved in a serious mishap on her hike down the mountain. I don't have any details yet. Etienne is finding out what he can from the hotel management, but—"

"Is she in the hospital?" asked Goldie.

"No." I shook my head. "No hospital. She...she didn't survive the incident."

Shocked silence.

"Are you telling us she's dead?" Ennis intoned.

I nodded. "I'm afraid so. I'm so sorry. I don't understand how it happened, but someone discovered a body on the mountain, and it appears to be Delpha's."

"Well, that's a no-brainer," wisecracked Bernice. "Bob's ape killed her."

Yup. Exactly what I feared would happen. Had I called that or what?

Helen glared at Bernice, her mouth falling open in disbelief. "Excuse me, but wasn't it you who just made a *huge* point of telling us that Bob's ape was fake news?"

"That was before the dead body showed up. It was the ape. Case closed."

"You can't just flip-flop like that," argued Helen.

"Why not? Haven't you noticed? It's the hottest trend in Washington."

"We're not *in* Washington," spat Helen.

Bernice offered an unapologetic smirk. "That's the thing about trends. They spread."

"As much as the academic in me would like to believe that Bigfoot is alive and well and roaming the mountain slope outside our window," Ennis interjected, "I'm quite certain that even if the creature is out there, it's a virtual impossibility that it would have caused Delpha's death."

"How do you know that?" asked Dick Stolee.

"Because given all the sightings of Bigfoot and creatures of its ilk, there has never once been a death reported in association with its appearance. The concerted opinion of scientists and others who've studied the literature is that despite the creature's genetic markers that indicate a relationship to the polar bear family, this particular specimen isn't carnivorous. It's a herbivore."

"So?" Bernice heckled. "Just because Delpha didn't qualify to be an entree on the ape's dinner menu doesn't mean he didn't kill her."

Collective *ewws*. Tsking. Sniffling.

"That is the vilest statement I have ever heard coming out of the mouth of any human being," sobbed Goldie.

Tilly pulled a face. "Actually, in comparison to some of the more despicable remarks she's made over the years, that one was relatively tame."

Alice nodded. "On a scale of one to ten, with ten being the worst, I'd give it a four."

"Six for me," said George.

"I'd rate it a solid five," said Dick Teig.

"Show of hands as to whether Bernice has lost her edge," Osmond called out. "Those voting yea, please raise your—"

"No voting!" I warned, stabbing my finger at him. I caught Goldie's eye. "I apologize for Bernice's insensitivity. She was raised by wolves."

Bernice doubled down on her smirk. "Numbskulls."

"This is all my fault," whimpered Florence, stiffening visibly as Thor snaked a comforting arm around her shoulders. "If I hadn't told her off for coming to my defense, she might not have ventured out on her own. She might still be alive."

"Why are you taking the blame?" chided Thor with his usual bombast. "It wasn't your fault. You didn't tell her to go running down that mountain on her own. The woman had a big mouth. You heard what she said to me. She mouthed off and she paid the consequences. I mean, I'm sorry she's dead, but it was her own fault."

Goldie let out a gasp. "Excuse me, Thor, but did you just have the unmitigated gall to make Delpha's death all about yourself?"

He raised his hand in a gesture of surrender. "I'm just saying, when people cross me, bad things happen."

"To them or to you?" asked Alice.

"To them!"

"That is so not true," confided Florence, looking embarrassed. "I don't know why you say things like that, Thor. People just end up laughing at you. When did anything ever happen to someone who crossed you? Specifically. I want names and dates."

"The hell you do. You don't need to know squat. All you need to know is, it happens. Believe me, just like clockwork, it happens."

Nana gave him a squinty look. "Sounds like one of them ancestral curses to me. You got any Scottish blood in you?"

"I'm one hundred percent Norwegian, pure and untainted, as far back as my ancestry extends."

"No kiddin'? Well, you might wanna look into that on account of I'm thinkin' that somewhere along the way, one of them relatives of yours mighta hopped a boat and gone rogue in Scotland."

And that just about clinched it. I waved my hands in the air to get the group's attention. "Can all of you please put your differences aside for the moment and try to refocus on the situation with Delpha? That *is* why you're here."

Downcast eyes. Silence. The appearance of contrition.

"So what happens next?" asked Ennis, his voice husky with emotion. "What…what do we do? Stay here? Go home? What?"

"This is so recent, we can't make any immediate decisions, so what I'm asking all of you to do is to just sit tight until we have more information, and then we can decide what our next move should be. Probably tomorrow morning sometime."

"Have you notified her family yet?" sniffled Goldie, her eye shadow leaving a trail of blue glitter across her face as she swiped tears from her eyes.

"I imagine we're going to have to coordinate that with the local authorities, so that's on hold for the moment."

"Her sister will be devastated," she choked out, her voice trembling. "Although she's traveling in Mongolia at the moment, so I don't know if you'll be able to reach her. Remember how she didn't want anything to do with the newspaper until Delpha sold it? And then she showed up with her hand open, wanting her share of the profits? The court case went on forever."

Orphie perked up. "I got to hear all the gory details because, as you know, Al's council meetings take place in the same building, so he used to pop into the courtroom and carry the latest scuttlebutt back home with him."

"The whole affair turned incredibly nasty," Goldie continued, "but I thought it was quite admirable that the sisters were able to mend their fences afterward. They really have quite a civil relationship now. At least, it appears to be civil." Her gaze drifted to Thor. "I mean, you can never really tell about relationships, can you? A perfectly nice outer layer might be hiding an inner core that's more rotten than month-old garbage."

Thor narrowed his eyes. "Why did you look at me when you said that?"

Goldie grinned coyly. "Because you're so handsome, Thor. I can't take my eyes off you."

"Alison's not here," Grover Kristiansen spoke up. "Have you told her yet? She deserves to know. She might have been with us for only a few hours, but I believe she's already established a warm rapport with the entire group, so I bet she'll be as devastated about Delpha's death as the rest of us are. I'll volunteer to tell her if you like. Save you the trouble."

I couldn't begin to imagine how thrilled Alison would be to become hostage to yet another of Grover's mind-numbing monologues. "Thanks anyway, Grover, but I'm taking care of that."

The sparkle fled his eyes at my refusal. "Okay, but let me know if you change your mind."

Why was I getting the feeling that Grover might become a nuisance for our pretty local guide?

"So I guess that's all I can tell you for now," I confessed as the ladies dried their eyes and blew their noses. "Hopefully we'll have more answers by tomorrow morning. So thank you all for coming on the spur of the moment like this. I just wish I'd had different news for you."

"But what about Bigfoot?" insisted Helen Teig, slanting a look toward the window. "What if he's really out there? What if he *did* have something to do with Delpha's death?"

I inhaled a calming breath. "Meaning no disrespect to either my father's photographic ability or Ennis's academic beliefs, I'm going to file Bigfoot's potential existence under 'mythology' and not give it another thought. And I recommend all of you do the same."

Wary looks. Skeptical expressions.

"Please trust me on this. You have nothing to fear from Bigfoot."

"Tell that to Delpha," mocked Bernice.

"About that!" I added as they began boosting themselves to their feet. "Please don't breathe a word about Delpha's death until the authorities make an official statement to the public. The last thing the police need to deal with is a social media circus pushing the theory that Dad's creature is responsible for Delpha's death."

"Too late," crowed Bernice, brandishing her phone over her head. "Already done."

I shot her a frustrated look. "You didn't."

She gave me a palms-up. "Hey, if you wanted to keep everything a secret, you should have said something sooner. Not my fault that your communications ability needs improvement."

Hisses. Boos. Razzberries.

"Yeah, yeah," taunted Bernice, dismissing the disapproval with a casual flip of her wrist. "Face it. You got scooped. You're all seeing green that I'm the one who flooded the internet with breaking news before the rest of you had the sense to think about it." She flashed a Cheshire cat grin as she waltzed out the door. "Better luck next time."

The group moved toward the door in slow motion, as if uncertain of their footing, Delpha's death definitely taking its toll. I intercepted Goldie as she rounded the bed.

"I apologize for not notifying you about Delpha first, Goldie, but as impersonal as a group meeting is, it seemed the best way to share the information." I squeezed her arm. "I know what a blow this must be for you. I'm so sorry."

She nodded as she dabbed her eyes with a tissue. "Thank you, Emily. And I appreciate your wanting to notify me first...but"— she regarded me with curiosity—"why would you want to notify me first?"

"Well, because of your friendship. Delpha told me that the two of you had been best friends since kindergarten."

"She did?"

"You bet. She said she was closer to you than she was to her own sister."

Her curiosity turned to confusion. "Why would she say something like that? We enjoyed each other's company in book club, and yes, we went through grade school together, but we're not close. We never hung out together. Never had sleepovers. Never called each other on the phone. We were planning to enjoy a spa date together tomorrow, but that didn't mean we were best friends. To be honest, our friendship was superficial at best. It's so odd that she made a comment like that. I really don't know what to make of it."

Neither did I, but if Delpha had lied to me, it shone a whole new light on the venomous look she'd directed at Goldie, Grover, and Ennis.

NINE

"GOOD MORNING, EVERYONE, AND thank you for taking the time to meet with me on such short notice. I'm Lieutenant Charlie Kitchen of the Alaska State Troopers, and, as Mr. Miceli has no doubt informed you, I'm here to ask you a few questions."

Etienne had returned to our room last night not knowing any more than when he'd left. "No one is able to tell me anything. They're drawing a curtain around the incident until the authorities can complete their initial examination of the scene. I asked who would be tasked with the investigation and was told the Alaska State Troopers would probably conduct the preliminary probe, so I called their headquarters in Anchorage and gave them my contact information, explaining my relationship to Delpha and urging them to share whatever details they can as soon as possible so I can make the necessary call to her family."

His cell had chirped at seven o'clock this morning, the officer on the other end requesting Delpha's emergency contact information and asking Etienne to gather his Destination Travel guests together for a group meeting at nine, which explained why we were all seated in one of the hotel's private conference rooms, eyes riveted on Lieutenant Charlie Kitchen with his short, compact build, blue uniform and tie, and wide-brimmed Dudley Do-Right hat. Everyone was looking a little rough this morning. Like me, they were probably suffering the effects of too little sleep precipitated by too much daylight.

"Did I allow you enough time to eat breakfast?" he asked.

Nods. Yups. A disgruntled "barely" from Bernice.

"Good. Before we get started, I'd like you to write your name and contact information on the sheet of paper I'm sending around the room." He handed a clipboard to Osmond. "And I'd appreciate your leaving the pen with the clipboard. I send them out but rarely get them back, so my supply is dwindling." He smiled pleasantly. "Let's begin, then. I'd like to review yesterday's timeline beginning with your tram ride to the top of the mountain and ending with your ride back down to the resort."

Florence popped out of her chair. "Against the advice of my husband, I'd like to confess."

"To what?" asked Lieutenant Kitchen.

Thor threw his hands into the air, followed by major head shaking and an irritated growl.

"I'd like to confess my part in Delpha's death. She went off by herself yesterday because I'd been mean to her."

"Don't listen to her, Officer," Goldie spoke up. "She wasn't *that* mean. Cross maybe, but certainly not mean."

"Perturbed," said Orphie.

"I got the impression that she was simply fed up with the status quo," theorized Tilly. "She was requesting a recalibration in her relationships, but I never saw any real anger."

"Florence doesn't get angry," Helen Teig attested. "She's a saint."

Lieutenant Kitchen's gaze bounced from one woman to the other. "I'm sorry. Florence is…?"

She waved her fingers in the air. "Me. I'll be sorry to miss the remainder of the trip, but I understand that you have a job to do." She raised her wrists in front of her face like a felon awaiting handcuffs. "Go ahead and arrest me. I'm ready to face the music."

Kitchen regarded her with a slightly dumbfounded expression before finding his tongue. "Florence," he said kindly, "I'm fairly certain that being mean, cross, or fed up doesn't constitute a crime necessitating your immediate arrest, so I'm going to suggest that you have a seat while we review yesterday's timeline, and we'll discuss your incarceration once we've finished. Is that okay with you?"

"Suit yourself," she said bravely, "but you're just postponing the inevitable." She sat back down while Kitchen took a moment to reboot, appearing a little off-kilter.

"So, if you could provide me with a bit of background information," he asked as he ranged a curious look around the room. "What type of tour is this exactly?"

"It's a tour for active Iowa seniors what's still got all their marbles," volunteered Nana.

"That's debatable," snorted Bernice.

"You're all senior citizens?" asked Kitchen.

"Not my daughter Emily and her husband," Mom said proudly. "They run the tour, so they're obviously much younger."

"So is Alison," added Grover Kristiansen as he gestured to the place she was sitting. "She's our local guide."

Kitchen nodded. "But all the rest of you are"—he paused, seeming to grapple for the right word—"older?"

Dead silence. Narrow stares.

"Something wrong with that?" asked Dick Teig in a tight voice.

"Uhh—no. Like I said. Background. So"—he leveled his gaze on Etienne—"perhaps I could ask Mr. Miceli to get the ball rolling. Did all your guests take the same tram up the mountain last night?"

"They did. We met in the lobby at six and walked over to the tram station as a group. Our dinner reservation was set for seven, so I wanted to frontload time for people to explore."

"I never tire of that ride up the mountain," admitted Kitchen as he removed a small notepad and pen from his shirt pocket. "The scenery's amazing, isn't it?"

"Bob got hisself a picture of Bigfoot on the way up," enthused Nana.

Mom made a gasping sound. Swiveling around in her chair, she stared at me with accusatory eyes. "Emily Andrew-Miceli, you *promised* me you wouldn't breathe a word about that to your grandmother."

"I didn't!"

"Then how did she find out?"

"Give credit where credit is due," cackled Bernice. "No one's faster at finding weird stuff on the internet than I am. In fact, my mental faculties are clicking with such lightning speed, I shouldn't even qualify to be on one of these Destinations Travel old-timers tours."

"I'll second that," hooted Dick Teig.

"Whoa!" interrupted Kitchen. "Back up a minute." He lasered a look at Nana. "Someone took a picture of Bigfoot? On the mountain? Last night?"

"You bet," said Nana, gesturing toward Dad. "Bob took the shot and uploaded it to one of them news websites, and now it's all over the internet. It's what you call goin' viral."

"You gotta be kidding me." Kitchen laughed. "I've been on the force for ten years without a single sighting. You're here for a day and one of you snaps a picture of the darned bugger. Anyone got the photo handy?"

They whipped their phones into the air like fencers brandishing their swords.

"It's in the lower left-hand corner," Nana indicated as Kitchen studied her screen. "Them folks at the news place was probably workin' with a magnifyin' glass, so they was able to see it a lot better than us."

"I'll be damned," Kitchen marveled, unable to contain his excitement. "I see it. The thing with the big head and hairy arms that could easily be mistaken for a tree. I'll be damned. Being something of a Bigfoot/Sasquatch enthusiast myself, I've gotta tell you, photographic evidence like this is huge." He lowered his brows at Nana. "It's not photoshopped, is it?"

"No, sir," answered Dad. "Doctoring stuff is way above my skill set."

Kitchen paused, his eyes signaling that his brain had kicked into hyperdrive. "So let me get this straight: When you were gliding over the treetops in your gondola yesterday, this *thing* was roaming around on the mountainside?"

Dad nodded. "Guess so."

"So...geez..." Kitchen rubbed the back of his head, his eyes rounding with enlightenment. "*Geez*...this is an added wrinkle I hadn't seen coming. Not that anyone's going to believe me."

"Why wouldn't folks believe you?" asked Helen Teig. "Bob's photo is plastered all over the web. It doesn't get more legitimate than that."

"I hate to disillusion you, ma'am, but not everything you see on the web is true. And something like this is bound to raise eyebrows, especially with my commanding officer. But hey, if this sighting is real, it'll send tourism through the roof. It'll be like the old gold rush days...only, this being Alaska, there won't be enough workers to fill the sudden boom in the hospitality sector, so things could really go to hell in a handbasket. It could collapse the whole economy."

"Did you want to resume your inquiry about our timeline, Lieutenant?" prodded Etienne.

Kitchen snapped his fingers. "Right. Sorry about the detour. But while I'm thinking about it..." He scribbled something on his notepad, ripped off the page, and handed it to Nana. "This is my email address. Would you mind sending those internet links to me? Okay, then, where were we?"

"The group had boarded the tram," repeated Etienne.

"Good. I don't have to ask about stops on the way because there aren't any. So once everyone exited the gondola, what happened next?"

"I'll answer that," offered Alison. "I instructed the group to follow me onto the observation deck, and then I provided them with several options as to how they could fill in their time before dinner.

Hike to the glacier, explore the immediate area around the restaurant, visit the museum, or enjoy a cocktail in the restaurant's bar."

"You never gave them the option of taking one of the hiking trails back down to the resort?"

"They would have missed dinner, so I never mentioned it. Besides, there were low clouds threatening to engulf us, so low visibility could have made the trails quite dangerous. I wanted to avoid putting ideas in anyone's head."

Kitchen made a notation on his pad. "So which guests went where?"

The room exploded in a cacophony of voices as everyone shouted out their destination at the same time.

"Whoa!" said Kitchen. He patted the air with his hand in a plea for quiet. "I don't want to squelch your input, but how's about we go about it a little differently. How many of you hiked out to see the glacier? Raise your hand."

Up flew the ladies' hands, proud and defiant, followed by the two Dicks and Etienne. Mom grabbed Dad's hand and hefted it upward for him. "He's talking about you, Bob," she scolded as she raised her own hand. "You saw the glacier."

"No, I didn't. The fog was too thick."

Dad had a habit of taking things kind of literally.

Kitchen smiled his surprise. "Ladies! Good for you. You really showed the guys up on this one, huh? You can lower your hands now."

Florence kept hers in the air.

"Yes, Florence?" he asked.

"I just wanted you to know that the reason why most of the ladies went to the glacier was to show support for me after I went off the rails."

"Thank you, Florence. I'll make a note of that. How many of you chose to explore the area around the restaurant? Raise your hands."

The Dicks shot their hands into the air.

Kitchen frowned. "Didn't you just raise your hands for the hike to the glacier?"

"We did some unscheduled exploring of the grounds before we went to the glacier," explained Dick Teig. "So we kinda did both."

Kitchen made another notation. "A show of hands for those who visited the museum?"

Up went Alison's hand, joined by the hands of the seven men who accompanied her to the museum, including the two Dicks, who became the targets of Lieutenant Kitchen's immediate scrutiny. "Let me guess, gentlemen. You visited the museum as well?"

"Only for a couple of minutes," confessed Dick Stolee. "It was pretty boring, which is why we ended up doing the other stuff."

With his eyes riveted on the Dicks, Kitchen hazarded his final question. "Did anyone spend their time in the restaurant bar?"

Bernice waved her hand. "That would be me. Me...and a sloe gin fizz that I could have bought anywhere else for half the price. You want to investigate something on that mountain? Investigate the price gouging in the bar."

"Thank you." He scanned his notes. "Did I miss anyone?"

I raised my hand. "I'm Emily Miceli. I operate the tour with my husband. I was fielding a call while everyone else was off exploring, so I spent most of my time in the restaurant foyer, waiting for a return call."

"And what about Ms. Spillum? When was the last time any of you saw her?"

"She high-tailed it to parts unknown after Florence was mean to her," Bernice volunteered.

"She was *not* mean," fussed Goldie.

"Show of hands," instructed Osmond. "How many people think—"

"This is not a votable issue," I warned.

"Ms. Spillum headed off toward the ski lifts as the group broke up into their various factions," Etienne disclosed. "And that was the last time we saw her, although it wasn't the last time we heard from her."

Kitchen poised his pen on his notepad. "You want to expand on that, Mr. Miceli?"

"I can answer that," I offered. "After the hostess told us our tables were ready, I texted Delpha because she hadn't rejoined the group yet." I flipped through a couple of screens and held up my phone as evidence. "I asked her where she was, and she texted back that she was skipping dinner and hiking down to the resort instead."

"She texted you on her cell phone." He made a quick notation. "What time was that?"

I eyed the screen. "7:06. And then at approximately 7:15 I texted her again. Her meal was already paid for, so I told her if she'd tell us what she wanted, we'd have the kitchen box it up and we'd deliver it to her when we got back to the resort."

"And did she reply?"

I nodded. "At 7:17. And that was the last I heard from her."

He scanned his notes. "And just to clarify, at 7:17 everyone else in the group was seated in the restaurant dining room. Correct?"

"We weren't all seated at the same table, but we were all there. Yes."

"May I see your phone, Mrs. Miceli?"

I handed it over to him, and while we watched, he captured screenshots of the texts with his own phone.

"Could you tell me if Delpha was carrying her phone on her person when you found her?" I asked with some hesitation as he returned my phone.

He paused a beat. "Why do you want to know?"

"Because I'm afraid that whatever happened to her might have occurred while she was texting me." I sighed self-consciously. "But if her phone was safely back in her jacket pocket, that would mean it didn't fly out of her hand on the hiking trail, so I might not be directly responsible for her death."

Kitchen glanced around the room, his mouth crooked at an odd angle. "Is everyone in Iowa like you folks? You're all practically champing at the bit to take the blame before you're even accused of anything."

"Not all of us," corrected Bernice.

"As for Ms. Spillum's cell phone, I regret having to tell you this, Mrs. Miceli, but I can't give you any specifics at this time."

"You can't? Not even if she was still carrying it?"

"I'm sorry. All information relating to her cell phone is part of our ongoing investigation."

"So…she *could* be dead because of me?"

"That's a pretty harsh assumption, Mrs. Miceli."

"Delpha was always texting people, Emily," Ennis spoke up. "All the time. She might have sent out a dozen more messages after she responded to you last night, so you shouldn't blame yourself. At least, not yet."

Despite Ennis's best intentions, if that was supposed to make me feel better, it failed miserably.

"Are you able to provide us some information about how she died?" inquired Etienne.

"I can't release those details yet."

"Was it an accident?" Margi called out.

"Can't comment on that," said Kitchen.

"Holy hell," blurted Dick Stolee. "Someone killed her."

"I didn't say that."

"Oh my god," cried Florence. "Delpha was murdered?"

"Whoa!" Kitchen waved off the question. "I haven't given you any indication that—"

"It's a dead giveaway," reasoned Dick Teig. "If you can't say it was an accident, it's always murder."

"We haven't determined a cause of death yet," admitted Kitchen, "and that's all I can say until we notify her next of kin."

"You might have a hard time with that," volunteered Orphie. "Her sister is touring Mongolia at the moment."

"Seriously?" Kitchen's expression morphed from surprise to sudden understanding. "Well, I guess that explains a few things."

"Did you find a murder weapon at the scene?" probed Helen Teig.

"Or was her death cleverly disguised as an accident?" George followed up. "We've run into a fair share of those."

Kitchen fell into momentary silence. "Who *are* you people? Retired detectives?"

"We've had the misfortune of suffering a few unexpected fatalities on our tours," I explained in a conciliatory tone.

"More like a boatload," croaked Bernice.

Kitchen arched a questioning brow at me.

"I—uh…I can't give you an exact number," I hedged. "It's been over a span of years, so…"

"There are four running totals," reported Alice matter-of-factly, sounding much the same as she had when she'd announced the price of pork bellies on KORN radio. "One exclusively for Windsor City guests, one for guests we hooked up with on larger tours, one for folks not on the tour, and one that tallies all four. Which one do you want?"

"Them numbers don't matter none," said Nana in what seemed like an attempt to soften the blow of Alice's calculations. "What's to blame is what you call our demographic, which is one of them fancy words what explains why guests what we're travelin' with drop dead so much. It's on account of we're old."

"Osmond's nearing the century mark," Margi pointed out as an example, "so you know he's not going to be with us much longer."

"Margi's right." Osmond nodded good-naturedly. "I could go at any time."

"Can we cut to the chase?" demanded Thor. "If you don't know what caused Delpha's death, then you can't charge any of us with anything because we all have alibis, right?"

Kitchen hesitated. "All of you have alibis. That's correct."

"But why is it important that we have alibis if Delpha's death was an accident?" asked Lucille.

"Hel-*looo*?" taunted Dick Teig. "Because her death *wasn't* an accident."

"Could we leave a bouquet of flowers at the site where she died, Officer?" Goldie inquired.

"Sorry, ma'am. We've cordoned the area off."

"A votive candle?" asked Florence.

"Same answer," said Kitchen.

"Besides which, you could start a forest fire of epic proportions," added Grover. "It just so happens I've studied the US Forestry Service statistics for—"

"I wouldn't have to light it," argued Florence.

"We're not letting you anywhere near the area, ma'am."

"What about a poem?" asked Margi. "It could be a group effort. And we could nail it to a tree so it wouldn't be mistaken for litter."

"The whole mountain is off-limits to everyone today," asserted Kitchen with ever-increasing volume. "Tourists, hikers, diners, everyone. We've even shut down the tramway, so no one is going to be traipsing on that mountain until further notice."

"What'd I tell you?" boasted Dick Teig. "It's murder."

"But why would anyone murder Delpha?" asked Grace.

Kitchen's face flushed with color. "Look, you can speculate all you want. I can't stop you. But I don't want to find Ms. Spillum's name in the papers or on social media until the department works through its protocol. We've told the local news outlets that a woman died on the mountain last night and that her identity will be released pending notification of kin. The department will release her name after we contact her sister"—he glanced at Orphie—"in Mongolia."

"Good luck with that," droned Bernice. "Internet bandwidth in that place probably sucks."

"But just so you know," advised Kitchen, "if I learn that one of you has leaked the victim's name prematurely, there *will* be consequences. Do I make myself clear?"

All eyes riveted on Bernice, who regarded her detractors with a complete lack of self-awareness. "What?"

Florence raised her hand. "Are you getting ready to wrap things up here?"

"I am." He slid his notepad and pen back into his pocket. "I'm done with you for now, but that doesn't mean I won't have more questions as the investigation progresses. Before I leave, though, I'd like to secure a copy of your tour itinerary from the Micelis."

"Did you want to lock me up now?" asked Florence.

"How about we hold off on that for a while. I have no idea how I'd explain you to the chief."

"So I'm free to go?"

"Everyone's free to go—after you hand over my clipboard and pen."

His dismissal caused a sudden flurry of indecision that prompted collective standing, staring, and dithering, so while Etienne spoke to Lieutenant Kitchen, I reminded everyone of their options for the day. "For those of you still keen on dog mushing, we'll gather at the tram station at ten to catch our ride. Alison and I will both be accompanying you. For those of you wanting to look around Girdwood, the shuttle leaves every half hour from the front of the hotel, but if you all want to go at the same time, we'll have Steele load you onto the bus and drive you. Some of you might not have the emotional energy to do anything today after hearing about Delpha, so I'd invite you to remain at the hotel where you can take time to meditate and begin the healing process."

They began shuffling toward the exit with uncharacteristic slowness, which allowed me to catch Bernice as she stepped off to one side to check her latest readout.

She gloated as she flaunted her phone. "Look at this: 658 likes and 96 shares. Bernice is on her way to going viral."

"For which post?"

She read from the screen. "'Bigfoot Kills Hiker on Alaskan Mountain.'"

"But that's not true!"

"*Au contraire.* If 658 people *think* it's true, it's true. It's called creating your own reality. Oops. Correction: 659 likes." She clutched her phone to her chest. "Every time I see the count go up, I get such a high, I feel like I've been injected with something illegal."

"Please tell me you didn't mention Delpha's name in your post."

She snorted derisively. "Mention a real name in an article so it can be verified? Be specific rather than vague? Do I look like I just fell off the turnip truck? Boy, you don't get the internet racket at all, do you? But since you asked, if you find Delpha's name on the web, it wasn't me who put it there. Happy?"

"Thank you. That's all I wanted to know."

A commotion in the hall drew my attention. Now what?

Hurrying out the door, I found myself confronted by a handful of people armed with cameras, lights, cell phones, and notepads. "KUTE-TV entertainment news," shouted a young man wearing a baseball cap bearing the same call letters. "We're looking for Bob Andrew."

"Can you tell us where to find him?" asked a brunette with official-looking credentials dangling from her neck.

"I'm Bob," said Dad, observing the reporters with polite calm.

"Stephanie Strange, *Talkeetna Tattler*," said the brunette by way of identifying herself. "Where were you when you shot your photo of Bigfoot, Mr. Andrew?"

"Were you on the mountain behind the resort when you spotted it?" prompted another man as the group of reporters crowded around Dad like pioneers circling their wagons, muscling out everyone else.

"How did you feel when you saw the creature?" demanded another guy who was filming Dad on his phone, the words *Alaska Entertainment Magazine* splashed across his jacket.

Dad shrugged. "Didn't feel anything."

"Not even a twinge of excitement? Really, Mr. Andrew, you had to have felt something."

"A little dizzy from the tower swing maybe."

"How did you manage to take his picture?" the gaggle shouted out in a blare of voices.

Dad shrugged again. "I was shooting scenery and the ape showed up in the frame."

Excitement amid the reporters.

"Did you get a close-enough look to determine if the creature actually was an ape?" asked the phone guy.

"I didn't see him."

"Would you say it looked more like a gorilla, a baboon, or an orangutan?" pressed the brunette.

Dad gave them a palms-up. "Dunno."

"But you called it an ape. What type of ape?"

"The kind that looks like a tree."

"A tree ape? So it resembled a chimpanzee rather than a great ape?"

"Or a gibbon?" suggested the TV guy.

The brunette guffawed. "How does KUTE's puff piece golden boy have time to learn about gibbons?"

"Nature documentary. On a competing network. Did it look like a gibbon, Mr. Andrew?"

"Did you hear me say I didn't see it?"

Bernice sashayed into their midst, hips swaying and eyes sparkling, causing a momentary break in the action. "My, my, my. What have we here? Lights. Cameras. Notepads." She primped her wire whisk helmet of over-permed hair. "Perhaps you've heard of me? Bernice Zwerg? Former magazine model?"

In less than a heartbeat, attention quickly shifted back to Dad. "Could we interview you in the lobby, Mr. Andrew?" asked the KUTE reporter. "We've got a whole slew of questions."

"And we'd like pictures of you posing with your Bigfoot photo," insisted the brunette. "This is huge entertainment news, Mr. Andrew. I hope you realize that you and your picture are in danger of claiming a glorious fifteen minutes of fame."

"No kidding?"

"Did you read the post on social media about Bigfoot killing a hiker?" interrupted Bernice as she stood on tiptoes outside the circle of reporters, struggling to breach their protective wall. "I wrote that. I was very nearly an eyewitness. And I'm available to be interviewed."

"Yah, yah," said the brunette in a dismissive tone. "We'll get right on that."

"It's not fake news! I have 659 likes to prove it."

The KUTE reporter peered down at Bernice. "Sorry, lady. We're the entertainment media. We don't do the hardcore stuff."

"So, Mr. Andrew," said the brunette, shifting her attention back to Dad, "are you ready for that interview? Should take a couple of hours. Entertainment junkies love lots of frilly details."

Dad checked his watch. "I'm supposed to go shopping with the missus in an hour."

"Then we'll wrap things up in forty-five minutes. Wouldn't want you to miss out on a shopping trip with your wife."

As the girlieness of the day's activity seared into Dad's brain, he registered the kind of panic common among men whose shopping skills were limited to the purchase of power tools and machinery... from a catalog. He checked his watch again. "Two hours should be about right."

And with that he was swept away like a swimmer in an undertow, trapped in the center of the reporters' phalanx as they stutter-stepped their way to the lobby.

With the hoopla over, the rest of the group scattered in an obvious rush not to be late for their next scheduled event, all except Mom, who stood rooted to the spot, looking perplexed.

"Well, that was unexpected," I said as I walked over to her.

"I'm torn," she confided, elevating her palms as if they were the scales of justice. "On the one hand"—she raised her right hand slightly above the left—"I need to make sure nothing happens to your grandmother in Girdwood with this Bigfoot creature on the loose, but on the other"—down went the right, up went the left— "I don't want to miss out on the opportunity to hear your father utter complete sentences."

"You should definitely listen to Dad," I encouraged, knowing that Nana would actually be able to enjoy her day if Mom wasn't around to form a protective wall around her. "You can go shopping anytime, Mom, but listening to Dad communicate with people for two hours? Potentially constructing compound sentences that might include subordinate clauses? Now that's a once in a lifetime event you can't afford to miss."

"He'll never last two hours. Two minutes maybe. Three, tops. And I won't hold out hope for the subordinate clauses."

"Don't be so sure. He could surprise you."

She worried her bottom lip. "Okay. I'll stay with your father, but you be sure and tell Etienne he needs to tail your grandmother as if she's a fugitive from justice—close enough so he can make sure absolutely nothing happens to her."

"You bet."

She took a half-dozen steps toward the lobby before turning back to me. "I suppose there's one upside of those reporters finding your father."

"What's that?"

"Once they finish their interview, maybe his phone will stop pinging."

Wanting to double-check the departure time for the shuttle once again, I headed for the concierge desk, where complimentary issues of what looked like a local newspaper were stacked in a tidy pile. Grabbing one off the top, I felt my stomach turn over in a slow, sickening somersault as I read the headline that appeared in boldface type above the fold.

Oh. My. God.

TEN

"*Recent Anchorage Homicide Might Be Work of Serial Killer.*" Back in our room Etienne read the headline aloud as I lingered beside him, watching him scan the article.

"Do you think this could be why the police are so hesitant to release any information about Delpha's death? Are they afraid they might be dealing with a serial killer?"

He continued to read, absorbing content like a human sponge, his former police inspector instincts kicking into high gear. "Serial killers often have rituals they follow in the execution of their crimes, bella. The same patterns. The same methodology. I assume that's what a forensics team might be trying to determine today. If they do find the pattern repeated in Delpha's death, it would make her his fourth victim. So they'll need to play their cards close to the vest. They won't want to slip up and divulge any pertinent evidence that would alert the killer that they're onto him."

He set the paper down and exchanged a sober look with me. "If Delpha died in a hiking accident, it'll be recorded as an unintended mishap. But if they discover it's the handiwork of their serial killer, it would mean he's expanding his territory, and that could well cause a public panic, especially among visitors during the height of tourist season."

A shiver tap-danced its way up my spine. "Ennis mentioned a baker who's still in prison for killing at least forty-nine women in the Anchorage area in the eighties. He also said the Pacific Northwest boasts a lion's share of known serial killers. It creeped me out when he said it, but I'm even more creeped out now because it looks as if he really knew what he was talking about."

Etienne hugged me against him, wrapping me in the protective circle of his arms, suppressing inspector Etienne to allow husband Etienne to surface. "Despite the newspaper article, bella, and contrary to your worst instincts, we don't know what caused Delpha's death. We're only grasping at straws. So can we refrain from drawing any conclusions until we learn the specifics? I can guarantee it'll save you hours of needless hand wringing."

"Easier said than done. It's genetic. You've met my mother, haven't you? The woman with the little moon face and the steamer trunk of worry grafted onto her back?"

"Listen to me, Emily. Based on my police experience in Switzerland, where mountains are the geologic norm and hiking is the national pastime, I can almost guarantee that Delpha's death was an accident."

"I hope you're right." I inhaled a calming breath. "Did you have to investigate many serial killer cases in Switzerland?"

"Uh…none, actually. Switzerland ranks rather low on the percentage chart of citizens who become deranged murderers."

Yup. That made me feel *much* better.

We parted company at the lobby, where a throng of tourists stood around watching Dad being interviewed and Mom displaying her heart on her sleeve as she offered him an assortment of encouraging facial expressions. I wasn't sure what the two of them planned to do after the interview, but at least Mom wouldn't be bugging Nana. And since all the ladies had decided to follow Nana's lead and spend the day in Girdwood shopping for souvenirs, we abandoned the shuttle idea in favor of the tour bus. So while Steele brought the vehicle around to the front door, I packed my mosquito spray and skipped out the back entrance to take the shortcut to the tram station, where Alison and the guys were already waiting.

"We're all here," she spoke up. "All eight of us, present and accounted for." Even though she was wearing nondescript jeans with holes in the knees, a generic short-sleeved tee, a baseball cap with her ponytail poking out the back, and off-brand sunglasses, she still looked like a million bucks, which was not lost on her admiring companions, who looked as if they were suddenly feeling decades younger.

"*Hush, you muskies*," barked Dick Teig as he cracked an imaginary whip into the air.

"Dude," chortled Dick Stolee, "you just failed Sergeant Preston of the Yukon 101. The command is *mush, you huskies*."

Dick bunched his features into a knot. "You sure?"

"Depends on what you're trying to do," needled George Farkas. "Spur a dog team forward or hush a bunch of fish."

"And you can lose the whip," lectured Grover Kristiansen. "Mushers don't use whips on canines. Ever. They're driving dog-sleds, not chariots. And speaking of dogs, did you know the only dogs allowed to run in the Iditarod are Siberian huskies and Alaskan malamutes? Interestingly, that rule came about because one fella had the idea of training a bunch of standard poodles to run in the race, so he—"

"Ho-lee Hannah," interrupted Thor Thorsen as he peered at the vehicle rumbling down the drive toward us. "I think our ride is here."

It arrived with a deafening blare of heavy metal music blasting out from the cab and a rack of humongous moose antlers perched above the windshield. Looking like a cross between an all-terrain vehicle and a jeep, it sported a closed cab, an extended flatbed with a canvas canopy, six wheels, and the word PINZGAUER stenciled on the glass beneath the moose rack. It was painted a brilliant fire-engine red because it was obviously too easy for drivers to miss a vehicle rumbling down the road with giant moose antlers mounted on the roof.

The vehicle screeched to a stop ten feet away and the driver jumped out with a clipboard, all teeth and energy. "Hey, folks, are you my pick-ups for the dog mushing adventure? Nine guests from Destinations Travel?"

"You bet," hooted the guys, who immediately began to circle the vehicle, oohing and aahing over its heavy steel construction as if it were the Batmobile.

"My name's Matt. I'm your driver today, and as soon as I check off your names, we'll hit the road."

"Is this vehicle military?" asked Thor as he ran his hand along the front quarter panel.

"Sure is. Austrian made and used by Delta Force teams for special operations behind enemy lines. A sweet ride, isn't she? With

125

mounts available for attaching weapons systems like M2 machine guns and MK19 grenade launchers. 'Course, we don't need those mounts right now, but it's a real comfort to know we could get them if we needed 'em."

Right. Like on those terrifying occasions when Alaska faced the threat of imminent invasion from Saskatchewan.

Whistles from the guys. Chests puffing out. Testosterone spiking.

Matt brandished his pencil in the air. "Okay, when I call your name, raise your hand."

Attendance taken, he shouted out final instructions before loading us into the back. "It'll take us about forty minutes to get there. Please keep your hands and feet inside the vehicle at all times. And like my grampa always said to his wife"—he offered his hand to Alison with a winsome look in his eye and a smile on his lips—"ladies first."

The music began blaring again when he started the engine, giving onlookers the impression that we were a traveling rock concert on six wheels. It blasted out with ear-piercing loudness as we sped down highways that snaked through primal forests…as we caught fleeting glimpses of houses that seemed to be cobbled together from hand-hewn lumber and spit…as we passed abandoned A-frames whose weathered signs might once have advertised dinner specials…as we spied cisterns and rain barrels, rusted pickups and tar paper privies…as we covered our ears to block the wind from puncturing our eardrums…as we jolted along uneven pavement until we hit the sign that warned End Road Maintenance…as we bounced down the teeth-clacking dirt road that led to the rutted cow path that meandered through flower-glutted meadows, over sparkling streams, and into a dazzling valley that was bounded on three sides by towering mountains with razor-sharp peaks.

Matt killed the engine inside the entrance of a compound that was enclosed on two sides by a plywood fence and was home to a couple dozen small wooden hutches whose occupants were barking frenetically at our arrival, causing me to wonder if I should have packed flea spray rather than mosquito spray. Dick Teig plugged his finger into his ear and gave it a rattle as Matt lowered the tailgate. "Anyone else lose his hearing on the way over here?"

"WHAT?" shouted George as he wiggled a finger in his ear.

"You gonna play any better music on the way back?" Dick Teig groused to Matt as we climbed out.

"Sure, man. What's your pleasure? Death Angel? Anthrax? Slayer?"

Dick stared at him, nonplussed. "How about something that'd be good in a more confined space? Say, like, an elevator."

As the dogs continued their chorus of howls and barks, the man who looked to be our host sauntered over to us with an easy stride and confident smile. "Welcome, welcome. I'm Jean-Claude, but it's these scamps"—he spread his arms wide to include all the animals in the broad gravel yard—"who are the real stars of our adventure."

He spoke with a slight accent I couldn't identify, but with a name like Jean-Claude, I figured he probably hailed from one of two places.

"You've got an accent," Grover pointed out in what might have been a cheesy attempt to shine the spotlight on himself in front of Alison. He elevated his chin at a jaunty angle. "You from Canada?"

"Brittany," said Jean-Claude.

"Is that near the Yukon?" enthused Dick Teig. "We're gonna be visiting Yukon Territory sometime while we're here."

I shook my head. "No, we're not."

"Yes, we are," said Dick. "It's on our itinerary."

I shook my head again. "No, it's not. The Yukon's in Canada."

"Brittany, where I come from, is a region," Jean-Claude clarified, "in France."

"So you're Canadian, are you?" asked Osmond as he turned his hearing aids back on. "I fought alongside Canadians in the war."

I hung my head. *Oh, God.*

My phoned chimed out Jackie's ringtone, which not only spared me from having to witness any more of this conversation, but filled me with admiration for the telecommunication giants who'd had the foresight to erect cell towers in the middle of nowhere. "'S'cuse me," I mouthed to the group as I slunk away to a more isolated spot.

"Hi," I whispered into the phone. "What's up?"

A pause. "Why do I hear dogs barking in the background? Are you at a greyhound racetrack?"

"Dog mushing adventure. The pooches are happy to see us. So how is Mildred? Did her face shrink back to normal size?"

"Not yet, which is why she's still in the hospital. The doc thinks something else is going on, so they're keeping her for further observation. But she's pretty perky because she's got company now."

"Aw, that's so sweet. Did her family drive down from Windsor City to visit her?"

"No. I mean, she's not the only tour guest in the hospital anymore."

A chill lifted the down on my arms as if the tiny hairs had been electrified. "Another guest has been hospitalized?"

"Uhh…actually, would you believe two guests?"

I fought to remain calm as I scanned the compound for somewhere to sit, but there was no bench. No stool. Nothing.

With gnawing fear and trepidation, I asked the question I had to ask. "But…the two guests are still alive, right?"

"Oh, sure. No chance of their dying from their injuries. They only suffered broken bones and bruises."

"How? What were they doing that they suffered broken bones? And which two guests are you talking about?" Jean-Claude must have invited the group to show the animals a little love because the guys had spread out and were wandering among the hutches, scratching and petting the dogs, who were leaping and barking in response.

"It's the two Toms. I knew they'd be trouble. They're just like the two Dicks—adult males who act like they're still in high school. So here's the scoop. They were in their tractor-cars, crashing into everyone on the floor at warp speed, when *boom!* They both hit a support beam at the same time, flew out of their little tractor-cars because they were both feeling macho and hadn't buckled their safety belts, and accidentally got run over by a couple of our tour members who couldn't remember which pedal to push to stop. These short-term memory issues are starting to create real problems, Em. How would you feel about making psychological testing a part of the sign-up process?"

"Explain 'tractor-car.'"

"Oh, remember the old bumper cars that were such a big hit at summer fairs—when you could hop into little electric-powered pods and ram the daylights out of all the other little pods? Well, Green Acres has resurrected the ride, only the cars look like little John Deere tractors and there's no electrical current sizzling across the floor or ceiling, threatening to electrocute you. Everything runs on battery, which really takes the fear factor out of it…except when someone runs over you at fifteen miles an hour and fractures your leg and pelvis and arm and—"

"How many broken bones do the Toms have?" I shrieked.

"Individually or collectively?"

"Jack!"

"Okay, okay. Tom number one has a broken tibia, arm, and nose. Tom number two has a broken fibula, pelvis, and wrist. And since neither of them can text one-handed, they're enlisting my thumbs to send messages for them. It's ruining my manicure. But you don't have to worry about who pays for their emergency surgery because they both bought the travel insurance. At least, they think they did."

"They had surgery?" My voice was a squeak. "Both of them?"

"Not yet. But there won't be any more TSA pre-check for them. They'll be packing more metal now than the Tin Man."

"Oh my god." Guests might have died on me, but at least none of them had needed emergency surgery. "Have you phoned their emergency contacts to speak to them personally?"

"Yup. Lots of family and friends headed in our direction. Isn't it good we're within driving distance and not stuck in Europe somewhere? Or Alaska?"

"Where are you now?"

"At the hospital."

"Who's watching out for the guests who are still at Green Acres?"

"Our van driver. Johnny's really good with people, Em, so I told him if he'd take over my escort duties while I was here, you'd settle up with him later, like, give him a bonus or something."

I nodded. "Sure. That's...that's fine. Will you call or text me later to give me an update on the Toms?"

"You got it. But...umm...there's one more thing I should probably mention."

I was so dazed already, what was one more bombshell? "What's that?"

"I told the Toms's families that if they wanted to stay in the area until the guys were released from the hospital, you'd pick up the tab for their hotel rooms, no matter how long they were here. That would be the classy thing to do, so I knew you'd insist I make the offer."

"Of course," I muttered, not knowing whether I should laugh or cry at how generous Jackie was being with our operating capital. "So maybe you could ask Johnny to direct the remaining guests toward the more risk averse rides?"

"Sure. The miniaturized cultivators look pretty tame, and the harvester ride looks about as dangerous as a merry-go-round, so I'm thinking we're home free." She let out a melodramatic sigh. "Try not to feel guilty about the tremendous hardships I've had to deal with, Emily. I'm quite happy to spend endless hours cooped up in a hospital. And not to toot my own horn or anything, but I've been told that my bedside manner is unparalleled." A pause. "So... would this be a good time to revisit the issue of my wardrobe allowance?"

"No. Thanks for the call, Jack. I'll talk to you later."

I disconnected, feeling as though I'd just been anesthetized. So while Jean-Claude gathered the guys around him to demonstrate the proper way to wrangle a harness over a sled dog, I questioned my idea of expanding our itineraries to two concurrent tours. The added revenue had looked attractive, but the reality was less rosy because instead of working myself into a lather over only one tour, I could now work myself into a lather over two.

As my brain started to clear, I cobbled together a mental to-do list and immediately got to work, starting with insurance. Rechecking the Toms's application forms, I discovered they had both bought our catastrophic travel insurance policy, so no matter what happened to them medically, they'd be covered. But in an effort to cover my bases, I called the company anyway.

After navigating my way through their menu, I got put on hold long enough to watch the guys wrestle harnesses onto the dogs, which was a bit like watching new dads try to dress overstimulated toddlers, but at least no one got peed on. By the time I finally connected with an agent, the huskies were in position at the front of the sled, attached to their rigging, with eight dogs on each line, jumping and howling in anticipation of their impending run.

Alison waved her arm to catch my attention. "Do you want to go with the first group?"

I shook my head and gestured for her to climb aboard with Thor, Ennis, and Grover, who'd already seated themselves. I still had another phone call to make before I could go anywhere.

As I ended my conversation with the insurance agent, Jean-Claude took off down the gravel drive like Santa with his reindeer, standing at the back of a compact wooden sled that sported wheels for runners and front- and back benches to accommodate a maximum of six passengers. Not knowing how long their jaunt would take, I put in a call to Etienne and spent the next ten minutes informing him of our forthcoming hotel room expenditures and repeating the mind-boggling misfires that were happening with Jackie in Iowa.

"But the prognosis is good for everyone concerned?" he asked as we were wrapping up.

"So far. I hope that doesn't change. How are you faring in Girdwood?"

"The situation is a bit dicey. Your dad finished up his interview right before we left, so he and your mom decided to join us, much to your grandmother's dismay."

I pinched my eyes shut and cringed. "I suppose Mom is breathing down Nana's neck?"

"Your mother attaches herself to your grandmother like static cling, bella, but Marion displays a remarkable aptitude for losing her. I've been running interference when I can, but your grandmother is quite self-sufficient. This isn't her first rodeo."

I blinked at his reference. "*Ooo*, unexpected catchphrase. Where did you learn that?"

"From your nephews. They insisted I watch an event being broadcast live from Las Vegas. Quite the curiosity. I'd never seen grown men scrambling around an arena dressed in such garish attire before. "

"You don't have calf roping in Switzerland?"

He paused. "No. We don't have clowns."

After hanging up, I wandered over to where the guys were taking selfies with the dogs that remained behind—or, more correctly, *trying* to take selfies. With the dogs straining at their leashes, pawing the ground, head-butting and leaping, they were a bit too frisky to pose for the perfect Kodak moment selfie.

"Here's a thought, guys. I could make myself useful and snap your pictures with the pups so you wouldn't have to struggle so hard to do it yourselves. Any takers?"

"You bet!" said Osmond as I watched one of the dogs bump his arm with such surprising force, it sent his phone flying out of his hand onto the gravel. Osmond picked the device up and brushed it off, and after inspecting it for damage, shoved it into his jacket pocket for safekeeping. He wagged a playful finger at the scamp who'd done it. "No more monkey business, you little whippersnapper. Now settle down and smile for the camera."

While the Dicks made a quick circuit of the compound, taking photos of each other, I took a series of photos of Osmond and George with their new canine buddies. "This Jean-Claude fella has run the Iditarod for five straight years," Osmond marveled. "And he's placed three times. Imagine: a thousand-mile race in the dead of winter where you're armed with a cook pot, an axe, and a sleeping bag, and contestants slap down big bucks for the honor of participating. I can see why it's a young person's sport. From where I'm sitting, even a Holiday Inn Express feels too much like camping."

"I thought the dogs were gonna be bigger," admitted George. "You know, like timber wolves or Sergeant Preston's dog King. But look at 'em. They're so small and wiry, they don't look strong enough to tow an empty toboggan much less a fully loaded sled and musher."

"They're lean and muscular," concluded Osmond with a wistful smile. "Kinda like I used to be before my legs turned to spindles."

"No poking fun of your legs," I scolded. "They still get the job done, don't they?"

"Yup. But I gotta keep moving. Standing in one spot for too long makes me stiff as a fence post—like in that museum on the mountain, I practically had to tap dance in place in order to finish reading all the materials."

I glanced at the huskies, who'd begun to whine with operatic drama at the sudden lack of human attention. "Did the museum offer any information on the beginnings of dog mushing in the area?"

George shook his head. "Nope. Plenty of other historical details and pictures though."

An idea suddenly bubbled up in my brain. "Hey, the book club guys have discussions every month about the latest book they've read. Maybe we can arrange a get-together where all the guests who visited the museum can share what they learned with those of us who did something else."

Osmond snorted. "It'd be an awful short meeting. The Dicks made the circuit of all the displays in about two minutes flat before ducking out, and the other fellers weren't there much longer. Once Alison left, it was like game over."

"Alison left early?"

George nodded. "Every time we moved on to a new display case, we lost someone else. But Alison left first."

"Then Grover." Osmond snorted. "That feller chases after that girl like his feet's on fire."

135

"Then the other two slunk out after that," said George. "Thor and Ennis. But I don't know if they left together or separately. One minute they were there, and the next they were gone."

This new revelation stuck in my brain like a monkey wrench in revolving gears. "Do you know where they went?"

Osmond shrugged. "Could've been anywhere around the building there."

Anywhere around the building, like the trail where Delpha was hiking? I felt an uncomfortable tightness in my chest. "Did you see the guys anywhere outside when you left the museum and trekked over to the restaurant?"

"Couldn't see a thing for the fog," said Osmond.

"Do you remember seeing them in the foyer of the restaurant when you arrived?"

"Yup," said George.

"Nope," said Osmond.

They eyed each other sharply.

"Why are you saying nope?" asked George. "Grover and Alison were already there. Center foyer. He was talking her ear off and she was standing there taking it. Remember?"

"Sure," defended Osmond. "He was making googly eyes at her. Hard to miss an old geezer like that making such a dang fool of himself. But I don't recollect seeing the other two fellers when we walked in. They arrived after we did, didn't they?"

George gave his head a bob that ended in a sigh. "Honest to Pete, I don't recall, but if you say they weren't there, I'll believe you."

Of course he would, because it was always safer to trust the memory of the guy who was pushing a hundred.

"Maybe we should call it a draw," I suggested. "Two guests definitely accounted for and two to be determined." Which meant both Thor and Ennis would have had plenty of time to catch up to Delpha on the hiking trail and...

And what?

Could Thor's simmering anger with Delpha have reached a boiling point while he'd been in the museum? Could he have tracked her down on the trail and...and...

Okay, Thor was mean-spirited and moody, but that didn't mean he was capable of committing cold-blooded murder...did it?

I looked from Osmond to George. "Do you think it might have been a good idea if one of you had mentioned to Lieutenant Kitchen that while Alison and most of the guys had gone to the museum yesterday, everyone left early except the two of you?"

Osmond shrugged. "I woulda told him if he asked, but he didn't ask, so I didn't think it was important."

"Me neither," said George.

Osmond studied me with squinty eyes. "Are you thinking it's suspicious that those folks left early?"

"Between you, me, and the bedpost, I'm not discounting anything."

George eyed me skeptically.

"I'm not making an accusation, George. I'm just saying that you've provided another avenue of investigation that Lieutenant Kitchen might want to explore. Another narrative."

"But what's the point?" asked George. "Thor and Ennis might have left the museum early, but they were sitting at a table right in front of you when Delpha died, so this new avenue might prove to be about as useful as a side saddle on a pig."

I'd gotten so far ahead of myself that for a brief moment, I'd forgotten it was my own phone that was providing the best evidence for Delpha's time of death. So why did this early departure from the museum bother me so much? And why was I being plagued by a niggling fear that not everything was as it appeared?

The sled rolled into the compound about ten minutes later. While Jean-Claude rewarded the dog team with doggie treats, Alison and the guys piled out, laughing, joking, and looking exhilarated from the experience. All except Ennis, who climbed off the sled in slow motion, his face pale, his motions fraught with unease.

"Bumpy ride?" I teased as I approached him.

He stared at me with a vacant gaze, as if he had no idea who I was. "I don't know. I..." He pulled his phone out of his jacket pocket, studying it intently. "I called Lorraine while the dogs were taking a break on the trail. I wanted to FaceTime with her so she could experience the ride for herself, but she didn't answer. So I said screw this and called the hospital where her mom's at—the one in Ames. I asked to be connected to her mom's room, and the receptionist told me there was no one by that name in the hospital."

"She's been discharged already? Wow, her surgery must have gone really well. What a relief, huh?"

"They hadn't discharged her."

I paused. "Did they lose her name in the computer?"

"They couldn't discharge her because they never admitted her in the first place. They had no record of her ever having been a patient."

"But she had a broken hip. Did the ambulance take her to another hospital? In another city maybe?"

"I went to the source. I phoned Lorraine's mother at her home in Story City. She picked up on the second ring."

"She's back home? That's incredible!"

"Not so incredible, really. She never broke her hip."

"What?"

"She didn't break her hip," he repeated. "She's been at home the entire time."

I peered at him, stupefied. "So if Lorraine's mom is at home, where's Lorraine?"

He stared at me, a haunted look in his eyes. "That's what I'd like to know."

ELEVEN

"SOMETHING BAD'S HAPPENED TO her," rasped Ennis. "I can feel it in my gut." He sat hunched over in the armchair in our room, elbows on knees, forehead braced on his palms. He'd already called every name on his speed dial list, asking if they'd seen Lorraine, and twelve times over he'd received the same response: "I thought she was with you in Alaska."

My group had arrived back from the mushing adventure at the same time the ladies had returned from their shopping spree in Girdwood, so I'd tracked down Etienne and told him that Ennis and I had an urgent matter to discuss with him in our room.

Twenty minutes later we seemed to be at an impasse, with lots of questions and no answers.

"She's been abducted." Ennis's voice was gravelly, his words strained. "That has to be it because I can't think of any other way to explain this. Someone sucked her in with that fake story about her mother, and when she was somewhere between our house and the hospital, the person grabbed her—maybe *at* the hospital, I don't know. But she's in trouble. The worst kind of trouble a woman can be in. There's nothing mythical about abductions. They don't have happy endings. Ever. And it's been four days since she disappeared."

The irony couldn't have been lost on him that his recent ruminations about the fate of missing persons in Alaska were being played out in his own backyard.

He dropped his arms between his legs and looked up. "I've gotta call the hometown police. I've waited too long already."

"We'll do that," Etienne assured him. "I'll make the call and talk to the chief myself. But give me a minute's worth of background. Who phoned Lorraine with the news about her mother?"

Ennis shook his head. "Don't know."

"But she thought the call was authentic?"

"Why wouldn't she think it was authentic? What kind of pervert makes up stuff like that?"

"Did she receive the call on your landline or her cell phone?"

He shook his head again. "Don't know. I was outside mowing the lawn, getting it clipped all nice and short before we left for vacation, so I never heard the phone ring." He frowned. "Why is that important?"

"It might help narrow things down. A stranger targeting Lorraine might call on your landline because those numbers are still available in a public phone book. But if the call came through on her cell, it might indicate that the caller knew Lorraine well enough to have her cell number, which would have a whole other subset of implications. How long after she received the call did she leave your house?"

Ennis focused on a spot on the wall, struggling to remember. "Not long—fifteen, maybe twenty minutes? We both knew there was no way in hell she'd be able to travel with her mom suffering a broken hip. There wasn't even any discussion. I told her I'd cancel our reservations, but she told me if I missed out on visiting a place that was at the top of my bucket list because of her mom's mishap, she'd never be able to live with herself, and neither would her mom, so she encouraged me to go without her. I told her that if she didn't go, I wasn't going either, but she said it was dumb for me to play martyr since she'd probably be with her mother for the next couple of weeks and wouldn't see me anyway. So she said I might as well hang out in Alaska with our friends. But she made me promise that if I fell in love with the place, we could plan another trip here next year." He regarded us with desperate eyes. "How do I not blame myself for this? If I'd been more insistent and stayed home, Lorraine might not be missing now."

"You don't know that, Ennis." I walked over to his chair and placed a comforting hand on his shoulder. "What happened to Lorraine might not have been within anyone's power to control."

"I should've gone with her to the hospital, but it didn't even occur to me. We've had so many medical emergencies with our parents that we agreed on a specialization of labor. She takes care of her mom's medical issues and I take care of my dad's." He exchanged a pained look with Etienne. "Can we call the police now?"

Etienne palmed his phone and flipped through his address book. "The chief will want to know a few basics. Lorraine's cell number. Make and model of her car. License plate number. How they can gain entry to your house. Can you write that information down for me?"

As Etienne dialed, I grabbed a pen and pad of paper off the desk and handed them to Ennis. "Could you use a cup of coffee? Latte? Cappuccino? Macchiato? Frappuccino? Wouldn't take me a minute to run down to the coffee bar."

"Thanks, Emily. That'd be great. I'm not sure caffeine is going to help my nerves, but it can't make me feel any worse."

"What's your preference?"

"Anything's fine. Surprise me."

I took the long way down to the ground floor to allow Ennis and Etienne the privacy they needed to make their call. Three flights of stairs and a maze of corridors later, I arrived at the conference room where we'd gathered with Lieutenant Kitchen earlier in the day, which seemed a lifetime ago now. Was it just me or was this tour shaping up to be one of those dreaded trips where we spent most of our time bouncing from one crisis to another?

I passed by the lounge, where I was happy to find Steele and Alison sitting side by side on a sofa, leaning into each other with casual ease, smiling flirtatiously. Thank goodness Steele had made a move. Maybe Grover would get the hint and back off now.

I arrived at the coffee bar as Goldie Kristiansen was leaving, her hand cradled around a tall plastic cup filled with a black raspberry-colored beverage. "That looks refreshing." I nodded toward her drink, which was floating in what looked like ten pounds of ice.

She elevated it in a toast. "Iced passion black tea mango lemonade. Today's special."

"For you or Grover?"

"For me, of course. He can buy his own." She laughed. "On second thought, maybe I *should* give it to him. 'Passion' being the operative word. Not that it'll have any effect on him. That ship sailed ages ago."

I forced an uncomfortable half-smile. *Uh-oh. Too much information.*

"But speaking of passion"—she nodded toward the lobby—"are the lovebirds still out there gazing deeply into each other's eyes? What's your take on the two of them? Is it young love or pure animal attraction? Grover and I were like that once. We could hardly keep our hands off each other. Don't ask me what happened."

"Speaking of animal attraction," I said in an undertone as I herded her away from the high-traffic area around the counter to a more secluded spot. "Have you noticed that Grover seems to be a wee bit smitten with Alison?"

"I'd be surprised if the whole world hasn't noticed. But he's not smitten, Emily. God, no. He's simply found a new audience to bore with all his useless trivia, so he's taking advantage of the situation."

"But that's pretty unfair to Alison, don't you think? She can't afford to be deliberately rude to the guests, but when Grover monopolizes all her time, he's preventing her from fulfilling her main purpose, which is to pay equal attention to *all* the guests. That's what we're paying her to do."

Goldie lifted one shoulder in a nonchalant shrug. "She looks like she'd know how to handle an irritating Iowa senior who never shuts up. In the meantime, I'm grateful to have someone else listen to him for a change. It makes me feel as if I'm truly on holiday. Now, if you'll excuse me"—she gestured toward the back of the hotel with her cup—"I have a date to meet Florence and Orphie for drinks and conversation at the pool before dinner, and I'm running late."

Toasting me once more, she hurried down the corridor in her flowy kaftan and flipflops. I returned to the coffee bar and placed my order for a latte, which the barista delivered after serving a half-dozen customers ahead of me. "Sorry to keep you waiting," she apologized as she handed me the drink. "I wouldn't ordinarily have this much foot traffic, but the tram and main mountain trail are closed down because of the hiking accident last night, so guests suddenly have time to kill."

"I know." I lowered my voice. "It was one of the guests in my tour group who died."

The young barista, whose nametag identified her as Gwen, clapped her hands over her mouth. "Oh, geez, I'm so sorry. I heard rumors that the victim was a guest at the resort, but management isn't telling us much…other than to alert guests that the tram will be starting operations again in about an hour, just in time for the dinner crowd to catch a ride up to the restaurant."

"Is the trail opening too?" If that happened, it would indicate that the forensics team had wrapped up their investigation, which might mean that Lieutenant Kitchen could be calling us with more conclusive information at any time.

"Haven't heard anything about opening the trail. Just the tram and the restaurant." Her eyes shifted left and right before focusing on me dead center, her expression one of breathless apprehension. "Do you know anything more than I do? I've worked here for three summers without anyone ever dying, fog or no fog." Her voice grew more hushed. "Have you been following the explosion on social media today? The picture of Bigfoot taken right outside here on the mountain? Some of us have been talking in the break room; crazy as it might sound, we're thinking the reason why management is keeping us in the dark is because there might be some connection between the dead hiker and…and the photo of Bigfoot. Have you heard any rumors about that?"

The girl was obviously worried, and justifiably so. But I wasn't about to tell her that the person who first gave voice to the concept was my own mother. "I'm sure it might seem natural to suspect a connection between the two, but I don't believe there's any evidence to support the theory that Bigfoot, if he exists, is aggressive toward humans. The rap on him is that he's a herbivore, which makes him a bit more shy and something of a wuss."

She arched a ring-pierced eyebrow. "Well, I'm an ovo-lacto vegetarian, which is kinda like being the human version of a herbivore, but that doesn't mean I won't bop someone a good one if I feel threatened. My mom's so worried about what's happening here, she wants me back home in Anchorage with her until the police make a ruling about how the hiker died."

Considering the disturbing headlines out of Anchorage, I wasn't sure moving back there would be any better.

When I arrived back at the room, Ennis was still slumped in the armchair, looking even more dazed than he had before, while Etienne paced across the floor, talking on his cell. I handed the latte to Ennis, who seemed to perk up a little as he boosted himself up in the chair. "Thanks, Emily. I feel like I've been hit in the gut with a two-by-four."

"Is Etienne still talking to the police chief?"

Ennis shook his head as he uncapped his drink. "Lieutenant Kitchen phoned when he was talking to Chief Burns, so he's returning the call."

"What did the chief have to say?" Etienne and Chief Burns played racquetball together, so they were buds.

"He took down all the information I gave him. He's planning to get my house key from our next-door neighbor so he can have a look around the premises and check our landline for messages. And he wants to find a photo of Lorraine to share with the local news—maybe put out an all-points bulletin."

"That sounds promising, huh?"

He stared at the foam floating on his latte. "You might not have paid any attention, Emily, but I was the recipient of an award the college handed out a couple of months ago. It's an annual award for excellence and it comes with a pretty hefty cash stipend, a hundred thousand dollars, which the news agencies picked up on and made public. So Chief Burns is wondering if Lorraine's disappearance might be connected to that. He says there's a possibility someone might be holding her for ransom, which is the main reason he wants to check our phone messages."

I didn't know what to say. Lorraine Iversen from Windsor City, Iowa, being held for possible ransom? Windsor City was a place that hosted Senior Olympics at the mall, financed county-wide corn shucking contests during harvest, and sponsored the annual Hog Queen and her float in the Independence Day parade. Windsor City was not a place that turned out home-grown kidnappers. "Did Chief Burns recommend that you fly home?"

"I offered to do that, but he's recommending that I sit tight until he has something concrete to offer me. He basically said there's nothing I'd be able to do back home other than worry, so I might as well do my worrying here instead of the police station, which is pretty much the same advice Lorraine gave me before she went missing."

Iowans were obviously of one mind about the sanctity of a person's summer holiday.

Ennis sighed. "I'll need to break the news to Florence, but I'm afraid how it's going to hit her. Coupled with the problems she's having with Thor, it could be the straw that breaks the camel's back. Any way you look at it, it's not going to be pretty."

"Do you need moral support? If you think it might help, I could go with you."

"Thanks for the offer, Emily, but I'll try going it alone. If Florence gets too emotional, though, I might give you a call. Handling emotional outbursts isn't my strong suit." He nodded toward Etienne as he stood up. "Thank him again for all his help, would you? Having him spearhead the interaction helps me feel a lot more positive."

Etienne ended his phone call just as I let Ennis out the door. Exhaling a sigh, he regarded me in frustration. "Lieutenant Kitchen extends his apologies, but at this time their evidence is too inconclusive to determine Delpha's cause and manner of death, whether it was accidental or a deliberate act. The only thing they're saying is that the circumstances are suspicious."

"So where does that leave us?"

"It leaves us with an open case. The medical examiner has completed his autopsy, but they're not going to make his findings available to the public until a later date, pending more investigation. In the meantime they're holding Delpha's body at the examiner's office in Anchorage, and they won't release it until her sister signs the authorization papers."

"Have they been able to track her down yet?"

He shook his head. "She's apparently as incommunicado as a human can be and still be on the planet."

"So now what?"

"Now, we wait."

I wrapped my arms around his waist and snuggled against his chest. "Incommunicado. Sounds heavenly, doesn't it?"

"Maybe we should include a new destination on our brochure— Off the Grid: a place where guests can be free from the constant assault of information from cell phones, iPads, internet alerts, Twitter, and cable TV."

I laughed. "Don't expect anyone from Iowa to sign up. A day without electronics would be worse than condemning the entire gang to hell—although I bet they'd even consider hell if it offered free Wi-Fi."

My phone chimed.

Etienne kissed the crown of my head and dropped his arms from around my back. "Perhaps we should consider taking the Off the Grid trip by ourselves."

I dug my phone out of my shoulder bag and read the incoming text. "Well, good news for a change. Jackie says the two Toms are recovering nicely from their surgeries, Mildred is continuing to improve, and the remaining guests got through the rest of the day without having to be transported to the hospital." I smiled with relief. "Isn't that great? Five guests on Jackie's tour aren't in the hospital yet." I typed an immediate reply.

"How did you respond?" asked Etienne as he began to unbutton his shirt.

"And I quote, 'Excellent. Keep up the good work.'" I watched with fascination as he peeled off his shirt, unfastened his belt, and kicked off his shoes. "Are you taking a quick shower before dinner?" I checked the time. "Better hurry. We have to be downstairs in thirty minutes."

His voice grew low, seductive. "That gives us plenty of time for what I have in mind." He stepped out of his slacks, electrifying every nerve-ending in my body as he flashed a slow, suggestive smile.

"Right now?"

"Right now."

As he backed me up to the edge of the bed, all reflective thought flew out of my head…except for one stickler. "Etienne? Would you tell me what you think?"

"I think you should stop talking." Off flew my top.

"No, this is serious. Remember all the guys who visited the museum before dinner yesterday? Every one of them except George and Osmond left the museum early for parts unknown. Do you think that could be significant?"

He feathered a kiss along the slant of my cheek and whispered his mouth over my lips. "Shhh."

"Don't you find it suspicious?"

He covered my mouth with his own, his breath warm, his voice husky as he found the zipper of my capris and worked downward from there. "No."

TWELVE

WE LOADED THE BUS at seven o'clock the next morning to begin the six-hour drive north to Denali National Park and Preserve, which boasts the tallest mountain in the United States. The peak, once known as Mt. McKinley, had its original name restored by our forty-fourth president, so it's now simply called Denali, which, loosely translated, is Athabascan for "really tall mountain."

Athabascans don't waste time with flowery language.

They cut right to the chase.

Given Ennis Iversen's concern with Lorraine, Etienne and I had checked the transportation options out of Denali and had discovered that if Ennis needed to fly back to Iowa in a hurry, we could book a flight for him on a private plane flying out of one of the area's nine smaller airfields. He'd been relieved to know he'd have a quick escape route, but that hadn't prevented him from dragging his feet and looking really strung out when he boarded the bus. I suspected he hadn't slept a wink all night.

Florence was no longer schlepping Thor's photographic equipment, but she didn't seem to be taking much pleasure in her victory. With her bloodshot eyes and barely combed hair, she was looking as ragged as Ennis. He'd told her about Lorraine's disappearance before dinner last night, informing her first before he made the announcement to the rest of the group, and true to his prediction, the news had upset her so much that she'd been unable to eat a thing at supper. Chances were she hadn't slept last night either, so maybe our six-hour ride would give both her and Ennis an opportunity to nap.

While Etienne and Steele posted themselves at the front and rear doors of the bus to help guests aboard, I hung out by the front door of the hotel with my clipboard, checking off names. Orphie hurried toward me weighed down with shopping bags that hung from her arms like shirts on a clothes rack.

I checked off her name. "Successful shopping trip in town yesterday, I see."

"You bet it was. I bought something for everyone. I even bought a souvenir for Lorraine. I just hope she gets to see it." She shook her head. "It rattles you to the bone when big city crime starts rearing its head right down the street from you."

"Did you and Al ever get your phone calls coordinated?"

"He called me last night—from North Carolina, of all places."

"No kidding? You never mentioned he was traveling south."

"I didn't know! It was a spur of the moment trip, actually. A developer contacted him about the possibility of having a hotel with an indoor water park built on the outskirts of town, so he offered to fly Al to North Carolina in his private jet so Al could tour the facility the developer built outside Asheville. It's all so out of the blue. But we could only talk for about three minutes because his phone ran out of juice, so I only got the bare bones."

"But we already have a water park."

"That's an *outside* facility. This one will be *inside*, so families will be able to use it all year-round. Think of the tourist dollars this could generate, Emily. Al is really going to make a name for himself if he can push this deal through."

A frisson of unease rippled through me. "Where on the outskirts of town is he talking about building it?"

"As far away from the outdoor water park as possible. On the opposite side of town."

"But that's all farmland."

"I know. Al mentioned something about eminent domain, but his phone died before he could finish. Isn't it exciting?"

I watched her head toward the bus in all her anticipatory bliss.

No, it wasn't exciting. That farmland belonged to my dad!

Goldie Kristiansen, her throat and wrists dripping in bangles that jingled like sleigh bells, was the last name I checked off. "Did you check off Grover's name already?" she asked as we walked to the bus.

"You bet. You're the last one to arrive."

"Well, I'm glad you've seen Grover because I had absolutely no idea where he was. I was rather getting my hopes up that we could leave him behind." She sighed. "Next time maybe."

As Etienne assisted her onto the bus, I spied Steele chatting with Alison and realized with chagrin how remiss I'd been about keeping him personally informed about all that had been happening.

"I'm so embarrassed," I apologized when I joined them.

"About what?" asked Steele.

153

"I haven't been keeping you in the loop. Things have been so crazy, I…" I stirred the air with my hand. "I'm really sorry. I promise to do better."

He laughed. "No worries. I'm up to speed." He tucked an errant wisp of hair behind Alison's ear—an innocent gesture that throbbed with intimacy. "Alison's been Johnny-on-the-spot."

"Thanks, Alison." I gave her forearm a grateful squeeze. "Uh… could I speak with you for a sec?"

"That doesn't sound good," Steele teased, "so I'll see you ladies on the coach." He winked good-naturedly and sprinted up the stepwell. I drew Alison aside, far enough away from the bus so that none of the guests would be able to hear our conversation, even if their windows happened to be down.

"I'll make this quick: Is Grover Kristiansen bothering you?"

"Grover. The small-boned guy who wears the wide-brimmed hat with the chin cord? The one who seems genetically incapable of allowing anyone else to talk? *That* Grover?"

"That's him. Has he become too much of a pest for you to handle politely?"

"Other than chattering like a magpie, he seems like a pretty good Joe. He's not obnoxious or bad-tempered; he just likes to talk. And to be honest, it's kind of a relief. I don't have to think of anything to say when he starts in on his lectures, so it's like a coffee break for my brain. I can figure out what I'm supposed to be doing next without listening to a single word he says. All I have to do is pretend I'm watching his lips move. But if he decides to test me on the information, I'm toast."

"You don't think you're the victim of overkill?"

She shook her head. "I'm cool with Grover. It's the grouchy guests I don't understand. They're on this great vacation with incredible scenery and really nice people and all they can do is complain. Who does that?"

She must have had a run-in with Bernice. "Okay, then. I'll take you at your word. But if he becomes too overbearing, let me know and I'll see what I can do about redirecting his attention."

"You got it."

"By the way, I like your tattoo." I wiggled my finger at the blue-winged butterfly beneath her ear. "I'm not sure I'd ever be brave enough to get inked."

She touched her neck as if reminding herself what was there. "You mean this old thing?" She laughed. "My cosmetology class decided we should celebrate our graduation by doing something a little wild but tasteful, so we all marched into the nearest tattoo parlor and got inked. Stupid, huh? When I'm eighty years old and my skin's all crepey, people will wonder why I have a shriveled Smurf on my neck." She smiled. "Try saying that eight times after knocking back a couple of margaritas."

I fished my phone out of my shoulder bag. "Will you stand in front of the bus so I can take a picture? It should be good advertising for the both of us. I'll send you the JPEG."

As Alison stood by the rear wheels, striking a pose with her hand sweeping toward the aurora borealis on the side of the bus, I carefully framed the shot to exclude the window above her head where Grover Kristiansen sat with his nose pressed to the window, staring down at her like a cat desperate to pounce.

"Before we get too far," Etienne announced as Steele revved the engine, "you might appreciate an update on the progress the police are making on Delpha's case." For the next several minutes he reiterated the same information he'd given me last night with relation to the police's inability to make a ruling on the cause and manner of death, their decision to withhold the results of the autopsy report, and their continued efforts to contact Delpha's sister.

"How long is Delpha's sister supposed to be in Mongolia?" asked Lucille Rasmussen.

"I think it was for a month," said Orphie. "If you're traveling halfway around the world, you can't be bothered with this long weekend stuff. And speaking of air travel, for those of you who haven't heard, my Al is in North Carolina right now on the verge of closing a huge land development deal with a fella who has his own private jet. He's being wined and dined at an exclusive—"

"Are you sure that's legal?" asked Dick Stolee. "Sounds like pay-to-play to me."

"Quid pro quo," said Tilly. "An exchange of favors. You give me something and I'll give you something in return. Never a good idea in the political arena."

"You scratch my back, I'll scratch yours," Dick Teig piped up.

"Exactly," Tilly agreed. "In many instances a prosecutable offense."

"No," Dick corrected as he angled his arms behind his head. "My back is really itchy. Can someone scratch it for me?"

"I'm sure Mr. Arnesen is conducting Windsor City's business in an ethical manner," Etienne offered in an attempt to calm the waters. "But if you have questions, I suggest you plan to attend the public meetings the council should be scheduling about the issue.

I'll now turn the mic over to Alison, who'll be entertaining you for the next several hours. Alison."

He handed her the mic as we pulled onto the road. "Morning, everyone. We have a long ride ahead of us today, but I aim to make it as enjoyable as possible for you. A little trivia, a little music, snacks, comfort stops, and, of course, spectacular scenery. We'll be traveling on a highway that parallels the route of the Alaska railroad, so I'd like to begin our journey by filling you in on a little history of that railroad project. Construction first got underway in 1904 and was financed by a private company whose ambition was to lay 470 miles of track between the interior of Alaska and the sea—Fairbanks to Seward. By 1912 a grand total of 71 miles of track had been laid, which was a good start, but unfortunately the company ran into financial difficulties and had to shut down, which is when the government stepped in. So in 1914 President Woodrow Wilson received authorization from Congress to—"

"This land development deal of Al Arnesen's," I whispered to Etienne as he sat down beside me. "Do you know what land is in his sights? Dad's farm! There's even talk of eminent domain."

Grasping my hand, he leaned close to my ear, his voice an undertone. "Nothing has been decided, bella. Try not to overreact."

"But what about Mom and Dad?"

"Do they know their farm is being targeted?"

"I don't think so."

"Then don't tell them."

"But what if Orphie tells them where the new attraction is supposed to be located?"

"Considering the blowback she received about Al's rather shady dealings, I doubt she'll ever raise the topic again."

That's right. She was probably kicking herself for trumpeting Al's trip in the first place. Temporarily relieved, I exhaled a breath and settled back in my seat. "Thanks," I whispered to Etienne, who pressed my hand to his mouth to grace it with a lingering kiss.

"Despite battling constant problems with permafrost and landslides," I heard Alison say as I refocused on her narration, "the railroad was officially completed on July 15, 1923, and President Warren Harding drove the golden spike at Nenana, whose location on the Nenana River gives it access to the Yukon River, which empties into the Bering Sea. Nenana is north of Denali, so you won't get to see the golden spike, but if you're interested in a replica, any souvenir shop—"

"I have a question," Dick Stolee shouted out. "How can the Yukon River be in Alaska if the Yukon's in Canada?"

My phone chimed with a familiar ring. I plucked it out of my shoulder bag before Alison could even finish her sentence. "What's up?" I asked in a hushed tone.

"Will you let me explain?" Jackie urged. "I neglected to take into account the Silo Slider."

"The what?"

"The Silo Slider. It's this waterslide thing that corkscrews inside a fake silo and extends outside the building over a long patio of concrete where the slide ends. It opened for the first time last night after I texted you—on a midnight run, something I might have known was scheduled to happen if I hadn't spent all day at the hospital."

"And?"

"And Pearl Peacock and Arvella Bly were first in line because the guys insinuated that the two girls would be too chicken to sluice down a slide on their backsides at umpteen miles an hour with a flood of cold water soaking them to the skin. So the girls thumbed their noses at the guys and climbed like a thousand stairs to the top of the slide." Jackie snorted into the phone. "The guys were so clueless, Em. Pearl and Arvella might be grammas, but they're no shrinking violets. They grew up on Iowa swine farms where they cut their teeth learning to castrate hogs. So I mean, once you've been that chummy with a three-hundred-pound pig, what's left to be afraid of, right?"

"I don't think the pigs weigh three hundred pounds at the time they're neutered."

"Whatever. So Pearl goes first. Spiraling down the corkscrew in twenty seconds of unobstructed gravity. Zooming out of the building under the lights…where she flies over the rim of the slide and smacks onto pavement and continues skidding over the concrete for at least ten more feet."

"Omigod, *no.*"

"And Arvella's already in route behind her and ends up zooming out of the building, over the side, and onto the concrete too."

The muscles in my stomach twisted into a Gordian knot. "How badly are they hurt?"

"Well, if they hadn't been wearing hiking pants made of quick-drying, tear-resistant microfiber—I am *so* sold on the toughness of microfiber now, Em. I'm thinking of having my sofa reupholstered in the stuff because, did I tell you? I'm thinking of getting a cat, and I haven't decided if I should have her declawed. There are two schools of thought on—"

"Jack!"

"Sorry. All these tour incidents keep interfering with my personal crises. Anyway, their injuries would have been a lot worse if they'd been wearing light-weight cotton or shorter pants or, God forbid, bathing suits, so they don't need plastic surgery for their scrapes, but the docs are keeping them in the hospital for observation because their CT scans showed some evidence of head trauma. Only minor concussions, but when you're in your late seventies, even a minor concussion can be problematic. Mildred, of course, is delighted. She's trying to organize a bridge game in her room this afternoon."

"So are you at the hotel or the hospital?"

"Hospital. And I've been up all night, so I actually have dark circles under my eyes that are proving to be resistant to concealer. I'm an eligible divorcee, Emily, in a hospital full of high income–earning doctors, none of whom are going to take a second look at me if I'm sporting circles as black as grease paint under my eyes. I look like an escapee from the morgue."

"I'm very proud of the way you're handling this, Jack. Talk about a baptism by fire, but you're doing everything right. And I'm sure your constant presence at the hospital is a great comfort to Mildred…and the Toms…and Pearl…and Arvella." I hesitated. "Is that everyone?"

"For now. And just so you know, Pearl's and Arvella's families are headed this way and they wanted me to tell you how grateful they are for your more than generous offer of free lodging while they're here. They think that's really upstanding."

"We wouldn't have it any other way," I wheezed as I thumped my fist against my breastbone to clear my windpipe.

"I am *so* wiped out. Would it be okay with you if I asked Johnny to fill in for me at the hospital while I catch forty winks back at the hotel?"

I nodded.

"What?"

"Fine," I said when I could breathe again. "Maybe he plays bridge."

"Wouldn't that be the bomb? He could be the fourth in Mildred's game. I'll call him right now. And one more thing. About my clothing allow—"

"No."

"But—"

"Hang in there, Jack, and call me with any updates." I slumped in my seat, my head still spinning. "Three healthy guests left," I said to Etienne, "and a new contingent of concerned relatives whose lodging we'll need to comp for an indefinite amount of time."

"Jackie's made all the right decisions so far, bella. There's nothing that generates goodwill like an offer of free lodging."

"Can we afford it?"

"We can't afford not to. But the upside is that the remaining guests only have two more days at the park. It's probably statistically impossible for anything else to go wrong."

Sure, sure. Where had I heard *that* before?

We spent the next six hours traveling on a highway that was amazingly devoid of traffic. We motored through endless miles of trees, crossed raging rivers and babbling brooks that were milky blue with glacial runoff, gaped at the endless parade of mountain ranges hunched on the horizon, watched birds with enormous wingspans soar above us, and passed pizzerias, liquor stores, RV centers, campgrounds, truck dealerships, storage sheds, one Walmart Supercenter near Wasilla, and not much else. It smacked of what the Scottish Highlands might look like with more trees and fewer sheep.

"Are we almost at the town yet?" Goldie Kristiansen called out after the group had finished singing the Iowa version of "A Hundred Bottles of Beer on the Wall," where the booze was replaced by "ears of corn on the plate."

"Denali isn't actually a town," admitted Alison. "By comparison, the largest city in Alaska is Anchorage, which is home to 41 percent of the state's population, or about three hundred thousand people. Denali Borough, on the other hand, has a permanent population of about nineteen hundred people, so we're not talking about a major metropolitan area. More like a flag stop on the rail line."

"We got more members in my church than that," said Nana.

"My grandson's got more players on his softball team than that," joked Dick Stolee.

"Are you saying there's no place I'll be able to have my hair professionally styled?" pressed Goldie.

"Not unless the Majestic resorts have in-house salons. I can check on that for you. Majestic Cruise Line is the big kahuna in the area. They offer the best hotel accommodations, the best restaurants, the best—"

"So why aren't we staying there?" demanded Bernice.

Alison didn't skip a beat. "Because the place Destinations Travel has booked you into offers a much more authentic Alaskan ambiance than Majestic Cruise Line's luxurious but unremarkable resorts. Unlike the Majestic properties, you'll have a woodland setting, an adorable cabin all your own, peace and quiet from the congestion of the park, easy access to—"

"Sounds like you're trying to put lipstick on a pig," crabbed Bernice.

"We're not staying in a place like the Bates Hotel, are we?" questioned Helen Teig.

"Heck no," defended Alison. "The Bates Hotel didn't have a hot tub or an onsite diner or free Wi-Fi or a gift shop."

"How many stars in the tourbook guide?" challenged Bernice.

Alison cleared her throat. "Uhh…multiple, I'm sure."

"Back in my day a place earned four stars if it had an indoor john," Osmond reminisced. "Five if toilet paper was included."

"What about mosquitoes?" asked George. "I've heard tell they're as big as dragonflies in interior parts of the state that are really remote."

I peered out the window. So basically everywhere.

Alison smiled. "They're not quite that big, but I have repellent that I'll be happy to share."

"Are Alaskan mosquitoes the dangerous kind?" asked Alice.

"I'm unfamiliar with the toxicity of Alaskan mosquitoes," Tilly said in her professor's voice, "but there are a substantial number of diseases that can be transmitted by the insect. Dengue fever, malaria, West Nile virus, filariasis, Western equine encephalitis, Eastern equine encephalitis, Venezuelan equine encephalitis, chikungunya."

"What if we all discover we're sick with this stuff when we get back home?" asked Dick Teig, who was already scratching his neck at the thought of future bites. "Will the clinic have the right antidotes? Will they be able to treat us or are we gonna be dead meat?"

"No need to panic," soothed Margi. "I'm pretty sure the illnesses Tilly just rattled off aren't on the Windsor City Clinic's list of most deadly diseases. The disorders that kill our patients usually have shorter names."

As we rolled into the parking lot of a sprawling complex of small log cabins, appropriately named Wilderness Cabins, I felt an undercurrent of anticipation ripple through the bus. "Welcome to Denali," trilled Alison as Steele cut the engine.

The cabins looked to be constructed of cedar and were perched on raised platforms that were connected by a network of plank sidewalks. As big as two-car garages, with petunias dripping from hanging baskets and lawn chairs arranged on outdoor decks, they were nestled amid towering fir trees and brought to mind a vision of what summer camp might have looked like if I'd ever attended summer camp.

"I thought you said we were going to be in the boonies," Thor Thorsen spoke up.

Alison laughed. "This isn't boonie enough for you? It's a long walk to civilization from here."

"So what's with the gridlock in the parking lot?" he challenged.

He was right. There was an unusual number of cars, SUVs, and vans in the lot, which made me wonder if scores of hungry tourists were eating in the cabins' onsite diner...until I realized that the side panels of each vehicle were emblazoned with eye-catching logos.

Uh-oh.

"They look like news vans to me," said George.

"Sure do," agreed Dick Stolee. "A bunch of them are even equipped with their own satellite dishes."

"What can possibly be newsworthy in the boonies?" scoffed Orphie.

"Do you suppose there's been another Bigfoot sighting?" asked Helen.

Gasps. Nervous tittering. Collective rubbernecking.

"Could it be the same one Bob saw?" asked Margi.

"I never actually saw it," Dad spoke up.

"Couldn't be the same one," asserted Dick Teig. "How'd he get here before we did? Helicopter?"

"There's no way a Cyclopean hominid would be allowed on a helicopter," argued Tilly. "Too many FAA regulations."

"There's gotta be more of them apes than the one what Bob seen," Nana chimed in.

"I didn't see it," repeated Dad.

"Maybe he's got relatives what live in the area."

"That ape is not going to book a helicopter ride," scoffed Bernice. "Do you know why? Two words."

"No money?" suggested George.

"No pants," said Bernice. "Who's gonna want to occupy a seat just vacated by a musty-smelling, tick-infested, flea-carrying ape? It's all about the upholstery."

"That's stupid," chided Margi.

"Is not."

"Is so."

"What kind of legal tender would an ape use?" mused Dick Teig.

"My money's on a credit card," said Helen. "American Express applications get mailed to everyone."

"My Mr. Fluffy received one last month," Lucille admitted. "He was even preapproved."

I listened to their discussion with some concern. They were actually arguing about whether a mythical creature qualified for an American Express card. Either they were being more eccentric than usual or they'd all managed to weasel out of the dementia screening portion of their annual wellness exams last year.

I popped out of my seat to address the group while Etienne and Steele scooted out the front exit door. "While Steele offloads your luggage, Etienne is going to run to the office to pick up your room keys and site maps. So once you have your suitcase in hand, head toward the office so Etienne can give you your key."

"Our suitcases aren't being delivered to our rooms?" questioned Helen Teig in a sour tone.

"Not this time. We're heading out again in a couple of hours to tour the park, so if you need access to anything in your suitcase, it'll be quicker if you roll it to your cabin yourself."

"I bet the guests at the Majestic resorts don't have to schlep their own luggage," taunted Bernice.

I threw a long look down the aisle at her. "If you'd like to ditch my tours for the Majestic brand, Bernice, I promise not to be offended."

"Show of hands," Osmond whooped as he waved his hand for attention. "How many people think Bernice should sign up for another company's—"

"No voting!" I cut him off.

"Say, the food in the diner must be pretty good," observed George. "Look at all the folks hustling outta that place."

They poured out of the eatery and crowded around the office that was located next door—a teeming mass of humanity with cameras and microphones and determined looks in their eyes. No newsworthy incidents had better be unfolding in the rest of Alaska today because it looked as if every news outlet in the state was camped out right here.

As my guys struggled to their feet with tired groans and an audible creak of limbs, I offered last-minute instructions. "Just to remind you again, the tour bus from Denali Park is scheduled to pick us up here in the parking lot at three o'clock, so please don't dillydally in your rooms. Find your cabin, freshen up, wander over to the office gift shop to look over the snack selection if you're hungry for a mid-afternoon nibble, then hightail it over to this building we're parked in front of so we can count heads." I gestured toward the cabin directly opposite us with the hot tub outside and rocking chairs on the porch. "I'm guessing that's the guest lodge. And don't forget to bring binoculars or other special photographic equipment you plan to use."

"What is it we're supposed to be seeing on this tour?" Goldie called out.

"I'll answer that," Alison spoke up. "The biggies are moose, caribou, and grizzly bear. This is the ultimate Alaskan wildlife experience, where you'll see animals up close and personal in their natural environment. So much better than a zoo. Trust me. This adventure is going to knock your socks off."

"Couldn't we get the same effect by simply watching one of those Disney nature movies?" questioned Helen.

"Looks like Steele has all the luggage compartments open," I said as everyone piled into the aisle in relative slow motion. "Be careful exiting. Watch your step."

I sprinted down the front stairs to assist with offloading, surprised when the gaggle of news people outside the office swiveled their bodies around to study our bus. As if controlled by one brain, they all looked down to check their phones at the same time, and when they'd finished reading and swiping, they looked up, paused for a heartbeat, then began to move all at once, like runners at the start of a marathon fighting to break out of the pack.

"Are you the Destinations Travel bus?" one of them shouted as they raced in our direction. "The group out of Iowa?"

They swarmed around the luggage bays, holding their cameras at the ready and firing up their microphones.

"That's him," someone else yelled as Dad descended the stairs.

Cameras whirred, elbows flew, and bodies bumped as they jockeyed for better angles.

"Mr. Andrew! Do you stand by your theory that the Bigfoot monster you saw in Girdwood was responsible for the death of the as-yet-unidentified woman who was a member of your tour group?"

Dad paused on the stepwell, looking gobsmacked. "I never said that."

"*I* said it!" cried Bernice, posing like the Statue of Liberty with her arm raised above her head. "Me! Bernice Zwerg. Former magazine model. It's *my* theory, not Bob's, and I expect you to give me full credit for it."

Brushing off Bernice as if she were a pesky gnat, the reporters refocused on Dad.

"Mr. Andrew, I'm sure you're aware that your traveling companion was killed on the very mountain where you took your now infamous picture, so if you were to devise a theory, what would it be?"

Dad blinked. "What?"

"The police haven't released any information about the circumstances surrounding your companion's death," another reporter called out. "Do you think that's because they found evidence that she was killed by Bigfoot and they don't want to scare tourists away?"

"Dunno."

"Would you agree that if a deranged ape is on a killing spree in the mountains around Girdwood, the police should inform the public immediately?"

Dad nodded. "Yup."

"How do you feel about the police department's refusal to share any details about this tragic accident, Mr. Andrew?"

"I figure that's their busi—"

"So you think it was an accident?"

"No!"

"So if you don't think it was an accident, do you agree she was deliberately targeted and killed by Bigfoot?"

Whirr. Whirr. Clickclickclick.

Dad raised his forearm like a shield in front of his face, squinting at the explosion of camera flashes.

"Can you be more specific about what Bigfoot actually looks like, Mr. Andrew? Height? Weight? Dermal composition?"

"I didn't see him."

"But what about your photo? How could you post a picture of the creature if you didn't see it?"

"I was showcasing the scenery."

"So you thought you were uploading photos of…what? Trees?"

Dad nodded. "They've got some pretty nice ones over on that mountain."

Whispers. Buzzing. Curious looks.

"Did you know the original tweet that claimed Bigfoot attacked a hiker went viral on Twitter, Mr. Andrew? Thirty thousand retweets? Over a hundred thousand likes?"

"That was *my* tweet," protested Bernice. "Those are *my* likes. *I* made that happen. Would you like to get a picture of me?" She slithered her way through the crowd to stand in front of Dad. Standing at an angle and sucking in her stomach, she preened for the camera. "Should I say cheese?"

The pool of reporters lowered their cameras and sidled uncomfortable glances at each other, which is when I stepped in, addressing them in an easygoing tone. "I hate to break this up, folks, but we're on a tight schedule, so if you don't move out of the way and allow my guests to pick up their luggage, our itinerary is really going to be messed up."

"What about my photo shoot?" complained Bernice as the throng of reporters took what I said to heart and shuffled toward the sidelines.

"Thanks anyway, ma'am," one of them shouted to Bernice. "Maybe another time."

"Oh, sure." She threw them a disgusted look. "You bozos will never make it as paparazzi."

"Grab your suitcases, everyone, and start heading over to the office," I instructed as I shooed them along. "Anyone not finding the right bag?"

With an assist from Alison and Steele, we aimed them in the right direction and watched them trudge to the office, where Etienne was waiting with their keys and site maps. With keys in hand they started to peel off in search of their cabins, but the reporters remained close by, loitering in the parking lot, looking as if they were waiting to pounce again, which they did when Mom and Dad struck out along the raised walkway.

"Mr. Andrew, would you take a minute to clarify?" a woman called out as she and her colleagues chased behind them. "Is it your opinion that Bigfoot killed the woman in your party who was hiking on the mountain trail in Girdwood?"

I wondered if one of the qualifications of being a good reporter was the ability to rearrange words in a sentence in such a way that they could ask the same question ten times in a row and not have it sound like the same question.

Mom and Dad picked up their pace.

So did the reporters.

"Mr. Andrew, from what you saw of the monster, would you classify it as a member of the bear or the ape family?"

Mom stopped abruptly, spun around, and, with hands fisted on her hips, confronted Dad's tormentors. "Stop it! I'm traveling with my elderly mother and you're scaring her half to death with this talk of yours, so I'm warning you to go away before you cause her to suffer a major heart event from which she'll never recover. God help you if you have to carry a burden like that around with you for the rest of your lives. How will you sleep at night?"

Penitent silence ensued for all of three seconds before someone threw out, "Are you Mrs. Andrew? Mrs. Andrew, did you see the creature too? Or was your husband the only person who got a good look at it?"

Etienne joined me near the office patio where I was watching the scene play out. "What do the newshounds want?"

"They want to conflate Dad's photo with Bernice's tweet so they can get Dad to hypothesize that Bigfoot killed Delpha."

"Are they having any luck?"

"Not with Dad. Bernice, on the other hand, is miffed that no one is asking her to pose for a photo shoot."

Mom and Dad scurried to a nearby cabin.

The media followed in hot pursuit.

Etienne shook his head. "Persistence is one thing, but what they're doing looks as if it's bordering on harassment. Shall I warn them to back off?"

I held up my hand to stall him. "Not quite yet."

Mom and Dad disappeared inside the cabin, leaving their pursuers to putz aimlessly around the grounds, swatting mosquitoes.

"Oh my god, this is the perfect solution. Mom is going to be so busy fending off reporters, she won't have time to stalk Nana." I pumped my fists in the air. "Yes."

Etienne's phone chimed. "Miceli."

He listened to the caller, his face unreadable as he uttered a string of throwaway phrases that included several "uh-huhs" and at least one "I understand." When he hung up, his handsome face had turned dour. "That was Lieutenant Kitchen."

I winced. "Bad news?"

"Based on the evidence they've collected, they're no longer treating Delpha's death as suspicious. They've ruled it a homicide."

THIRTEEN

"OH, NO."

"He's driving up here tomorrow to conduct further interviews with the group. He's apparently discovered a number of gaping holes he needs to fill in."

"Uff-da." I sucked in my breath. "The guests who left the museum early? The ones Osmond and George spoke to me about? I *told* you there was something suspicious about that. Maybe Lieutenant Kitchen found out about their early departures and wants to know where they went afterward."

"He didn't say which guests he plans to question, bella."

"It has to be them: Thor, Grover, Ennis, and Alison. Kitchen knew which guests visited the museum, but he never asked how long they stayed or if anyone left early. Don't you find it curious that no one volunteered to tell him? Other than the Dicks, and they don't count."

"So are you suggesting that one of the four may have slipped into the fog, hunted down Delpha on the hiking trail, and killed her in such a way that the police couldn't determine it was murder until today?"

I twitched my lips. Why did my theories always sound so dopey when they came out of his mouth? "Well, there was no love lost between Thor and Delpha. He might have decided to get even with her for the embarrassment she caused him."

"And the other three?"

I gnawed my bottom lip. "I don't know what their motive would have been. Everyone seemed to like Delpha—Thor being the exception."

"Hard to pin a murder on people who lack a motive."

"Except"—I speared the air with my forefinger in a eureka gesture—"I might not have mentioned this to you, but on our first night at the resort, when we were all in the lobby, I noticed Delpha staring at Grover, Goldie, and Ennis, and it was pretty unsettling. You wouldn't have believed the look in her eyes. They were spitting pure hatred."

"You're sure she was looking at *them* and not something else?"

"I'm positive." I gave my head a definitive nod. "At least, I'm pretty sure." I pinched my eyes shut in order to reexamine the memory, but it was suddenly fuzzy around the edges. "I thought she was looking at them at the time, but—" My voice faded as my level of confidence plummeted. I heaved a sigh. "What else could she have been looking at?"

Etienne caressed the back of my neck. "Why don't we leave that to Lieutenant Kitchen to determine?"

We grabbed our suitcases and rolled them to our cabin with its cheery basket of pink wave petunias hanging from the eaves and a matched set of Adirondack chairs bookending the door. The room

174

was northwoods rustic with natural cedar boards covering the walls and ceiling, a wildlife quilt spread across a queen-size bed, a small flat screen TV perched on the dresser, heavy-duty blackout curtains, a coffee maker with disposable cups, and a sheet of paper on the desk that read:

Urgent Notice—

Due to a pipe failure in our main well, water to your cabin is temporarily unavailable. We apologize for any inconvenience this might cause and trust that the problem will be resolved quickly. The public restroom in the guest lodge is not affected by the shutdown, so we invite you to use those facilities should the need arise. During this emergency, bottled water will be available in the lodge at no extra charge. We hope you enjoy your stay.

—The Management

"Uh-oh." I shot a desperate look at Etienne as he walked out of the bathroom. I held the paper up for him to read. "There's no water."

"Ah. The explanation for why nothing happened when I turned on the faucet."

I regarded him with alarm. "The water can't possibly be off in the whole complex, can it?"

The pounding on our door was loud and insistent. *Bam bam bam bam.*

Etienne stared at the door. "I suspect the answer to that is… yes."

Ennis Iversen waved his cell phone at us the moment Etienne opened the door. "I just checked my bank account. Don't ask me why. It just seemed like a smart thing to do. I've been wiped out. All the award money I deposited in our money market account? It's gone. The checking account hasn't been touched, but my nest egg is gone. This is the newspaper's fault! They never should've reported the dollar amount of my award. It made me the target of every crazy for miles around. It made Lorraine a target!"

He tapped the screen of his phone. "See the date here? It was withdrawn the day Lorraine disappeared. Someone *has* her. How many times have we seen scenarios like this play out on the evening news? Remember that grisly case in Connecticut some years ago?" His face crumpled onto itself as if it had suddenly been deprived of gravity. "They must have forced her to withdraw the money under threat of her life and once they got their cash, she became disposable. They could have killed her already and…and dumped her body in a field or the woods. Isn't that what always happens? They can't risk being identified, so they…they kill the hostage…or worse." His eyes welled with tears. "Jeesuz. The minute I think this can't get any worse, it does."

Etienne ushered him into the room and sat him down on the bed. "Have you called Chief Burns?"

Ennis shook his head. "I saw you and Emily come in here, so the only thing I could think of was to tell the two of you."

"Did the chief ask for your bank account information?"

He shook his head again. "No."

Etienne fished his cell phone out of his pocket and tapped the screen. "This could be the break the police are looking for. If Lorraine was coerced into withdrawing the money, it should show up on the bank's surveillance cameras, so let's hope they still have the footage." He held his forefinger up to pause the conversation as his call went through. "Etienne Miceli for Chief Burns. Tell him it's urgent."

Ennis stared at Etienne, his face a road map of utter misery. I sat down on the bed beside him. "So here we find ourselves again, Ennis. Can I do anything for you?"

"You got anything to calm a man's nerves?" He held his hands out in front of him, doubling them into fists when they wouldn't stop shaking. "You're not packing any brandy, are you?"

"The strongest thing I have is chamomile tea. You want to give it a try?"

"I'll try anything."

"But what I don't have is water, so if you give me a minute, I'll run over to the guest lodge to get some." I hopped to my feet.

"You don't need to do that, Emily. Water out of the bathroom faucet is fine."

"It would be if there *was* any. Didn't you get a notice?" I retrieved the paper from the desk and handed it to him. "Maybe your cabin wasn't affected."

He scanned the sheet. "No water? Well, isn't that great. The day just keeps getting better. I remember seeing a paper on the desk in my cabin, but I didn't take the time to read it."

"Okay, then, so you just sit tight, and I'll be back in a jif." I scooted around Etienne, grabbed my shoulder bag, and headed out the door only to be greeted by the sight of a string of guests already hotfooting it toward the guest lodge, arms swatting the air around their heads violently enough to fend off entire squadrons of mosquitoes, which made me realize that the *real* danger in the wilds of Alaska wasn't from disease-transmitting mosquitoes but from torn rotator cuffs.

Nana poked her head out the door of her cabin and looked both ways before tiptoeing onto the deck.

"Are you headed for the guest lodge?" I asked as I approached her.

She pressed her forefinger against her lips as she continued to eye her surroundings. "Where's your mother?"

I gestured toward the opposite side of the complex. "Do you see that crush of reporters hanging out over there? They have Mom surrounded in that cabin."

"The coast is clear, then." She looped her arm through mine and shuffled full speed ahead, pulling me with her. "C'mon, dear. Let's get outta here before she sees me. I kept losin' her yesterday, so she'll probably be on a tear today wantin' to make up for lost time."

"Etienne tells me you pulled quite the vanishing act in town yesterday."

"Yup. Don't know how I done it, though. Guess I'm not such a big target no more on account of I keep shrinkin'."

"Did you buy anything good?"

"You bet." Opening her jacket, she held the flap wide so I could see the pink camouflage hip holster and belt that hugged her waist.

I laughed as I eyed the cylindrical bulge in the holster. "What are you packing? Room freshener?"

"Somethin' better." She removed a canister with a bright orange trigger from the sheath. "Bear spray."

"Seriously? There's a commercial product on the market that repels bears? Who knew?" Iowa wasn't exactly a hotbed of rogue bear activity.

"Yup. The fella what was in the outfitters store said that one sustained blast on the nozzle and you got yourself a fog of super-hot, oil-based mist what covers an area up to thirty feet."

I slowed my steps as I pondered her description. "A fog of super-hot mist? Holy crap, Nana, that's not animal repellent, it's pepper spray! That's like…like carrying a loaded gun around with you."

"No kiddin'?"

"That stuff has the potential of being really dangerous. Are you sure you want it strapped to your waist? I mean, one accidental discharge and you could be looking at an emergency room visit with serious eye, nose, and lung damage. And you'd probably get socked with a slew of out-of-network medical bills that your supplemental insurance won't cover. I get that you'd like to be prepared in case of attack. We're in the middle of the woods where *we're* the intruders. But do you really think this is the way to go?"

"I didn't buy this stuff to waste on no bear. I bought it to use on your mother."

"Excuse me?"

"You know…if she don't keep her distance."

I sucked in enough air to turn my lungs into balloons. "You will *not* blast Mom with pepper spray, Nana. Do you hear me? That is so unacceptable." I held out my palm. "Hand it over."

"How 'bout I just threaten her."

"No."

"What if I see a bear?"

"Run."

"Spoiled sport." She slapped the canister into my palm with reluctance. "You want the belt too? It's adjustable. Fits any body type."

"You can keep the belt." I dropped the container into my shoulder bag.

"Maybe I'll give it to George. His wardrobe could use a little sprucin' up."

"You think he'd wear a pink belt?"

"Won't bother him none. He's color-blind."

As we stepped through the door of the guest lodge, Margi Swanson greeted us armed with a pad of sticky notes and a pen. "Are you here for the water or the potty? Potty people have to take a number. It's only a one-seater. Water people can just grab and go."

I scanned the gathered attendance. The Dicks competing against each other at the foosball table. George and Osmond picking over pieces of a half-completed jigsaw puzzle. Grace and Lucille watching TV on a sofa in the far corner. Goldie and Orphie setting up pieces on a checkerboard while Florence stood over them, coaching. Helen standing guard by the restroom door.

"Potty," said Nana, holding out her palm. "How long's the wait?"

Margi perused the room as if she were a hostess gauging wait times for tables. "About twenty minutes." She lowered her voice. "The fellas snagged all the low numbers, so it might be longer, especially if any of them forgot to pack their meds. But with my numbering system, we don't actually have to stand in line, so we're freed up to enjoy other activities while we wait."

"Isn't that somethin'?" marveled Nana. "Just like Disneyworld. I swear, Margi, the more birthdays you celebrate, the smarter you get."

Margi beamed as she ripped off a note and handed it to Nana. "Number thirteen, Marion. I hope this isn't an omen that the bathroom tissue is going to run out before you get your turn. What about you, Emily?"

"I'm only here for water." I spied a cooler brimming with bottled water on the floor just inside the door. "Does it matter how much I take?"

"Serving number four," Helen Teig announced in a robotic monotone as Alice Tjarks exited the restroom. "Number four? Serving number four."

"Bingo!" said Osmond, waving his sticky note above his head. As he shuffled happily toward Helen, Thor Thorsen barged through the front door like an angry wind. "Great place we're booked into. Not even enough water to flush the toilet. Where's the head?"

Margi stared at him wide-eyed. "It's over by Helen, but you have to take a—"

He blew past us, storming across the floor like a Sherman tank. "Outta my way," he snarled at Osmond before darting in front of him. Helen stepped calmly into the doorway, filling the space like an NBA center working the paint.

"You heard Margi," she warned, standing her ground. "It's first come, first serve. You can't use the facilities without a number."

"The hell I can't."

"It's the rule."

"Says who?" With a Mexican standoff in the offing, he glanced toward the far corner of the room. "Whoa! Is that a rat?"

"*Eeeeeee!*" cried Grace and Lucille as they hoisted their legs off the floor and onto the sofa.

"*Eeeeeee!*" cried Goldie and Orphie as they upended the checkerboard while jumping out of their chairs.

"*Eeeeeee!*" cried Helen as she fled across the floor in a desperate attempt to escape.

Thor walked into the restroom and slammed the door behind him.

George glared at the closed door, his mouth hanging open in disbelief. "That's just wrong."

"Do you see the rat?" cried Helen as she sheltered behind Margi.

Nana bobbed her head toward the opposite wall. "He's in the potty."

"Please, everyone," Florence apologized as she began picking up checkers off the floor. "He's not like this all the time. I'll be happy to forfeit my number to make up for his cutting in line ahead of all of you."

Indignant sniffs. Cold stares. Stony silence.

Thor Thorsen was proving himself to be much more disagreeable than I'd imagined. Which begged the question: Was a man who felt entitled enough to flout small conventions the kind of person who could easily flout more significant conventions? Like…the Sixth Commandment?

The front door banged open and Bernice sashayed in, sporting an oversized tote bag over her shoulder and what could almost pass as a smile on her face.

I hung my head in a pitiful show of surrender. Yup. Just what I needed right now. A scathing tongue lashing from Bernice Zwerg on the inadequacies of our accommodations.

Pausing just inside the threshold, she ranged a suspicious look around the room. "Why is it so quiet in here? Did someone else die?"

"Are you here for the water or the potty?" asked Margi in a breathless rush.

Bernice narrowed her eyes to a curious squint. "Why is Alice standing on a chair?"

"Potty people have to take a number. It's only a one-seater. Water people can just grab and go."

Shifting her gaze to the cooler against the wall, Bernice arched one thinly plucked eyebrow. "I don't know what's going on here, but I don't need a number. I just want to collect a few bottles of water." Standing over the cooler, she began grabbing bottles and stuffing them into her tote. One…two…six…eight. "Isn't it lovely here? The crisp air? The quaint cabins." Ten…twelve. "The feeling of being one with nature." Fourteen…sixteen. "The complimentary water."

Nana cocked her head. "What are you fixin' to do with all them bottles? Fill the hot tub?"

"*Au contraire*, Marion. The poor souls who've posted themselves outside Margaret and Bob's cabin look so parched that I consider it part of my Christian duty to offer them free beverage service. Who knows? They might be so appreciative, they could decide to write a feature story about a member of the tour group who actually wants to talk to them." Eighteen…twenty.

"That's bribery," scolded Margi.

Bernice shrugged. "Whatever works." Twenty-four. Twenty-six.

Nana shuffled over to the cooler to peek inside. "You didn't leave no water for no one else."

Bernice rolled her eyes. "There's obviously more where that came from. Just tell the management the cooler needs to be refilled."

Nana fisted her hands on her hips and glared at Bernice over the tops of her wirerims. "I'm not tellin' them management folks no such thing."

"All right, all right. Geesch." She pulled a bottle out of her tote and placed it back in the cooler. "Happy now?"

"Are you sure you don't need to take a number for the little girls' room?" Margi asked as Bernice heaved the tote bag over her shoulder.

"I'm sure," she grunted. And with that, she headed out the door, listing to port at a 30-degree angle.

Nana snatched the bottle out of the cooler and handed it to me. "You'd best take this before she decides to come back."

"I can't *believe* she had the nerve to take all the water," complained Margi as she eyed the empty container.

"I can't believe she said something nice about our accommodations," I quipped.

"I can't believe she didn't need to visit the potty," said Nana. "Say what you want about Bernice Zwerg, but for someone as short as she is, she's got some long pipes."

By the time I arrived back at the cabin, Etienne was off the phone, but Ennis still looked as if he was about to suffer a nervous breakdown. "Got the last one," I said as I twisted the cap off my bottle of water and poured the contents into the reservoir of the coffee maker. "So did the chief have anything noteworthy to say about the missing money?"

"He's expanding the investigation from a missing person case to a possible kidnapping," said Etienne. "The surveillance footage from the bank will be invaluable if it hasn't been automatically taped over, and this would provide him with a definitive timeline. He's also going to check with the businesses across the street to see if any of them have security cameras he might access. He hadn't covered the bank angle yet, so Ennis's discovery has given him a new avenue to explore. All in all, he sounded hopeful that there might be a break in the case soon."

Shoulders slumped, neck bent, Ennis shook his head. "Not soon enough to save Lorraine. I've got a feeling in my gut…a feeling that I'm never going to see her again."

"Please don't think that," I pleaded. "They'll find her, Ennis. You'll see."

"But what kind of condition will she be in? Are they going to find her in the same condition they found Delpha?"

A pang of dread slithered through me, coiling into a fist in my stomach. *Dear God, I hoped not.*

FOURTEEN

"THIS IS THE NATURAL History tour of Denali National Park and Preserve," announced the young man who'd just seated himself behind the steering wheel of our bus, replacing the young female driver who'd picked us up at the cabins. "So if you signed up for the Tundra Wilderness Tour or the Kantishna Experience, you've boarded the wrong bus. My name is Kyle, and I'll be your guide for the next four hours." Outfitted with a wireless mic, he pulled away from the park's visitor center and banged a sharp right onto the paved roadway.

Our coach was vintage mini school bus with genuine Naugahyde bench seats, no overhead racks or cupholders, no side exit door, and no lavatory, which could prove to be an enormous problem for everyone except Bernice. Ennis had agreed to join the group after downing three cups of chamomile tea that calmed his nerves considerably, although I didn't have the heart to tell him that his cell phone probably wouldn't work inside the park, so he'd be incommunicado for a lot longer than he wanted to be. Mom had emerged from her cabin like the Marvel Comics version of Mary Poppins, prepared to swat reporters away from Dad with her umbrella, but happily, Bernice had proved to be such an annoyance with her bottled water ploy that the entire press pool ran back to the diner en masse to escape her, so Mom and Dad were spared having to run the gauntlet.

After an agonizing discussion, Etienne and I decided to hold off informing the group that Delpha's death had been ruled a homicide. They'd received so much bad news already that we wanted them to be able to enjoy a few hours of calm before Lieutenant Kitchen showed up tomorrow, and with no cell towers in the park threatening to deliver the latest news to their phones, a short blackout period might be achievable.

Ahhhh. Peace. Quiet. Tranquility.

I could hear them complaining about it already.

"There's only one road going in and out of the park," Kyle continued. "It begins at the park entrance and ends at mile marker 92, where there's a few private lodges to accommodate overnight guests. We'll only be going seventeen miles into the park on this tour, but if you keep your eyes open, there's a good chance you'll spot the big five of Alaskan animals: grizzly bears, moose, wolves, caribou, and Dall sheep."

"What kind of sheep?" Dick Teig called out.

"Dall," said Kyle. "They're a breed of—"

"I know what they are," interrupted Grover Kristiansen with obvious excitement. "They're a close relative to bighorn sheep and are sometimes mistaken for mountain goats because of their ability to navigate rocky terrain."

"That's right," said Kyle. "Dall sheep—"

"—have whiter coats than mountain goats, and their horns are lighter in color," Grover interrupted again. "Mountain goats have black horns that are slightly curved, while Dall rams have massive horns that can curl into full circles. And both animals have cloven hooves, which is the main reason why they're able to scale steep ter—"

"Thanks for sharing that." Kyle cut him off as he eyed him in his rearview mirror. "As I was saying, the animals are roaming out there in the tundra, so if you think you see one, tell me to stop so I can pull over to the side of the road and give you a chance to take pictures."

"What should we say if we want you to stop?" asked Helen.

"How about *stop*," said Kyle.

"How specific do we have to be?" Goldie followed up. "Like… should we say, *Stop! I see a moose!* Or *Stop! I see a mountain goat!*"

"Weren't you listening?" chided Grover. "There *aren't* any mountain goats in Denali. Only sheep that *look* like goats."

"How can we tell the difference between the two?" questioned Dick Stolee.

"I just got through explaining," bellyached Grover.

Thor Thorsen guffawed. "Waste of time, sparky. No one was listening. No one ever listens."

I sidled a glance at Etienne and rolled my eyes. Maybe a few intermittent cell towers wouldn't be such a bad idea after all, just to keep them occupied.

"You're making this more complicated than it needs to be," reasoned Kyle. "The process is simple. Yell stop if you want me to stop. I'll pull over to the side of the road, if I can, and then the person who asked me to stop can tell the rest of us what he spotted and where he spotted it."

"What's going to prevent us from getting thrown from our seats when you stop?" asked Margi. "We don't have seat belts. Are there any urgent care clinics inside the park?"

"The maximum speed limit for this bus is thirty-five miles per hour, ma'am, and I rarely even hit twenty, so seat belts aren't really a concern."

"What are we supposed to be looking for again?" asked Osmond.

Oh, God.

"I'll start you out with a few statistics," said Kyle as we drove through an area of new growth birches and aspens. "The park covers approximately six million acres, which makes it about the size of Massachusetts—maybe a little bigger. But unlike Massachusetts, much of the ground is underlaid with permafrost, which is basically ground that's remained frozen for thousands of years. You'd think that only a few plants could grow in the thin layer of topsoil that thaws above the permafrost every summer, but the park supports over 650 species of flowering—"

"Would someone please tell Thor to close his window?" Helen Teig demanded. "He's letting in all the mosquitoes."

I turned around to see Thor kneeling on the seat behind the Teigs with his camera poised at the open window. "Dig out your repellent," he griped. "I didn't buy a boatload of expensive camera equipment to shoot a picture through a closed window with glass too dirty to see through."

Dick Teig raised an orange canister and pressed hard on the nozzle, blasting Thor with a sustained shot.

Psssssssssst!

I froze in place. *Omigod. Please make that be something other than bear spray. Please make that be something other than bear spray.*

"What the hell!" yowled Thor, flapping his arms through the air as if he were battling a swarm of midges.

Psssssssssst!

Dick got him again.

"Cut it out!" yelled Thor as he chased away lingering traces of mist. "What is that stuff?"

"Bug spray," said Dick.

"It stinks!"

"It's generic. Generic repellents don't have the same fresh scents as the name brands, but they're a lot cheaper, so I've learned to live with the stench."

"Spray that stuff at me again, Teig, and I swear I'll twist you into a pretzel."

"Hey, this is the thanks I get for saving you from an excruciatingly painful and potentially fatal insect-borne disease? Okay, have it your way." Dick faced front again, a satisfied grin on his face. "From now on, you're on your own."

"Everything okay in the back of the bus?" questioned Kyle.

"It will be in a minute," responded Etienne, who stood up and made his way down the aisle to Thor's seat. Oh, wow. Talk about a diplomatic nightmare. How did one go about chastising a guest for rude behavior while still making him feel a welcome part of the tour?

Thirty seconds later Etienne returned to the front of the bus with Thor following close behind, weighed down with all his photographic equipment. Uff-da! Did Etienne just kick him off the bus?

"Mr. Thorsen has agreed to change seats with us, bella."

I stared up at Etienne. "What?"

"Having a window open in the front of the bus doesn't affect so many passengers." He nodded toward the stepwell. "Fewer seats around it."

"But…what about the mosquitoes?"

"I've never had a problem with mosquitoes on the bus," Kyle spoke up. "We don't usually stay in one place long enough for them to find us."

"Oh. Well…" I stood up, annoyed that we were rewarding Thor for his bad behavior by giving him a front seat but proud of Etienne for realizing that the best way to keep the peace was to isolate Thor from the rest of the group.

Thor slid onto the front seat and dumped his equipment beside him. "All right!" He looked over his new surroundings like a king acquainting himself with his throne. "This is more like it."

On our way back to our new seat, we passed Florence, head bent, hand shielding her eyes in obvious embarrassment. And my heart went out to her that she had to live with the profound disappointment that the man she *thought* she married wasn't the man she'd married at all.

As Kyle resumed his narration, touching on the retreat of the glaciers and the revegetation of the area with fungi, mosses, lichens, and algae, the landscape morphed from a forest of shrubs and young hardwoods to panoramic vistas of broad, flat valleys whose backdrop was a muscular range of craggy, snow-drenched mountains. Shallow rivers cluttered with pulverized rock meandered through the flattened plains, carving out new channels that flowed outward like tentacles. Meadows lush with ground-hugging wild-flowers swept to the water's edge, sprinkling color like flakes of crushed candy. It was a frontier wilderness of grand proportions, untouched by commercialism, serene in its isolation, but thriving in the distant shadow of the cloud-covered behemoth known as Denali.

"I haven't spotted any caribou yet," Kyle continued as we bounced along the park road, "but if we see one, we'll see a whole herd because they travel in groups. And an interesting factoid for you: unlike other members of the deer family, both male and female caribou have antlers. A typical herd size numbers around—"

"Stop!" yelled Thor. "Bear! Right side of the bus." He thrust his hand out the open window to indicate the rise that sloped upward from the valley toward another mountain range.

Kyle hit the brakes gently and pulled the bus to the side of the road where he came to a full stop. "Can you tell what color it is? Grizzlies are kind of a dirty blond."

Thor stuck his camera with its comically long zoom lens out the window, directing it toward an expanse of low bushes that were interspersed rather sparingly with tall, pointed spruce trees. "It's halfway up the hill here. At about three o'clock. And as far as I can tell, it's brown."

He might as well have fired a starting pistol.

Passengers occupying the aisle seats on the right side of the bus sprang to their feet and clambered over their seatmates in a desperate attempt to stake out a place at the window.

Passengers on the left side of the bus jammed into the aisles to peer out windows that were being blocked by their traveling companions' heads, arms, torsos, and cell phones.

"You people who are hogging the windows need to sit down so the rest of us can see something," insisted Dick Teig.

"I don't see any bear," scoffed Dick Stolee, his face glued to the window glass.

"Right up *there!*" barked Thor, his camera whirring as he snapped shot after shot. "Three o'clock. Take the blinders off!"

"Is that three o'clock Iowa time or Alaska time?" asked Margi. "My watch has dual time zones, so I get both."

"Which way's twelve o'clock?" questioned George. "How are we supposed to figure out where three o'clock is if we can't locate twelve?"

"Can't help you there," lamented Osmond. "My watch is digital."

"I can't see nuthin'," fretted Nana as she stood on tiptoe amid the tall timber in the aisle.

"No one can see nothin'!" complained Dick Teig. "Guess they forgot to tell us we'd need x-ray vision to see out the damn windows."

"Too late now," blared Thor, his camera suddenly silent. "It just disappeared over that first ridge. Excitement's over, folks."

Disappointed and grumbling, everyone in the aisle returned to their seats on the left side of the bus. Kyle started the engine again and pulled onto the road, creeping along at about fifteen miles an hour. "The deeper we drive into the park, the more likely you are to see grizzlies, so I'll tell you a little about them. They're not fussy about what they eat. Anything goes: plants, berries, rodents, moose, carib—"

"Stop!" cried Thor. "Right side of the bus. Bear foraging by that big boulder on the hill."

"Is it a grizzly?" asked Kyle.

"Nope. It's black."

The lefties clogged the aisle again with renewed excitement, bobbing their heads, weaving through the crush of bodies, stretching to make themselves tall, crouching to make themselves short, aiming their phones toward the windows that were being monopolized by the righties.

"Grover, will you move your damn head?" sniped Dick Teig as he waved his phone in frustration.

Grover didn't budge. "Why do I have to move? My seat, my window."

Grover's mulishness didn't surprise me. I'd noticed he'd been a little out of sorts ever since he'd learned that instead of joining us for the excursion, Alison would be remaining at the cabins to manage details of our meal at the diner this evening.

"Hey, the bear's got two cubs with her," announced Thor, his camera whirring frenetically as he squeezed off a flurry of shots.

"Where's he seeing bears?" fussed Goldie as she knelt on the seat behind Grover, peering over his shoulder. "I don't see anything moving out there."

"I see a black dot," Mom called out from the back.

Thor lowered his camera. "That's the bear. But if you don't have binoculars or a telephoto lens, that's all you're gonna see."

"Why are we looking for dots?" asked Helen Teig.

"Have we decided where twelve o'clock is yet?" asked George.

"I'm not takin' pictures of no dots," grumbled Nana as she returned to her seat.

"Come on, people," I chided. "Share the windows with your friends. This isn't like you. Does anyone have binoculars they want to share?"

"I do," boasted Thor, "but I'm not going to share because they're way too expensive to just pass around. Oh, look at that! The cubs are romping around like puppies. It's really too bad the rest of you can't see this." Whirr. Whirr. Whirr. Whirr.

Throwing in the towel on the wildlife photography, the lefties dragged themselves back to their seats, and as Thor continued to shoot pictures, they resorted to their favorite pastime—taking pictures of themselves—which seemed to boost their spirits considerably.

"Okay," Thor said after another five minutes, "I'm done here. Let's get going."

We'd gone no more than five hundred yards when he yelled, "Stop!"

A collective sigh went up from the group.

"What is it this time?" droned Lucille.

"Probably another dot," said Mom.

Thor peered through his viewfinder. "Right side. Top of the ridge. Big blond-colored bear lumbering in the low bushes. Gotta be a grizzly." Whirr. Whirr. Whirr. "This is awesome."

"I think I see it," whooped Dick Stolee. "At the ridgeline. A little yellow speck."

"That's it," affirmed Thor.

Dick swiveled around to snap a headshot of himself in front of the window. He showed the screen to his wife. "Grace, when we get home, in case I forget, would you remind me that this is the picture with the grizzly in it?"

The afternoon wore on the same way, with Thor making Kyle stop every one to two hundred yards so he could photograph wildlife that no one else could see. After three hours, having traveled a grand total of four miles out of the seventeen we were supposed to cover, Kyle decided to turn the bus around so he wouldn't be late making it back to the visitor center.

"I'm really sorry we haven't seen any caribou herds," Kyle apologized. "They're usually out there in force. Maybe if we could have made it farther into the—"

"Stop!" shouted Dick Teig.

Kyle pulled over and killed the engine.

"Right side of the bus," Dick enthused. "Down by the river. Near that gravel bar. A huge black blob."

We shot excited looks out the window. Searching left. Searching right. Searching left again.

Helen harrumphed. "What black blob?"

He swatted his hand in front of his eyes. "False alarm! It's a floater."

"Is anyone getting cell service?" Ennis Iversen called out as Kyle restarted the engine.

"No bars for me," Osmond responded.

"Me either," a smattering of voices agreed.

"You'll be able to get service once we're back at the visitor center," Kyle assured them.

"Have you had any updates on Lorraine since last night?" Florence asked in an anxious voice. "We're all really worried, Ennis, but none of us want to pester you with questions when you're in the middle of a personal crisis like this."

"Well, the crisis got worse this afternoon," he admitted, sounding as if he couldn't allow the burden to fester inside him any longer. "Lorraine is more than just missing. The police think she might have been kidnapped or abducted or whatever terminology they're going to use."

"The difference between the two is in the intent," Grover spoke up. "Kidnapping is the forceful seizure of a person against their will for either ransom or other criminal motives, and it usually involves false imprisonment. Abduction, on the other hand—"

"Will someone shut him up?" barked Thor.

A suggestion proving that even wankers like Thor could come up with constructive ideas every once in a while.

For the next five minutes Ennis reported on the latest news about Lorraine, his depleted money market account, and what it all might mean, ending with a confession that he never should have left his cabin this afternoon. "Chief Burns might have news, and here I sit…holding a phone with no bars."

"I'm glad you decided to come with us," Florence reassured him. "We're all glad you're here, aren't we, everyone?"

Nods. Fist pumps. Scattered claps.

"It doesn't make any sense for you to suffer by yourself when you're surrounded by all your friends," she continued. "And you just wait and see. I bet when we get within range of a cell tower again, you'll find a voicemail on your phone from Chief Burns with good news for you."

Ennis sighed. "Hope so."

"It'll happen," encouraged Florence. "I can feel it in my bones."

"*Stop!*" shrieked Bernice, leaping out of her seat. "Right side of the bus." She aimed her phone toward the side of the road.

Kyle pumped the brakes and glided to a full stop.

"What's there?" urged Dick Teig.

"Squirrel! Right over there." She stabbed the window.

Accompanied by excited oohs and aahs, everyone scrambled toward the windows again, angling their phones at the glass in the hopes of photographing what looked like a common gray squirrel.

Thor's boisterous laughter echoed through the bus. "Why are we wasting time stopping for a squirrel? We have squirrels back home."

Bernice sniffed with disdain. "That squirrel is the only photo-worthy thing we've stopped for today."

"Oh yeah? Why's that?"

"Because it's the only thing in this whole damn park we can see without a telephoto lens!"

FIFTEEN

It must have been arthritis Florence had been feeling in her bones when she'd made her prediction because when we arrived back in civilization, Ennis discovered no new message from Chief Burns in his voicemail. Alison greeted the bus in the parking lot at the cabins with goofy waves and smiles, and when we were safely offloaded, she gathered us around her to give us our immediate instructions.

"Your meal is all ready, so if you'll march directly over to the diner, they'll start serving. No waiting necessary. They were expecting you about twenty minutes ago, so they're doing their best to keep everything hot."

"We decided to use the comfort facilities at the visitor center in case the water was still off here," I explained.

Alison nodded. "Good decision. We're still without water."

Boos. Hissing. Razzberries.

"To the diner, everyone!" She raised her arms and pointed to the eatery as if she were an airport technician guiding an incoming jet to its gate. "And cue up your photos because I want to see each and every one of them at dinner."

The media vans had vacated the parking lot, which was good news for Mom and Dad but not such good news for Nana, who was right back where she started, having to figure out innovative ways to avoid Mom's overprotective clutches. All I could say was Mom owed me big-time for taking Nana's bear spray away from her.

The waitstaff started serving as soon as we sat down—a fixed meal of chicken fingers, cole slaw, and fries, which had sounded Happy Meal enough to order for everyone, except that each "finger" was big enough to be classified as a hand.

"What kind of fish is this?" asked Osmond as he poked at the two claws of meat on his plate. "Walleye?"

"Looks like a largemouth bass to me," said George.

Helen picked a hunk up by two fingers, studying it from front to back. "It's got a mouth?"

"It's actually chicken," said Alison as she flitted between tables, handing out extra napkins. "And it's really pretty tasty once you get past the outer crust."

"You want to join our table?" Grover asked her, his face alight with anticipation as he gestured to the empty chair across from him.

"Thanks so much for asking, but I ate earlier with Steele. I couldn't let him eat by himself, could I?"

A flicker of irritation crept into Grover's eyes as he tried to mask his disappointment. "Then have a seat and I'll show you the pictures I took this afternoon."

"What kind of fish did you say this is?" fretted Margi in alarm. "It looks like it might have a lot of bones."

"There's no way I'm going to sit here picking bones out of my entree," complained Orphie. "I'll have the chicken instead."

Etienne cleared his throat. "That *is* the chicken."

"Then how come it looks like fish?" asked Osmond.

"I bet it's a muskie," concluded Dick Teig.

Lucille examined her plate. "Funny they didn't serve tartar sauce with it."

I hung my head. *Oh, God.*

While the group continued to quibble about whether they'd been served fish or fowl, Alison made good on her promise to peruse the day's photos, starting with Dick Stolee. "Oh my," she gushed over the image on his phone. She paused. "I'm sorry. Is that a picture of a dot?"

"It's a bear," said Dick.

"Can you zoom in?"

"It is zoomed in."

Alison crooked her mouth. "So…how can you be sure that dot is a bear?"

"Because it's black. But wait'll you see my money shot." He swiped the screen and angled it toward her. "*This*…is a grizzly."

Alison stared at the screen, bewildered. "That's a headshot of yourself."

"Yeah. The grizzly's hard to see because he's out of frame."

Alison displayed both patience and good humor as she made the rounds at each table, and when she was through, she basically lied through her teeth. "Great job, everyone. Looks like the ground squirrels were out in force today."

"Squirrel," said Nana. "We only seen one."

Alison squinted as if she'd heard incorrectly. "Excuse me?"

"We all took pictures of the same squirrel," clarified Tilly. "It was the only wildlife that wasn't a dot."

A dog barked loudly nearby, which might lead a person to believe that a dog was actually barking loudly nearby, but in this era of whacky cell phone ringtones, it meant that Ennis Iversen's phone was ringing. "It's the Windsor City police," he choked out, clutching his cell as he pushed away from the table. Rushing outside to take the call, he returned ten minutes later, looking as unnerved as a vegan at a bratfest.

"The police don't think Lorraine was kidnapped," he announced in a hollow voice.

Claps. Whooping. Cheering.

He gazed around the room with vacant eyes, waiting for the commotion to die down. "They've reviewed the surveillance footage from both the bank and the businesses across the street and… and they've come up with no evidence that would indicate anyone was coercing her to do anything. She entered the bank looking calm and composed and left with a huge smile on her face. In fact, the police can't find any hint of criminal activity anywhere. So it's looking pretty much like…Lorraine might have run away. All on her own."

Gasps. Wheezing. Dropped jaws.

"I don't understand," cried Florence. "Why would Lorraine run away? What was she running away *from*?"

"That's pretty clear, isn't it?" admitted Ennis. "Me."

"That can't be true," challenged Goldie. "The two of you have the perfect marriage. You're kind to each other. You laugh at each other's jokes. You treat each other with respect. You have two-sided conversations. You still *like* each other."

"How do we know it wasn't all for show?" Thor taunted smugly. "How do we know that behind closed doors, the two of them didn't treat each other like dirt?"

Grover snorted with laughter. "As opposed to treating each other like crap in *front* of everyone? Which is, as we all know, *your* preferred style."

"Quiet, you little pipsqueak, before I—"

"I'm so sorry about Lorraine," Orphie cut him off. "I can't begin to imagine how you must feel, Ennis, being married to the same woman for so many years, living in the same house, sharing the same bed, but finding out decades later that you didn't really know her at all. That has to be so gut-wrenching."

"Ennis knew her," defended Florence. "We all knew her."

Orphie shook her head. "If that were true, she'd be here vacationing with us. I hope you don't mind my saying this, Ennis, but if you're contemplating divorce, I just want to warn you that this is going to be no picnic for all your mutual friends. What's going to happen to us? You'll have to divide us up between you like community property. And I have no idea how this is going to affect the status of the book club. Without Lorraine's input, this could spell the end of a long, glorious tradition."

"I don't give a damn about the book club, and I'm not entertaining any thoughts of divorce," snapped Ennis. "I'm just sorry that if Lorraine had grievances, she didn't share them with me. I mean, maybe we could have worked it out. Maybe we can still work it out."

Orphie nodded. "Maybe if she ever comes back, you can try what Al and I do. We set time aside every single day to talk to each other about the stuff that really matters. Hopes. Fears. Proposed Medicare cuts. The latest episode of *Game of Thrones.* "

Thor guffawed. "Al must love that. Trapped by the missus for an indeterminate amount of time on a daily basis. *Eww.*"

"Go ahead and laugh," she fired back, "but I'm quite convinced that our little tête-à-têtes are what's kept us together all these years. We know each other inside out, which is apparently more than some folks around here can say about each other."

"I hope you're not blaming Lorraine's behavior on Ennis," huffed Goldie.

Orphie rolled her eyes. "I'm not blaming anyone for anything. I'm just saying that if you want to know the secret of a happy marriage, it's simple: communicate with each other."

"I've gotta agree with Orphie," Bernice piped up, which caused everyone to quit chewing what was in their mouths to stare at her. "My folks talked every night for forty-two years, but it was mostly my mom who did the talking because she found more to complain about than my dad. So she aired out her grievances night after night, and Dad just sat there in his favorite rocking chair, smoking his pipe, taking it like a man."

"He didn't have no objection to bein' read the riot act every night?" asked Nana.

"Nope," said Bernice. "Not once. Of course, it helped that he was stone deaf."

An uptick in traffic noise outside drew our attention to the open windows, where I noticed a convoy of media vehicles returning to the parking lot.

"Well, would you lookit that," mused Nana. "It's them reporters again."

"Jesus, Mary, and Joseph. Come on, Bob." Mom sprang from her chair and bolted toward the door, dragging Dad with her. "Hurry up before they see us."

Mom and Dad fled across the deck as car doors started to slam, but they weren't quite fast enough. "Hey! It's him!" someone shouted, sounding the alert with a whistle that was loud enough to pierce eardrums. "Mr. Andrew! Mr. Andrew! Will you admit on record that your photo of Bigfoot nails down the theory that your tour companion was killed by the monster on the hiking trail in Girdwood?"

I sighed. As much as the paparazzi's unrelenting presence was saving Nana from Mom, there was such a thing as critical mass, and I think we'd just hit it. Mom might be a thorn in Nana's side, but she was still a paying guest and didn't deserve to have her holiday ruined. Removing my napkin from my lap, I stood up and placed my hand on Etienne's shoulder. "Excuse me for a minute, would you?"

Mom and Dad were halfway to their cabin with the reporters hot on their heels when I let fly my own ear-splitting whistle. "Stop right there!" I ordered, a little unprepared when they actually did.

They turned around in unison to stare at me. "What?" a guy with a camera balanced on his shoulder asked.

"I hope you realize this is private property. Unless you're registered guests or have the owner's permission to be here, you're trespassing. Are you registered guests?"

Shrugging. Head shaking.

I smiled inwardly as I went in for the kill. "Do you have permission to trespass on private property?"

"The guy in the front office said we could have the run of the place," said a woman in a baseball cap. "Look around you, lady. We're in the middle of nowhere. Other hotels around here would kill for the kind of exposure we're giving this place. It's called free advertising."

I narrowed my eyes in suspicion. "Is that the truth or are you just saying that to get rid of me?"

"Don't take my word. Stop at the front office. Ask for yourself."

Nuts. "Look, guys, this is a dream vacation for my parents, and you're harassing them. Do you think that's fair?"

"Who said life was fair?" cracked the cameraman. "This is our job. We've got bills to pay too."

"They're almost back at their cabin," advised another man. "Geez. Hey, Mr. Andrew!"

I watched in frustration as they took up the chase once again, surprised when the woman in the baseball cap jogged back to me, looking mildly repentant. "I'm really sorry we're spoiling your parents' vacation, but I'd like to try to make it up to you with a dietary tip. There's a great roadside diner ten miles north of here. Down home cooking. Good service. It's called the Hungry Grizzly Cafe. Tell the manager that Patti sent you. Might even be worth a discount." Her chest swelled with pride. "He's my brother."

"Thanks." I flashed a smile. "That's nice of you. The food here isn't what I was expecting."

"That's an understatement. You want another tip? Whatever you do, don't order the fish fry." She lowered her voice a few decibels as if she were passing along state secrets. "It tastes suspiciously like chicken."

SIXTEEN

"After our ziplining adventure, we plan to stop at a road-side café for lunch before heading back to the cabins." Exulting in our fourth straight day of brilliant sunshine and temps in the seventies, Etienne made his announcement as we pulled onto the road the next morning, leaving the press vehicles that had arrived before breakfast in the parking lot. I'd wasted my breath on them last night. They were staying put until they got a story, so there was only one sure way to outmaneuver them.

Leave.

"By my estimate, we should arrive back here around one o'clock," Etienne continued, "which is about the time I expect our friend Lieutenant Kitchen to join us to conduct another round of questioning."

Groans. Whines. Jeers.

"He's traveling all the way up here to ask us more questions?" puzzled George. "Why?"

"Because he's looking for more information. Their investigation has uncovered evidence that indicates Delpha died at the hands of someone who acted intentionally, so they're ruling her death a homicide, which means they need to shine more light on details they might have initially overlooked."

"So…it wasn't an accident?" asked Florence in a tremulous voice. "Someone killed her?"

"Regrettably, Mrs. Thorsen, that's the consensus."

"Do they have any suspects?" questioned Grover.

Etienne shook his head. "If they do, they haven't shared that information yet."

"Jesus, Mary, and Joseph," protested Mom. "But why do they want to question *us*? They should be questioning Bigfoot."

"Really, Margaret," admonished Tilly. "Even if the creature exists, his lack of verbal skills would be problematic, so questioning him would be a complete waste of police time."

"Maybe he knows sign language," Margi tossed out.

"Why would he know sign language?" countered Lucille. "Is he deaf?"

"Is Lieutenant Kitchen planning to question us again because he thinks one of us killed Delpha?" asked Ennis. "Someone on this tour? One of her friends?"

Talk of Bigfoot ceased dramatically as an uncomfortable silence settled over the bus.

"The lieutenant has more questions," Etienne explained without fanfare. "I think we should leave it at that for now."

But Ennis's question obviously gave rise to a period of soul-searching, self-reflection, and internet surfing because the bus was unnaturally quiet for the half hour it took us to reach our ziplining venue.

At an indistinct break in the trees on a nondescript part of the highway, Steele turned off-road, driving the bus down a short gravel lane where a couple of muddy vehicles that resembled modified jeeps were parked. Two twentysomething young men in hiking pants and hoodies hopped out of the vehicles to direct us to the preferred parking spot, and when we'd come to a full stop, they climbed aboard to greet us. I shook their hands, introduced myself, told them how excited we were to be here, then stood back as they took over the show.

"Hey, everyone! Welcome! I'm Morgan and this is Josh, and we're the dudes who'll be driving you to the site today"—he gestured toward the jeeps—"in those two outstanding vehicles."

"They're awfully muddy," Margi observed with some distaste. "Is there a car wash nearby?"

"We had a lot of torrential rain last week that's turned our access road to slop," lamented Morgan, "so we're getting showered with mud. But that's what makes our vehicles so outstanding. They can plow through just about anything. Mire. Mud. Sludge." He thrust his hand at the dividing line where the gravel ended and the road into the forest began. "It's three miles to the site and the ride's pretty bumpy, so I've gotta ask now before we take off: Does anyone here suffer from knee pain, hip pain, joint pain, back pain, neck pain, heart problems, asthma, or have a detached retina?"

Everyone's hand went up.

"Oh man." Morgan's features collapsed in horror. "Uh…" He exchanged a glance with Josh, who whispered something in his ear. "Okay then. No worries. We'll drive slow."

"This place you're taking us to won't unnerve someone with a slight aversion to germs, will it?" asked Margi.

"No, ma'am." Morgan gave his head a vigorous shake. "It's a bit muddy on the way in, but it's clean mud."

"Clean mud." Tilly laughed. "That's an oxymoron, young man."

"I don't know what that is, ma'am."

"It's a self-contradiction in terms. Like...jumbo shrimp? Living dead?"

His eyes lit up. "Oh, yes, ma'am. Zombie flicks are my favorite movies. So here's how this is gonna work. Josh and me can take eight passengers apiece in our vehicles, so we'll make one run with sixteen of you, then I'll come back to pick up who's left. I'll let Mrs. Miceli decide who gets to go on the first leg, so once you figure that out, mosey on over to the jeeps and we'll strap you in. See you in a minute."

After dumping the selection process in my hands, the two guys made a quick exit, leaving me to wrestle with the usual headache of who should go first and whether they should line up by age, height, or social security number. But I had no intention of dithering. I was going to be strong and decisive and simply lay down the law, and if someone complained, I'd be uncharacteristically forceful and... and...

Someone always complained and I never did anything about it, so who was I kidding? But on the upside, this couldn't have worked out any better. By manipulating the roster, I'd get a chance to do something I'd wanted to do since yesterday.

"So here's the scoop." Accessing the list of guest names on my phone, I made a few quick calculations. "Alison and Etienne will ride along with the first two groups and I'll stay behind with the remaining guests. So when I call your name, you can head out. First group goes with Alison."

I read off seven names and waited until they were safely off the bus and hustling across the gravel with her.

"Second group goes with Etienne." I read off seven more names and watched them go, then did my best to ignore the peeved looks being directed at me from the six guests who remained.

"How come we got picked to go last?" taunted Thor as he eyed the book clubbers still on the bus. "Nothing smacks of favoritism more than showing partiality to your regular travelers. I hope you have the decency to be embarrassed."

"The reason you guys are going last is because you're not my regular travelers," I explained in the most tactful fib I could think of. "You've seen the gang in action. They go bonkers if they're not first out of the starting gate. I chose you to go last because I know you're more patient than they are, so I figured you wouldn't mind."

"What a nice thing to say," gushed Goldie Kristiansen. "I'm not sure the 'patience' moniker applies to all of us"—she slanted a look at Thor—"but I'll accept the compliment."

"So will I," Florence chimed in. "I pride myself on my patience. So you called that right, Emily. I don't mind waiting at all."

"You wouldn't," snarled Thor. "Miss Goody Two-shoes."

"You shouldn't knock my patience," Florence retorted in a slow, even tone. "It's the only thing that's allowed me to stomach you all these years."

"Zing!" hooted Grover. "Truth hurt much, sparky?"

Thor unfolded himself from his seat and stepped into the aisle, pausing only long enough to skewer his detractors with a menacing look. "I'm waiting outside where the air's not so foul."

"Good!" Grover called after him. He ranged a look around the near-empty bus. "It was too crowded in here anyway."

"What about mosquitoes?" questioned Orphie as Thor stormed out the exit. "Does he risk being eaten alive if he stands out there?"

"What do you care?" asked Grover.

"Well, if he gets bitten and dies from one of the diseases Tilly warned us about, we won't be able to needle him at our next meeting for not reading the book. Watching him make up excuses is the best part of the entire evening."

"I'm not seeing any mosquitoes," Steele sang out helpfully. "In years when they're bad, you can usually see 'em swarming around the front windshield, but I'm not seeing anything today. Not a one."

Goldie smiled. "Oh, good. I have to agree with Orphie. As much as I dislike Thor, book club is much less boring when he's there."

I nodded toward the group. "Would the five of you like to stay in here until we get picked up? Steele, would you have any problem with that?"

"They can stay if they want. I'm not going anywhere. Gonna sit here, drink some coffee, and read my book."

"You're a reader?" Florence called out. "How wonderful."

"What are you reading?" asked Goldie, deserting Grover to head to the front of the bus.

"Lemme dig it out."

"Is it anything we've read?" inquired Orphie, popping into the aisle excitedly and pulling Florence out of her seat to investigate with her.

I smiled at the trio gathered around the steering wheel, then peered down the aisle at Grover and Ennis.

Perfect.

"This news about Delpha is terrible." Ennis shook his head as I approached. "I could understand an accident, but this? This is beyond belief."

"Hard to believe no one saw anything, isn't it?" I commiserated. "You guys were in the museum. Was the hiking trail visible from there?"

The two men exchanged blank stares. "It might have been," said Grover, "but I didn't really notice." He swiveled toward Ennis. "Did you?"

Ennis shook his head. "Nope. I don't even know if the place had windows."

"It was bright inside," Grover recalled, "but to be honest, I can't remember if the source was from overhead lighting or natural light. It's getting harder to figure out what's real and what's fake anymore, especially with the new LED color temperature bulbs."

Ennis shot him a droll look. "You probably could have figured it out if you'd stayed longer."

"I stayed long enough."

"Yeah, right. Until Alison left. If your goal is to stalk the girl, you're doing an upstanding job of it."

"For your information, I was not stalking Alison. My diuretic had just kicked into overdrive, so I needed to use the restroom."

"Which one did you use?" I asked. "The one in the restaurant or the more public one by the express take-out place?"

He stiffened, spooling out his answer with some hesitation. "I'm...I'm pretty sure it was the one in the restaurant."

"Well, you must have sneaked right by me because I was sitting in the restaurant foyer for about forty-five minutes and I never saw you."

"You must have been distracted," he shot back, his expression growing irritated. "Or, who knows? I could have come and gone before you got there. Or maybe I'm just not remembering correctly. Maybe I used the public restroom after visiting the museum and the one in the restaurant during dinner. I bet I'm just mixing them up."

I smiled. And maybe the dog ate his homework.

"That hole in your alibi is so big, I could walk through it," taunted Ennis. "Better think about lawyering up, Grove. Kitchen will have a field day with you otherwise."

"Why should the lieutenant care about my bathroom habits? Delpha was alive when all of us went in to dinner, remember? So what I did or didn't do after I left the museum is of no consequence, is it?"

Ennis lifted his brows. "It might be of consequence to Alison. Maybe she'll decide to file a restraining order against you when Kitchen arrives."

"That's low."

"I call 'em like I see 'em."

"So what about *your* alibi?" bristled Grover, pivoting like a savvy political hack practicing avoidance tactics. "How much time did *you* spend looking at those old pictures in the museum?"

Ennis shrugged. "It had to have been a good long while because I remember looking at every exhibit. Must have been at least a half hour. Maybe longer."

"Actually," I said, hoping not to sound like a prosecuting attorney, "Osmond happened to mention that he saw you and Thor leave just a few minutes after Grover."

"You left right after me?" hooted Grover. "Well, well, well. Looked at every exhibit, did you? I bet. For a nanosecond maybe."

Ennis paused. "Osmond might have seen Thor and me leave, but he sure as hell didn't see us leave together. Exiting at the same time is entirely different than leaving together."

Sure it is. Like…having words come out of your mouth is entirely different than talking.

"You and Thorsen hooked up after the museum?" accused Grover. "Why would you want to go anywhere with him?"

"I didn't *go* anywhere with him. Once we were out the door, he went his way and I went mine."

"And where was that?" I prodded.

"Where did *I* go?" repeated Ennis. "Just…around. Explored the grounds. Wandered around the deck. Watched the fog roll in."

"And you thought *my* alibi had a hole in it?" mocked Grover. "You better think about hiring your own lawyer."

"I don't think so." He fixed Grover with a piercing look. "You said it yourself: Delpha was still alive when we sat down to dinner, so what difference does it make where I went?"

For two men who supposedly had nothing to hide, they sure seemed to be taking great pains to avoid transparency.

"Grover!" Goldie called from the front of the bus. "Come see what Steele's reading. You'll never guess, not in a million years. Hurry up. I'm dying for you to see."

Grover executed a major eye roll before dragging himself out of his seat. "Coming, dear." Then, to Ennis: "See what you're missing by not having Lorraine on the trip with you? A word to the wise. Enjoy your freedom while it lasts."

Which seemed like a pretty insensitive thing for Grover to say considering how upset Ennis was about his wife's disappearance, but maybe Grover Kristiansen was a lot more self-centered than I realized.

Ennis glared at Grover's retreating back. "Putz."

"So. I'm not sure how much longer we have to wait to get picked up, but I want to pop outside and speak to Thor before we leave."

Ennis gave me a nod. "Better you than me." He waved his phone. "I'll be checking for news back home."

Thor was standing at the edge of the woods chucking stones at the ground cover when I came up behind him. "Are you aiming for anything in particular?"

"Mosquitoes."

"You can actually see them?"

"I can't see 'em, but I might be crippling a few inadvertently." He picked up another handful of rocks from the ground and launched one into the forest. "Did you want something?"

"Yeah. I was wondering what your thoughts were about the exhibits in the Roundhouse Museum. Osmond and George really enjoyed the displays, so I'm canvassing the rest of you to see if you agree. I'm trying to do a little advance planning for future brochures."

"I wasn't impressed. I've seen old black-and-white pictures before. These were nothing special. And you had to read way too much junk."

"Don't say that too loudly. You'll offend the avid readers in your book club."

"In that case, I should yell it out. Nothing makes me happier than to upset those little prigs." He skipped another stone into the trees.

"Did you take the time to read everything?"

"I told you—there was too much, so I left. Iversen followed me out. I think he was trying to spy on me, but I lost him quick enough."

"Why would Ennis want to spy on you?"

"Don't tell me you haven't noticed that they don't like me. They're trying to find ways to oust me from the group, gathering any dirt they can find anywhere they can find it. And the more dirt they have, the easier they think it'll be for Florence to file for divorce. It's a conspiracy. They're all in on it. But they're in for a big disappointment because I'm not going anywhere."

"So how were you able to lose Ennis?"

"I—" He paused mid-throw to stare at me. "Why do you want to know?"

"No reason. I—"

"Oh, I get it. You wouldn't be on a fishing expedition to see if I happened to follow Delpha down that hiking trail, would you? What do you think I did to her? Rough her up? Kill her?"

"That's not why I—"

"Tell you the truth, Emily, I don't recall where I went. I kind of lost track of time. But here's the thing: since you're not the police, you don't get to ask the questions." He narrowed his eyes to hostile slits. "You've drunk the Kool-Aid, haven't you? Decided to join the conspiracy against me. They're always looking to recruit new members, and it looks like they've succeeded. Well, bully for them. Now do me a favor and get out of my sight." He side-armed the remainder of his rocks into the air with an angry slice. Ping! Thunk. Ding!

"You bet." As I scurried back to the bus, I bemoaned the fact that I still didn't know where the guys had actually gone after they left the museum, but their responses sent up a red flag that could have life-threatening implications. If their vague recollections of their surroundings were typical of the entire group, it left me to draw one very troubling conclusion.

Half the time they were walking around, they didn't have a clue where they were.

SEVENTEEN

"YOU'RE DOING GREAT SO far," our zipline instructor commended us. Her name was Sydney Ann and she was an elastic-
limbed millennial with a southern drawl, a long braid that trailed
down her back from beneath her helmet, and a knack for remembering names. "Now what y'all need to do is step into the harnesses
that're right in front of you."

The harnesses she was referring to were laid out on the deck like
industrial-size cobwebs, only with straps and hooks and shiny
metal rings.

"I don't understand where we're supposed to step," complained
Goldie as she studied the maze of nylon webbing at her feet. "Are
we ziplining or parachuting?"

"Watch the way I do it, hon. It's easy as pie. Place your feet in
these two openings"—Sydney Ann positioned her feet in what
looked like two random spaces—"then reach down and pull the
straps up between your legs, over your shoulders, and across your

chest, like this." With the skill of a master magician she hoisted the harness upward and into place in about three seconds flat.

I guess she'd done this before.

"Could you do that again?" asked Grover. "In slow motion?"

"Tell you what, Grover, how about I come 'round and help each one of y'all. That might be easier."

Nods. Relieved sighs. Smiles.

The equipment hut where we were standing was about the size of our cabins. It was located in the middle of a clearing surrounded by skinny fir trees and a network of cables that anchored a series of zipline structures to the ground. The structure closest to the hut resembled a towering jungle gym that might have served as a staging area for the Flying Wallendas' highwire act. Two sets of upright posts as tall as ships' masts faced each other like opposing goalposts about thirty feet apart, with railed platforms built onto them at rising elevations. Narrow suspension bridges with cables for handrails and wooden slats for stairs connected one platform to the other in a succession of switchbacks, each bridge climbing ever higher to the final jumping-off point.

Uff-da. The bottoms of my feet started tingling in anticipation.

"Al's never going to believe I did this," gushed Orphie as she waited her turn to get harnessed up. "Imagine: at my age, flying through the air like Peter Pan." She looked suddenly worried. "Is anyone planning to take pictures? If I don't document this, Al might not believe me."

Al. Just the person I wanted to discuss. "Has Al had any more news to share with you about the indoor water park deal?"

"I'm afraid not. He's so busy negotiating the deal of the century that he's had very little time to chat on the phone. People like Al have more important priorities than the rest of us, Emily."

"Would you let me know if you hear any updates?" I asked as Sydney Ann finished cinching the straps on Goldie and moved down the line to Grover. "The acreage the developer wants to build on? It belongs to my dad. It's his farm."

"Really? Well, can you imagine how happy he'll be when he finds out what Al plans to do with it?"

"That's not going to make him happy, Orphie. He loves farming, and as far as I know, he's entertaining no thoughts of retiring."

"But all those cornfields are such an eyesore—and so monotonous. Just think what an improvement a big, beautiful resort hotel will be. It'll put Windsor City on the map...and Al Arnesen in the political spotlight just in time for next year's elections. Can you picture Al as our next mayor? Or state senator? Or governor?" She clutched her throat with excitement. "The governorship even comes with a mansion, doesn't it?"

"Would you do me a favor and not mention the resort's proposed location to either Mom or Dad? I don't think they're going to be as thrilled with the project as you are."

She locked her lips with an invisible key and dropped it down her blouse. "My lips are sealed. But you need to face reality, Emily. They'll find out sometime. There's no stopping the wheels of progress."

Maybe not, but wheels weren't indestructible. Sometimes, they even fell off.

After trussing us up like Thanksgiving turkeys, Sydney Ann stood back to assess her handiwork. "Any of y'all's straps too tight?"

I made a T of my arms as I peered down at myself. It looked as if someone had strung me up in a cat's cradle, with straps criss-crossing my chest and shoulders and snaking between my legs under my tush. A couple of orange straps were attached to the webbing across my chest, and at the end of these hung two sturdy D-rings that resembled the clips mountain climbers use.

"These metal clips are called carabiners," Sydney Ann informed us as she demonstrated the spring-loaded action of the D-rings on her own harness. "We use two as a safety precaution, so when we fasten one clip to the zipline cable, you'll still be attached to the stationary cable on the platform until we fasten your second clip to the zipline. We never allow any of y'all to stand on a platform without having at least one of your carabiners attached to a cable to anchor you. It's how we prevent y'all from taking that unexpected swan dive to the ground, so we've got you covered. The site has ten zips of varying lengths and heights for y'all to try, each one more fun than the last. Y'all ready?"

Cheers. Fist pumps.

"Okay then. Helmets on!"

We picked our helmets up from the deck and snugged them on our heads. All except Goldie, who turned it over in her hands as if it were a reject from a thrift store fire sale. "Do we have to wear a helmet?"

"Sure do. It's another safety precaution."

She primped her flame-red hair with a bejeweled hand. "But it'll ruin my hairdo. I'll have helmet hair."

"Will you just put the damn helmet on so we can get this show on the road?" bellowed Thor.

"How about you have more respect for the ladies," Ennis challenged.

"How about you stop acting like my mother," Thor shot back.

Florence stomped her foot on the deck in front of her husband. "Can I never enjoy just *one* activity without you ruining it for me?"

"Ruin it for *you*?" spat Goldie. "How about ruining it for *everyone*?" She thwacked Grover's arm. "Are you going to stand there and let him talk to me like that?"

"Ennis already chewed him out. What else am I supposed to say?"

Goldie's eyes turned to ice. "You're such a prince."

"Maybe you could postpone this conversation until after you complete the course?" I suggested. "I'm sure Sydney Ann has a schedule to maintain."

"I've got a group of Majestic Cruise Line guests coming in right after y'all, so Emily's right: we gotta keep moving. Don't want to inconvenience our patrons by making them wait." She flashed a sympathetic look at Goldie. "I'm sorry about your hair, hon, but if you don't put your helmet on, you don't get to go."

Goldie grunted her frustration. Wincing, she lowered her helmet onto her head, fastened the chin strap, then looked to Florence for positive affirmation. "How do I look?"

"What does it matter?" snorted Thor. "No one looks at you anymore anyway."

"Are you planning to give us some instruction about what we're supposed to do?" Orphie interrupted.

Sydney Ann swung her arm toward the jungle gym structure in the distance. "That's our first zip. When y'all finish climbing to the top platform, I'll tell you what to do next. My teammate Mindy is already up there waiting for us, so let's get cracking so y'all can meet her."

We trekked single file down the manmade gravel path, Sydney Ann in the lead with me pulling up the rear. After climbing up a short flight of stairs, we arrived at the first platform, but making our way to the next platform looked a little more complicated.

"Take your time on the skybridge," Sydney Ann instructed as she demonstrated her ability to navigate the thirty-foot length of rope-ladder that floated upward to the next platform. "Hold on at all times," she shouted over her shoulder while gliding her hands along the cable rails, "and walk at your own pace, but be sure to step carefully." This as she scrambled over the close-set wooden slats with the sure-footedness of a gazelle. She executed a little pirouette for our benefit from the opposite platform. "So who wants to go first?"

Not waiting for anyone to cut in front of him, Thor barreled up the skybridge more like a bull than a mountain goat, causing the slats to bounce from his weight and the ladder to ripple like incoming waves. "Can I keep going?" he asked when he reached the first platform.

Sydney Ann gestured toward the next ascending skybridge. "Be my guest. See you up there." She glanced back down toward us. "Who's next?"

I insisted that the three girls go next, so with deep breaths and great trepidation they crept over the bridge, shuffling so slowly that the slats hardly moved. Grover and Ennis followed, and when they'd cleared the bridge, I made my way across, feeling a bit like a pirate being made to walk the plank, only without the water.

"Excellent, y'all! Only three more to go."

The first skybridge was the easiest. The next three rose at a steeper incline and the slats were wider apart, so the ladies proceeded at an even slower pace, stopping to catch their breath more than once.

"We're really high up," marveled Orphie in a tense voice. "Did I mention I'm afraid of heights?"

"Don't look down," suggested Florence.

"Whoever is making this thing bounce, cut it out," urged Goldie.

"If you three don't speed it up, we'll never get to the top," whined Grover.

But we eventually did make it to the top platform, where we met Mindy, whose eastern European accent was so thick, she might have done the voice-overs for both Boris Badenov and Natasha. "Goud for you," she greeted us, gripping our orange straps as we stepped onto the platform. She immediately clipped our carabiners to a stationary cable that encircled the utility pole–like beam in the center of the decking, kind of like a hitching post. When we were all secured, Sydney Ann walked to the departure point at the edge of the platform and tapped a brick-sized block that was attached to the zipline.

"This block here is what's gonna slow y'all down at the end of each zip. When your carabiners hit it, it'll prevent y'all from crashing into the deck." She nodded toward the fairly distant tower that was nestled in the trees opposite us. "That's your first destination. I'm gonna zip over first so I can help y'all onto the platform when you arrive. Mindy'll stay here to get y'all on your way. And just one word of caution: after she clips your carabiners to the zipline, don't fiddle with 'em while you're flying through the air. We don't want anyone accidentally unfastening themselves, 'cuz that would do it"—she paused for effect—"and it's a long way to the ground."

Orphie grabbed my hand. "I'm not sure I can go through with this, Emily."

"A little late to be having second thoughts now, isn't it?" chided Thor. "What a wuss."

"You're going to be fine, Orphie." I squeezed her hand. "Stay beside me and we'll do this together, okay? I'm not crazy about heights either, but if we can master the first one, I know we'll be fine. I bet we might even enjoy ourselves."

Orphie looked skeptical. Thor smirked. "Take a good look at how far it is to the ground, Orphie. Awwwful long way to fall. Bet you'd make quite the splat."

Ennis's expression soured with disgust. "You really are a louse."

"*I'm* a louse," howled Thor. "I'm not the one whose wife left him. Sounds to me like you need to look in the mirror to discover the real louse."

Noticing that Sydney Ann and Mindy were raising their eyebrows at each other, I let fly a long, shrill whistle that sliced through the air like a knife, rousing birds from their nests and causing everyone on the platform to cringe.

"C'mon, guys!" I warned like a kindergarten teacher to her classroom. "If you don't care to listen to Sydney Ann and Mindy's instructions, I'd invite you to leave right now."

Sydney Ann smiled. "Now's the only time you can leave, y'all, 'cuz there's no stairs on any of the platforms. Only way down once you're on the course is either by zip or by rope." She nodded toward a wooden box that was nailed about nose-high on the center pole. "There's a box like this on every platform with mountaineering rope inside, in case of emergency. But in all the time the course has been open, none of our teams have ever had to use it. Just one of those regulations we gotta follow."

Sydney Ann tugged on her harness, readjusting the straps. "I think y'all are just nervous," she teased. "That's okay. Lots of folks are nervous their first time out. So…here we go."

Mindy detached one of Sydney Ann's carabiners from the hitching post and clipped it to the zipline. When both carabiners were in place on the cable, Sydney Ann let out an exhilarated "*Wheeee!*" and took a flying leap off the platform, sailing along the zipline with her arms thrown wide, head back, and legs splayed, as if she were doing a back float in zero gravity. When she neared the tower, she assumed a sitting position, slowed down as her carabiners hit the block, then cruised onto the platform, grabbing hold of a thick rope that dangled from the cable to pull herself in. Scrambling to her feet, she looked back at us and waved with jazz hands before detaching herself from the zipline and securing her carabiners to the hitching post. She then walked to the edge of the platform and encouraged us to join her with a huge "come on over" sweep of her arm.

"You." Mindy stabbed a finger at Thor. "You go first. Stand here. No talking."

She positioned him near the cable, attached his clips to the zipline, then gave him a little push off the deck. While Sydney Ann had back-floated along the zip, Thor spun around like a top, round and round, twisting uncontrollably in the wind, legs askew, hands pulling on his straps to stop the dizzying rotation. "Whoaaaa!" he yowled in semi panic.

"You not want to spin?" counseled Mindy. "Grab hold of straps just under clips." She nodded toward Thor. "Not like heem."

I detected a mischievous little sparkle in her eye suggesting that despite being from another country, she'd gotten Thor's number very quickly.

"Frightened lady." She curled her forefinger at Orphie. "You next."

Orphie shuffled forward reluctantly, dragging me with her. "Goodbye, everyone. I've so enjoyed knowing all of you. If Al asks if I had any last words, tell him—"

"Stand here," directed Mindy. "Let go woman's hand. I tell from looking at you, you going to rock this."

Orphie released my hand as Mindy sorted through the array of carabiners and straps on the hitching post, separating Orphie's from the others. When both carabiners had been attached to the zip, Orphie took a deep breath, glanced over her shoulder at the rest of us with puppy dog eyes, inched close to the edge, and, by dint of will, pulled her legs up into a fetal position and propelled herself forward, which sent her skating down the zipline like a sled down a bobsled run.

"Oh my GAWWWWWWDd*ddddddddddddddddd*!"

She spun around once, but by the time she hit the block, she'd gained enough control over her equipment to make a graceful feet-first landing onto the platform. "Now that's the way it's done!" Sydney Ann yelled back to us.

Mindy arched her brows in a smug smile. "I knew lady would rock. Woman with red hair, you next."

Now that the ice had been broken, the whole idea of sailing above a strip of real estate fifty feet in the air seemed a lot less daunting. The rest of us completed our first zip with hoots, whoops, and laughter, and I even felt brave enough to let go of my straps and allow myself to rotate like a slow-spinning top.

Each zip presented a new challenge. Some were high off the ground with a short distance between towers. Others were closer to the ground with a longer-distance zip cable. And Sydney Ann and Mindy always made it interesting, setting up little competitions that had us vying against each other for who could yell out the word "Geronimo" to make it stretch for the entire length of the zip, who could scream the loudest, who could do the best imitation of an animal while flying through the air, and who could traverse the length of the zip the fastest. And each platform was different. Some were rectangular-shaped with railings, some were square-shaped without railings. But one feature that remained standard was the stationary hitching post that circled the main upright pole of the tower with our carabiners always secured to it, like streamers in a maypole.

Platform number six was unique in that it reminded me of a crow's nest set high on the mast of a clipper ship. It was perched at a dizzying height off the ground, and the decking around the central post was round and uncharacteristically narrow, with no guard rails around the edge. *Eww.* While Sydney Ann awaited us on platform seven, Mindy stood ready to attach our harnesses to the zip. "Who's up?"

"Where are you from, anyway?" Goldie asked her as we huddled around the central post while checking out the next course. "I can't quite place the accent."

"Belarus."

"Where's that?"

"You know Russia? Belarus share border with Russia and Ukraine and Poland and Lithuania and Latvia."

"Sounds like it's landlocked," said Orphie.

"Like pit in middle of peach."

"Just like Iowa!" enthused Goldie. "Do you grow sweet corn?"

Mindy shook her head. "No corn."

"What about hogs?" asked Grover. "Do your farmers raise pigs?"

"No pig."

"How did you end up in Alaska?" Ennis followed up.

"Work visa. Spent summer as maid at lodge in Denali Park. Met Prince Charming. Got married." She wiggled her ring finger to flaunt the gold band around it. "Plan to become citizen. Have many babies."

"So you came for the work and stayed for the romance," said Florence in a wistful voice. "That's so sweet. It's like a fairy tale."

"I snagged the leading role in a stage play with a premise like that years ago," Goldie reminisced. "It was called *From Russia with Love*."

"That's not a stage play," corrected Ennis. "It's a James Bond novel."

"This was an original stage play," explained Goldie. "The scriptwriter merely lifted the title off Ian Fleming to attract a wider audience. Titles can't be copyrighted."

"I remember seeing that play," mocked Thor. "Florence dragged me to see it. It wasn't about a spy with a license to kill. It was some girly type soap opera with a bunch of third-rate actors with bad accents flouncing around the stage. And if you played the lead, I hate to tell you, but you stunk up the place."

Goldie dismissed him with a flick of her wrist. "If your opinion meant anything, Thor, I'd be crushed, but since no one values what you think, I'll accept your words as high praise."

"No more talk." Mindy held up her hands. "You peoples hurt my ears. So...ladies first, yes?"

"How about guys first?" demanded Thor. He detoured around Florence on the outer perimeter of the platform, stepping wide to avoid running into her but so dangerously close to the end of the platform that if he hadn't been tethered to the hitching post, he might have—

Losing his balance when Florence accidentally bumped into him, he stutter-stepped toward the edge and windmilled his arms, stumbling off the edge in unexpected freefall and plunging head-long to the earth below, his all-important orange straps and cara-biners streaming outward like dangling appendages.

I shrieked in horror, the words he'd used to torment Orphie ringing prophetically in my ears.

He'd been right.

It was an awfully long way to the ground.

EIGHTEEN

"I REALIZE YOU'VE ALL just witnessed a traumatic event, but I need to take preliminary statements while the details are still fresh in your minds, so if you'll find a seat for yourselves somewhere, we can begin."

We were in the equipment hut with Alaska State Trooper Sergeant Patrick Quinn, surrounded by an array of harnesses, helmets, carabiners, rope, rain gear, boots, cables, and winches. Quinn had arrived first on the scene after Sydney Ann had made the 911 call, but he'd needed his four-wheel drive to maneuver through the muddy access road and an assist from a couple of the other instructors to locate Thor's body at the base of platform six on the course. Mindy and the rest of us had been left stranded at the top of the platform while Sydney Ann had rappelled to the ground from platform seven and raced to check on Thor's status. But it had been apparent to me even before she arrived that he hadn't survived the fall.

In the midst of the chaos and confusion I'd hammered out arrangements with Etienne to have him and Alison escort their groups back to the cabins to await Lieutenant Kitchen, urging them to return directly to our lodgings rather than stop at the roadside café we'd promised. I suspected no one would be happy about missing this fabled watering hole, but circumstances had changed, so we needed to adjust. After dropping the group off, Steele could drive back here to pick us up when the authorities were through with us.

Florence had remained remarkably calm throughout the incident. "She's in shock," Goldie and Orphie had confided to me as they'd comforted her atop the platform. But the level of calm that Florence was exhibiting smacked of more than just shock.

It smacked of relief.

Per Trooper Quinn's request, the six people in my group sat down on folding chairs and metal footlockers while Sydney Ann and Mindy sat cross-legged on the floor, looking even more stunned than the rest of us. Seating himself on an available folding chair, Quinn removed a pen and notepad from his shirt pocket, and after jotting down all our names, he put a bead on Florence.

"So let me start out by saying that I'm very sorry about your husband's accident, Mrs. Thorsen."

Florence nodded. "Thank you."

"And since I've never ziplined, I'd like to have one of the instructors tell me how the process is supposed to work."

Sydney Ann jumped in with the information about the guest harnesses, the stationary cable that served to anchor everyone, and how guests' carabiners were always tethered to a hitching post until an instructor attached both clips to the zipline. "It's against our regulations to allow any guest to be present on a platform without being anchored by two carabiners."

Quinn canted his head. "And yet Mr. Thorsen fell to his death because neither of his carabiners was attached."

"I attach him to center cable when he finish fifth zip," argued Mindy. She pantomimed the motion of detaching his first carabiner from the zip and fastening it to the hitching post. "*Click.*" And then the second. "*Click.*" She held Quinn's gaze. "Impossible for him to fall."

"So how do you explain what happened?"

"I no explain. Man must have fiddled with carabiners. Detached himself. But Sydney Ann warn before first zip, 'No fiddle with carabiners. Very dangerous.' Maybe he not listen."

"Why would he want to detach himself?" prodded Quinn.

Mindy shrugged. "This man act like beeg shot. He not like following instructions."

Quinn glanced at the rest of us for confirmation. "Is that true? Did Thor Thorsen take pleasure in acting like a big shot?"

Glances fired back and forth between the five remaining book clubbers. "Thor was…difficult," offered Goldie, "and quite hard to like."

"He didn't think rules applied to him," added Orphie, "so he always ignored them."

"He was obnoxious," said Ennis.

"He didn't like me," confessed Grover. "In fact, he always went out of his way to insult me. Anything he could say or do to ruin my day, he'd do it. He thrived on making me feel miserable. Made him feel powerful."

Quinn's face softened as he regarded Florence. "I'm sorry you have to listen to this, Mrs. Thorsen."

"I don't mind, Officer. It's all true. Thor was toxic. My one regret is that I didn't discover his shortcomings until after I married him. He kept the real Thor under wraps until I had a ring on my finger."

"There's always divorce."

Florence shook her head. "There was no divorcing Thor. Even if I'd gone through with it, I'd never be rid of him. He would have found a way to torture me until I died."

"So...his death today," questioned Quinn. "Would you label this a way out for you?"

Goldie sucked in her breath. "Are you suggesting that Florence might have had a hand in killing her own husband?"

He kept his gaze riveted on Florence. "Why don't you tell me exactly what transpired right before your husband fell, Mrs. Thorsen?"

She folded her hands in her lap and lowered her eyes to focus on a random spot on the floor. "We were all bunched together on the platform, listening to Mindy tell us how she'd ended up in Alaska. And as usual Thor demanded to be first across the next zip, so he circled around me on the outside edge of the platform, but we accidentally bumped into each other. I remember him throwing his arms in the air to regain his balance, but the next thing I knew he wasn't brushing past me." She looked up from the floor to make eye contact with Quinn. "He was tumbling over the side."

"You accidentally bumped into each other?" pressed Quinn. "Or did you give him a well-placed push on purpose?"

"No, I didn't push him," cried Florence. "He was the one who did the initial shoving so he could get to the front of the line."

"So you deny being the person who unfastened his carabiners, Mrs. Thorsen?"

"Of course I deny it. I wouldn't dare monkey with those things. Besides, they looked so tangled, I wouldn't have been able to figure out which carabiner went with which harness."

"Carabiners *not* tangled," challenged Mindy. "I know which clip belong which guest." She made a V of her index and middle fingers and directed them at her face. "I have good eye. Never make mistake with harness, even if woman say straps tangled."

As he studied Mindy, Quinn clicked his pen to retract the point, then clicked it again to advance it. Retract. Advance. Retract. Advance. "How long have you been an employee at Last Frontier Ziplining, Mindy?"

Her eyes shifted nervously. She held up her forefinger as if it were a roman numeral. "One week," she said in a small voice.

Quinn's voice rose an octave, cracking with disbelief. "Seven days?"

"Not full seven. I have weekend off. But I make no mistake all that time."

He stared at Sydney Ann, nonplussed. "Just how long has this outfit been in operation?"

"Counting today?" She forced a smile. "A week."

He made a notation on his pad. "With a flawless performance record until today. I suppose congratulations are in order. You avoided any fatalities until day seven." He shook his head. "How much training were you required to go through before you earned your instructor's status?"

Mindy and Sydney Ann exchanged dubious looks, accompanied by slow shoulder rolls. "Zipping," reflected Sydney, ticking the list off on her fingertips. "Rappelling. Knot tying. CPR. Safety tips." She crooked her mouth at Mindy for validation. "About two weeks?"

"Ten days," corrected Mindy. "They give us weekend off."

"Almost two weeks," repeated Quinn. "Two weeks to qualify you to be entrusted with the lives of countless tourists."

"We move clip from one cable to another," Mindy fired back, demonstrating the process in slow motion for him. "One cable to another. It not like brain surgery."

"And you couldn't possibly have made a mistake and failed to tether Mr. Thorsen to the anchor cable. Is that your claim?"

Mindy shook her head adamantly. "If I not attach to cable, man's carabiners would be flopping from harness. *Boomboom, boomboom.* Man's carabiners not floppy. They fastened to hitching cable."

"Until they weren't," Quinn pointed out. "What line of work were you in before you were hired here, Mindy?"

"I work as chamber maid in lodge at Denali."

"And before that?"

"In Belarus? I work for family company what make room freshener. All organic. Very healthy. I make up name for scents. Cinnamon Potato," she said proudly. "Alfalfa Garlic."

Which probably explained why she'd needed to seek alternative career opportunities in another country.

"I'd love a job like that," mused Goldie. "Only instead of room freshener, I'd like to be able to give names to eye shadow and blush. *Whisperberry.*" She pronounced it slowly and sensuously, as if she'd been dying to say it out loud for a long time. "What color do you think that sounds like?"

"Shell pink," fantasized Orphie. "With maybe a hint of bergamot."

"Bergamot?" Goldie gave her a squinty look. "What's bergamot?"

"I think it's a town in Germany," said Florence.

A sharp knock sounded on the door.

"What?" Quinn called out.

A man poked his head through the opening. "Need to speak to you for a sec, Sarge."

Quinn left the room for a quick two minutes before returning. I suspected he'd been on the receiving end of unwelcome news because when he rejoined us, his body language screamed of exasperation. Retaking his seat, he ranged a long look at us and sighed. He nodded at Mindy. "After Mr. Thorsen fell, why didn't you rappel to the ground immediately to check on his condition?"

"It against company regulation to leave guest on platform without instructor, so I no could leave. Sydney go instead. She by herself on platform seven."

He lasered a look at Sydney Ann. "And how long did it take you to reach Mr. Thorsen?"

She puffed out her bottom lip. "Ten minutes? Maybe less? I made the 911 call, then rappelled to the ground, but it seemed to take me forever to reach him because I had to fight through a whole bunch of scrub brush."

"What was his condition when you reached him?"

She spoke her words slowly, self-consciously. "He landed face-down, so I rolled him over and checked the pulse in his neck, but I couldn't find it. So I detached his harness and pulled his jacket and shirt apart to listen to his heart, but when I still couldn't hear a heartbeat, I knew…you know…that…that he was dead. That's when I sent out an SOS text to the other instructors on the course. So they converged on platform six to help get the stranded guests through the rest of the zips so they could get down."

Quinn jotted something onto his notepad before returning his gaze to Mindy. "So, to reiterate: it's your opinion that Mr. Thorsen detached his carabiners merely to showboat?"

"Showboat?" Mindy's features puckered in confusion. "What you mean, showboat?"

"A showboat is the same thing as a big shot," interjected Grover, "only on a grander scale."

Mindy crossed her arms and nodded her head emphatically. "Man was showboat."

"Excuse me, Officer," Ennis called from his perch on a footlocker at the back of the room. "If Thor did release his own carabiners, won't his fingerprints be all over the metal?"

"They would be," said Quinn, "if all trace of prints hadn't been obliterated when his harness was detached. From what I was just told"—he bobbed his head toward the door—"the prints on the carabiners are smudged beyond our capacity to lift them."

It took Sydney Ann a couple of heartbeats to comprehend what Quinn had just said, but when enlightenment struck, she rounded her mouth into an O of indignation. "Are y'all saying you can't get any fingerprints because of *me*?"

"I'm saying the fingerprints are unsalvageable," Quinn responded in an even tone.

"Well, what'd y'all expect me to do?" she huffed. "Are y'all saying I shouldn't have touched him? That I shouldn't have bothered to check for a pulse or listen to his heart? I spent a whole half hour of training time breathing into the mouth of a plastic dummy to get CPR certified. I know what to do to revive someone, but he was beyond any help I could give him."

"Sydney Ann did the right thing," applauded Goldie. "I'm sure it was pure accident that she screwed up the way she did."

"Does that mean we'll never know the real reason why Thor detached himself from the anchor cable?" asked Florence. "I can't imagine what he was trying to prove—I mean, other than showing off." She fluttered her fingers in the air. "Look, ma. No hands."

"What if none of this had anything to do with showing off?" suggested Orphie in a conspiratorial tone. "What if Thor was trying to detach someone else's hooks and detached his own by mistake?"

"You think Thor was trying to kill one of us?" squealed Grover.

Orphie shrugged. "Why not? He didn't like any of us. Maybe he saw this as the best chance he'd ever have to get rid of one of us. It wouldn't have been too hard, what with the straps being tangled like they were."

"Straps not tangled," charged Mindy between gritted teeth.

"Unhook the clips," Orphie continued, "leave them draped over the hitching post thingie, and no one's any the wiser…until they step too close to the edge."

The group pondered her theory as they crossed glances. "But which one of us did he want to kill?" whispered Florence.

"By the same token," Quinn spoke up, "if all of you despised Mr. Thorsen as much as he despised you, what would have prevented one of you from deciding that this was the perfect opportunity to take advantage of getting rid of *him*? Quite successfully, I might add. And by a serendipitous twist of fate, there are no fingerprints to link any of you directly to his death."

Sydney Ann threw her arms into the air. "Go ahead," she railed at Quinn. "Why don't y'all just shoot me now and get it over with."

Goldie gasped. "Oh my god. Is she confessing?"

"I believe she's referring to the unwitting part she played in corrupting the fingerprint evidence," explained Ennis.

"I didn't do that on purpose!" swore Sydney Ann.

"So are you going to arrest her?" asked Orphie.

Quinn ranged a look around the room, his flinty expression cowing everyone into silence. "As I told you when we began, I'm only taking preliminary statements this morning, but I'm ruling this as a suspicious death, and none of you are above suspicion. Whether this is a case of criminal negligence on the part of the instructor or an intentional homicide remains to be seen. I've just begun my investigation, so you can expect to see a lot more of my face in the days to come."

I hung my head in despair. No problem there. Maybe he and Lieutenant Kitchen could form a tag team.

"I don't know what your itinerary looks like, Mrs. Miceli, but you'll need to remain in Denali until further notice. That applies to the Last Frontier instructors also."

I stared at him, dumbstruck. "But…we're planning to leave tomorrow."

"Not now, you're not. I'm sorry."

"But…but…it's going to be impossible to book accommodations for all our guests on the spur of the moment at the height of tourist season. What are we supposed to do, sleep on the bus?"

"You work in the travel industry, Mrs. Miceli. I'm sure you'll find some way to resolve the problem."

Easy for *him* to say. I knew I should have packed more antacids. But as he stood up, summarily dismissing us, I realized I had much more to worry about than overnight accommodations.

Two guests dead in four days.

Two book clubbers dead in four days.

Oh my god. Were they killing each other?

I cast a wary look at the faces around me. Whether I wanted to believe it or not, there was a good possibility that someone in this room was a cold-blooded murderer.

"Do you think Thor's death might be related to the death of one of our other tour members in Girdwood a few days ago?" Goldie called out as Quinn made his way to the door.

He stopped in his tracks. "Are you talking about the Bigfoot homicide?"

"Is that what they're calling it?" asked Orphie. "Oh my goodness, wait until Emily's father finds out. Won't he be surprised? He's the one who saw it, you know."

"He didn't actually see it," I corrected.

Quinn regarded us in an obvious fluster. "The victim was a member of your tour group? You've suffered two deaths in how many days?"

"Four," I said in an undertone.

"Okay, folks." He herded us back to our seats. "Sit yourselves back down. No one's going anywhere yet."

NINETEEN

"LIEUTENANT KITCHEN AND SERGEANT Quinn have decided to coordinate their investigative efforts," Etienne informed me when I arrived back at the cabin.

Tag team. I knew it.

Because Quinn's additional questioning had delayed our departure by another hour, we'd missed Lieutenant Kitchen's scheduled interview session, which was unfortunate for his investigation because the people whose alibis were the flimsiest were all with me. We'd had to stop for lunch on the way back—despite the trauma of the morning, everyone was starving. When we pulled into the cabins' parking lot, things didn't improve because we had to fend off reporters who were skulking about in search of a story about this latest incident.

"Two of your guests have died under suspicious circumstances in four days. Do you think you're cursed or just incompetent?"

"Would you advise future travelers to avoid Destinations Travel on their next vacation because of your curse?"

"Do you think Bigfoot had a hand in this most recent death?"

Etienne had enveloped me in his arms when I'd opened our cabin door, hugging me tight against his chest, which is when he'd sprung the news about the coordinated investigation.

"I figured as much." I snuggled against him. "Does that mean they'll hold joint interview sessions rather than schedule them one after the other all day long?"

"That's the idea. And since you missed Kitchen's earlier session, he's arranged for a special meeting to take place at four o'clock this afternoon for you and the book club members, with Sergeant Quinn in attendance. I've already sent a text to the affected guests to request their presence in the lodge at the appointed time."

"Uff-da." I dragged myself across the floor and belly flopped onto the bed. "My head's about to explode from all the questioning. And you know what they've come up with so far? Diddly-squat."

Etienne joined me on the bed. "Tell me."

It took twenty minutes, but I told him exactly what had happened on the zipline platform, ending with Quinn's theory that the incident most likely would be categorized as either criminal negligence or homicide. "Someone unclipped those carabiners. If Thor didn't do it himself, someone else did—with the obvious intent of killing either Thor or another member of the group."

Etienne intertwined his fingers with mine, his flesh warm, his touch reassuring. "I'm not sure what I would have done if you'd been the person who'd fallen, bella."

I'd tried to avoid going there mentally, but thinking about it now caused a tingling sensation to slither up my spine. Omigod. Did one of the book clubbers want *me* dead? But...but...what did I do? I probably didn't even read the same kind of books they read.

"Do you suppose you could hold me for a little while?" I asked as I crawled into his arms. "Just until my heart stops racing?"

It took forty-five minutes, but by the time we needed to gear up for our next wave of duties, I was operating on all cylinders again.

"Our meeting is in precisely one-half hour," Etienne reminded me as he rolled to the side of the bed. "Can you manage that?"

"You bet. But would you do me a favor? Would you stop by Florence's cabin to see how she's faring? Maybe escort her to the meeting so she won't have to go by herself? Although, for a woman whose husband died only a few hours ago, she's doing remarkably well."

"Really?" He stood up. "Is that a good thing or a bad thing?"

"I don't know what kind of thing it is. It's an observation. She's sure not shedding any tears over Thor. Does that mean she could have killed him? I don't know. But if it turns out that she did kill Thor, does that increase the likelihood that she's a person of interest in Delpha's death too?" I blew a puff of air toward the ceiling. "Did you pick up any new details from Lieutenant Kitchen at the meeting?"

He shook his head. "The Dicks repeated their alibis. George and Osmond linked their phones to the television so they could show the whole room the pictures they took during their forty-five minute museum tour. They mentioned that was your idea. Alison shared for the first time that she left the museum after five minutes because she found herself experiencing a flare-up of an intestinal disorder that rears its head when she's under stress, so she headed for the ladies' room and stayed there until just before dinner. Lucille Rasmussen empathized with Alison's plight by informing the room that she'd suffered from the same disorder for years when her husband was alive, but she hadn't suffered a single flare-up since she'd cut back on fiber and buried Dick."

He paused. "I'm still not sure if she meant that to be a commentary on low-fiber diets or marital bliss. Everyone else was otherwise occupied at the glacier, which Kitchen knew about from our first meeting. So if our book club members aren't more forthcoming when he questions them, I'm afraid no one is going to learn anything new."

"Here's something new, and you're not going to want to hear it. Because of Sergeant Quinn's investigation into Thor's death, we have to stay in Denali."

"But we're scheduled to leave tomorrow."

"Not anymore. We have to find new accommodations until we're given the okay to leave."

He muttered something in exasperated Italian before planting a kiss on my cheek and heading out the door. I remained inert for another ten minutes before heading for the bathroom, where, to my utter delight, I discovered the water had been restored.

After washing my face, freshening my makeup, and spritzing my hair with styling gel, I returned to the bedroom to change out of my ziplining clothes. As I pulled on clean jeans and a V-neck top, I tried to anticipate Lieutenant Kitchen's line of questioning, but it seemed that no line of questioning, no matter how clever, could negate the fact that all our guests had been at dinner when Delpha died, so none of them could have killed her. She'd been alive when she'd responded to my texts, so that cleared everyone of suspicion. No one could have been in the restaurant and on the hiking trail at the same time.

Unless Delpha was already dead when you received those texts, said a little voice in my head.

I yanked my top over my head and stood very still for a moment, bowled over by the suggestion. Already dead when the texts were sent? But...how...?

A recent conversation began flirting with my memory. Just on the edges. A conversation with Jackie. And then I recalled something she'd said. How the Toms with their broken appendages couldn't text one-handed, so they'd enlisted her thumbs to send their messages for them, to the detriment of her manicure.

So...like in the case of the Toms and Jackie, what if Delpha wasn't the one who'd replied to my texts? What if the person who'd responded had been her killer?

As if caught in the blowback of an explosive blast, I sank back onto the edge of the bed, my mind going off in six different directions.

Uff-da. I never considered that possibility. But...but...is that why Lieutenant Kitchen hadn't been able to give me any specifics about Delpha's phone at our first meeting? If there'd been no phone at the scene, he wouldn't have even known she was carrying one until I told him. Had her killer stripped her of all her valuables after he'd attacked her? Phone? Jewelry? Cash? Credit cards?

I stared into space as the gridlock in my brain shifted ever so slightly.

This was making more sense now. If Delpha's killer had stolen her phone, the timeline for her death could be altered drastically. She could have died long before I texted her, and her killer could have rejoined the rest of the group at the restaurant, set her phone on vibrate, and responded to my unexpected text right from the dinner table. Who would have noticed? They all texted relentlessly.

So under this new paradigm, no one escaped suspicion. Was my theory solid enough to present to Lieutenant Kitchen?

But what if the police *did* have Delpha's phone? What if they'd had it from the start?

Then I'd look like a complete fool with egg all over my face.

Unless…

I slanted a look at the shelf perched above the clothing rod of our exposed closet. At Etienne's soft-sided messenger bag.

I'd look like a fool…unless I could prove that Delpha's responses to me had been written by someone else.

Energized by a sudden surge of adrenaline, I pulled the messenger bag off the shelf and fished out the file folder that contained our guests' handwritten medical history forms. "Spillum…Spillum…" I muttered as I riffled through the wad of papers. It would have been easier to check the document online, but I needed to use my phone to check out something else. Finding Delpha's form, I set it on the bed, then accessed my text messages from two days ago, rereading the questions I'd asked and her responses.

In answer to my question "Where are you?" she'd told me she was hiking back to the resort.

A random killer wouldn't have known where she was staying, especially since the resort's name wasn't printed on our key cards, but it would have been an easy question for anyone else on the tour to answer.

I'd asked her about the fog and she'd replied that it was clearing farther down, which revealed absolutely nothing and could easily have been a lie.

I'd suggested she select an entrée that I could bring back to the resort to her and she'd nixed the lamb, salmon, beef, and duck in favor of the crab.

Nuts. I wished I could find something surreptitious about that, but I couldn't. Salmon and crab were Alaskan specialties that all tourists were encouraged to sample.

It seemed there was no "there" there.

With my adrenaline flagging, I scanned the first page of Delpha's medical history form, taking note of her name, address, occupation, doctor's name, and emergency contact. Page two listed her medications, over-the-counter supplements, disabilities, dietary restrictions, and—

My heart started racing as I read the last line on the form.

Omigod. Omigod, omigod, omigod!

I grabbed my phone to skim the readout screen again.

I reread the last line on the medical form.

Eureka!

With phone and medical form in hand, I grabbed my shoulder bag and ran outside, banging through the front door of the guest lodge like a charging bull. "Delpha never sent me those texts," I announced in a breathless rush to the handful of people in the room.

Lieutenant Kitchen and Sergeant Quinn, their Dudley Do-Right hats still sitting atop their heads, glanced across the floor at me.

"It couldn't have been Delpha." I waved my phone at them. "She ordered the crab. Delpha never would have ordered crab." I brandished her medical form in my fist. "She was allergic to shell-fish."

TWENTY

THEY STARED BACK AT me, speechless—Kitchen and Quinn, Goldie and Grover, Florence and Etienne, Ennis, Orphie, and Alison.

"Delpha must have died *before* we went into dinner," I blurted out, "because when I texted her, it had to have been her killer who responded. He must have stolen her phone and thought he'd be clever by jerking me around. But he gave himself away because he didn't know about her allergy. Do you know what this means?" I searched the faces in the room with barely contained excitement. "It means that *anyone* at dinner in the restaurant that night could have killed her."

I paused as I listened to my own voice, wondering if I should be quite this euphoric about casting shade on every member of the group.

"A phantom text from the killer?" questioned Lieutenant Kitchen. "An intriguing suggestion, Mrs. Miceli, but highly improbable if Ms. Spillum's phone was locked."

"Delpha never locked her phone," Ennis spoke up.

"None of us do," revealed Goldie. "It's a precautionary measure."

"Against what?" asked Sergeant Quinn.

Silence ensued as the group shot awkward glances at each other.

"Against wanting to use our phone and suddenly forgetting what our password or code is," confessed Florence. "It's happened to all of us. Senior moments. They make you feel so stupid. But if we don't lock our phones, we avoid the problem. Crisis averted. It's so much less stressful."

"What Florence said," commended Orphie.

Nods of assent. Scattered applause.

Lieutenant Kitchen regarded me soberly as he motioned me farther into the room. "Would you care to have a seat and join us, Mrs. Miceli?"

"Do you want to see Delpha's medical history form?" I hurried toward him, handing him the pages. "It didn't occur to me until a few minutes ago to check her medical forms. I should have thought of it before."

Kitchen studied the information. "This could be significant, Mrs. Miceli. Thank you."

His approval gave me confidence to offer more advice. "So it should be easy from here. All you have to do is find the person who has Delpha's phone. And it's pretty easy to spot because it has a custom-ordered black-and-white newspaper print case."

The two troopers exchanged wary looks before Kitchen nodded toward an unoccupied chair. "While you're taking a seat, Mrs. Miceli, Sergeant Quinn and I need to step outside. We won't be long."

"What do you suppose that's all about?" asked Goldie as we watched the two men kibitzing outside the window.

"Has anyone noticed that every time we mention Delpha's phone, Lieutenant Kitchen gets a little twitchy?" questioned Ennis. "He didn't want to discuss the phone issue in Girdwood either."

"I expect he has his reasons," said Etienne, who was seated beside Florence. "Probably none of which are for public consumption at the moment."

I made eye contact with Florence as I sat down. "I'm sorry you have to sit through more questioning, but if it becomes completely unbearable, you just raise the alarm and I'll get you out of here, whether the police like it or not."

She forced a half smile. "I'll be okay, Emily. I want to find out who killed Delpha as much as the rest of you."

Alison caught my attention. "Etienne just told me about the change in our itinerary. Are we really going to have to stay in Denali longer?"

"According to Sergeant Quinn we are." I heaved a sigh before regarding her in confusion. "How come you're at this meeting? Didn't you already attend the earlier one?"

"Yeah. But since my alibi is intimately connected with all the guys who visited the museum, he asked me to come back when he questioned them. So here I am." Her ponytail bounced as she bobbed her head with the inconvenience of it all.

As Kitchen and Quinn stepped back into the room, Etienne tossed out a question. "Before you begin your questioning, officers, my wife has informed me that you've requested we remain in Denali for longer than we'd scheduled."

"That's right," Quinn spoke up. "You got a problem with that?"

"I do: lodging. Where do you suggest twenty-three tourists find last-minute accommodations in an area where No Vacancy signs are posted a year in advance? I appreciate your request, I simply question our ability to implement it."

Kitchen threw a long look at Quinn. "You told them they couldn't leave?"

"A man fell to his death at the zipline site and I haven't even scratched the surface yet of why it happened, so yeah. I told them they couldn't leave."

Kitchen nodded. "Good." Then, to Etienne, "I might have a lead for you, Mr. Miceli. I got an alert about an hour ago that one of the Majestic cruise ships has reported an outbreak of the norovirus and is returning to Vancouver immediately. So you might want to contact their resort here because, according to the press release, Majestic was supposed to be bussing a whole slew of folks from the ship to Denali tomorrow. Might be the resort would be willing to rent those rooms out to another group rather them leave 'em vacant. Just a suggestion."

Etienne removed his cell phone from his pocket and stood up. "Thanks. I'll see what I can do. Would you excuse me?" And out the door he went.

Kitchen removed his hat and set it on the jigsaw puzzle table before returning to the center of the room and plucking his notepad and pen from his shirt pocket. "So folks, here's what we've decided to do. I'm dispatching Sergeant Quinn to search all your rooms for Ms. Spillum's cell phone."

A collective gasp from the others. An elated smile from me.

"Don't you need a warrant to do that?" questioned Ennis.

"Sure do…unless you folks give the sergeant permission to perform his search without it. It'd save us loads of time. If you've got nothing to hide, I don't see any reason why you'd insist on a warrant. But we're gonna end up searching your rooms one way or the other, so you decide. It's just that this way will be a lot quicker."

"You can search my room," Orphie spoke up. "I've got nothing to hide."

Kitchen flipped back through the pages of his notepad. "We don't need to search your cabin, Mrs. Arnesen. I've already documented your whereabouts during the time in question."

"Does that mean you don't need to search my cabin either?" asked Goldie. "I was with Orphie and Florence at the glacier."

"We'll need to search your cabin because of your husband, Mrs. Kristiansen." He referred to his notes. "The Kristiansen cabin, Ennis Iversen's cabin, Alison Pickles's cabin, and Florence Thorsen's cabin."

As he rattled off names, Quinn scribbled notes on his own notepad.

"Why do you need to search my cabin?" asked Florence. "I was with Orphie and Goldie. Besides which…my husband is dead."

"I'm sorry for your loss, Mrs. Thorsen, but I don't have an accurate account of where your husband went after he left the museum, so it's necessary." Kitchen directed a questioning look at his audience. "So what's the verdict?"

"You can search Thor's things *and* mine," Florence relented in a tired voice, "but I can guarantee you won't find Delpha's phone. Thor might have been a louse, but he wasn't a killer."

"I won't force you to apply for a warrant," said Ennis. "Go ahead and search my stuff. I'm not hiding anything."

"Me either," said Alison. "Knock yourselves out."

Kitchen leveled a look on Grover. "That leaves only you, Mr. Kristiansen."

Grover shifted uncomfortably in his chair, eyes downcast, tongue drifting out of his mouth to wet his lips. Goldie thwacked his thigh. "Tell him it's okay, Grover. What are you waiting for?"

Grover hesitated before giving his head a reluctant nod. "You have my permission. But my suitcase is arranged in very specific order so I'd appreciate your not messing things up. I have a system."

"You hear that, Sergeant?" needled Kitchen. "Make an effort to be neat."

Quinn looked less than amused as he addressed the room. "If you're carrying your cell phone with you, please hold it up. All of you, not just the guests whose cabins I'm going to search."

We pulled them out of pockets and handbags and held them in the air.

"Do any of you have more than one cell phone with you?"

Head shaking. Scattered nopes.

"So I shouldn't find any extra cell phones in your rooms, right?"

Nods all around.

"All right, then, I need to collect your room keys, please."

"Even if you're not going to search our cabin?" asked Orphie.

Quinn read off his notepad. "I need four keys: Kristiansen, Iversen, Pickles, and Thorsen."

He made a quick pass around the room to gather the old-fashioned metal keys with their attached cabin number tags. He paused in front of Alison. "You're not part of the zipline contingent."

255

"There were three groups of zipliners. I was in the one that escaped any fatalities."

"And you're here why?"

"I asked her to be here," Kitchen replied for her. "I need her to corroborate the alibis in the Spillum investigation."

Quinn took the key from her hand, but he lingered as she smiled up at him, acting as if his feet were suddenly buried in concrete.

"How long are you gonna keep us locked up in here?" Grover snapped, his gaze fixed on Quinn.

"I'd like to know that too," complained Ennis. "I've got ongoing problems of my own to take care of back home. I need to be making phone calls."

"You'll be here as long as it takes," warned Kitchen as Quinn wrenched himself away from Alison and headed out the door. "Longer if you don't lose the attitude. So"—he grabbed a folding chair and sat down—"don't spare me any details, gentlemen. I'll start with Mr. Kristiansen. Where did you go and what did you do after leaving the Roundhouse Museum on the evening Ms. Spillum was killed?"

Not surprisingly, Grover launched into the same explanation he'd given me earlier in the day, saying he'd left the building shortly after Alison because his diuretic had kicked in and he needed to find a restroom. But he still couldn't recall which of the two facilities he'd used.

"And afterward?" asked Kitchen.

"I just wandered around. But I'm remembering now that I spent a lot of time watching the gondola go up and down the mountain. That's quite the operation, but noisy as all get-out."

"Ms. Pickles, did you run into Mr. Kristiansen again after you left the museum?"

"Not until I left the ladies' room and saw him standing near the hostess podium in the restaurant. Like I told you earlier, I needed to spend a lot more time in the restroom than I would have liked."

"Did you run into any other tour guests after you left the museum, Mr. Kristiansen?"

"Not a one. Not until I stepped into the restaurant foyer."

Kitchen flipped a page on his notepad. "Did you harbor any animosity toward the victim? Grudges left festering? Scores you wanted to settle?"

"No! Delpha was a friend. Her reading tastes were different from mine, but we never let that affect our friendship. She got along with everyone in book club, except maybe…Well, let me put it this way: the only person I ever saw her have words with was Thor."

Kitchen nodded. "Mr. Iversen." He redirected his questioning. "Would you please repeat your alibi, including any added details you remember?"

Ennis offered the same version of his whereabouts that he'd given me. He'd left the museum at about the same time as Thor, wandered the grounds, hung around the deck, and watched the fog roll in.

"You didn't see Mr. Kristiansen in your travels?"

Ennis shook his head. "I saw a lot of tourists milling around, but I didn't see Grover, no."

"And you didn't see Ms. Pickles?"

"She was in the ladies' room," Orphie said helpfully. "Didn't you hear what she said?"

"I didn't see anyone I knew," Ennis confirmed. "Including Alison."

"Do you agree with that, Ms. Pickles?" asked Kitchen.

"I couldn't see anything from my stall in the ladies' room, especially our male guests, so yeah, I agree."

Lieutenant Kitchen narrowed his eyes at Ennis. "Do you have any reason to want Ms. Spillum dead, Mr. Iversen?"

"Delpha and I were good friends, Lieutenant. We shared similar intellectual pursuits, had the same political leanings, enjoyed the same movies. A conversation with Delpha was always a lively one. She pushed you to think. I'm going to miss that. So no, I certainly had no reason to want her dead."

"What about Thor?" Goldie spoke up. "How are you planning to find out where he was? He's the one you should be focusing on. It ticked him off that Delpha wouldn't kowtow to him, so he had it in for her. You could tell just from the way he treated her. Never any respect. Always mouthing off to her. Trust me, if anyone killed her, it was him."

"Thank you for your opinion, Mrs. Kristiansen." He eyed the rest of us. "Anyone else?"

I raised a tentative hand, uneasy about poking a hornet's nest, but uncomfortable about what might get swept under the carpet if I didn't speak up. "I have a comment…for whatever it's worth. Maybe someone can explain it to me. When our group was gathered in the hotel lobby our first night in Girdwood, I saw Delpha glare at Grover, Goldie, and Ennis when they stepped off the elevator. And it wasn't just a passing look. It was intense and filled with loathing and disgust. When I asked Delpha if she and Goldie had had a falling out, she told me that the two of them were the best of friends and that Goldie had been like a sister to her ever since kindergarten. But when I spoke to Goldie, she told me that she and Delpha shared a cordial but basically superficial relationship. So you can see my confusion. If Delpha was such good friends with everyone, what was up with the hateful look? And if that look mirrored the true depth of her feelings, did it also factor into why she died?"

Kitchen studied me for a long moment. "Intriguing questions, Mrs. Miceli." He ranged a look at Goldie. "Do you know of any reason why Ms. Spillum would have regarded you with animosity?"

"No! We've always been on good terms. It's hard for me to believe she'd ever look at me that way." She lifted her chin at a haughty angle. "Emily could be wrong, you know."

Kitchen nodded toward Grover. "Mr. Kristiansen, same question."

Grover gave two palms up. "I'm with Goldie. I think Emily was imagining things."

"Mr. Iversen?"

"There's no reason in the world why Delpha would give me the stink eye. Whoever she was looking at, I can say with some certitude that it wasn't me."

"Alrighty then." Kitchen flipped to a fresh page on his notepad. "Now that we have that over with, let's try again, only this time I want specifics. And I hope you'll try real hard to give me something other than you were wandering around like zombies for an hour because that's just not going to cut it. So, Mr. Kristiansen, with as much detail as possible please, where did you go, who did you see, and what did you do after you left the museum?"

Kitchen plied them with questions, testing both their alibis and their short-term memories. Clever questions. Tricky questions. But

259

their responses were no more detailed on the second telling than they had been on the first. So he subjected them to a third round, then a fourth. By the time Sergeant Quinn walked through the door again, not only were we worn out from the constant barrage of questions, but Kitchen had nothing new to show for the hour and a half he'd been interrogating us, and his mood reflected the failure.

"I hope you've had more luck than I've had," he barked at Quinn. "Did you find the phone?"

"No, sir."

Nuts. I was so sure it'd find something. I slumped in my chair, discouraged that my brilliant idea had proven to be not so brilliant after all. But it had made so much sense at the time.

"I'm through for a while," admitted Kitchen, slapping his palms on his thighs and rising to his feet. "Show's all yours."

"Thank you, sir." Releasing his handcuffs from his belt, Quinn crossed the floor to where Alison was sitting. "Alison Pickles, I'm placing you under arrest on suspicion of murder."

The room erupted in gasps and cries of shock.

Omigod! Alison? But…but…no. It couldn't be Alison. She'd been holed up in a restroom stall with intestinal distress!

"I didn't kill that woman," Alison cried as Quinn cuffed her right wrist. "How could I kill her? I didn't even know her!"

"I'm not arresting you for the death of Delpha Spillum," he said as he slapped the cuff on her left wrist. "I'm arresting you for the death of Ralph Henry Carter."

I choked back an emerging gasp to stare at Lieutenant Quinn.

Ralph Henry Carter?

Who was Ralph Henry Carter?

TWENTY-ONE

"Are you out of your mind?" shrieked Alison as she fought against her restraints. "I don't know any Ralph Henry Carter."

"You married him," Quinn said calmly. "Ring any bells now?"

Grover lasered a look at her, his mouth and eyes rounding like moons. "You're married?"

"Not anymore, she's not." Quinn braced his hand on her shoulder, anchoring her in her seat. "You're not so big on the whole wedded bliss thing, are you, Alison?"

She gritted her teeth so hard, her cheeks bunched into knots. "I don't know what you're talking about. I told you. I don't know anyone named Ralph Henry Carter."

Quinn shrugged. "Older guy? Nearing retirement age? Lived in Kansas? Obsessed with the over-fifty dating sites after his wife died? I guess he was pretty lonely, so he was ripe for the picking."

"I don't know what this has to do with me," huffed Alison.

"Ralph died as a result of a fall in the shower. Skull fracture. Died immediately. His young bride wasn't home when it happened.

She mentioned to friends that she was taking a few days to visit her parents across the border in Missouri. The authorities found him after he failed to show up at work for two days running, but when they tried to contact his wife, they discovered her cell phone was no longer in service, and—surprise surprise—all Ralph's bank accounts had been cleaned out."

"Sounds familiar," grumbled Ennis.

"And even more curious," Quinn continued, "there were no parents in Missouri. They were fake. Just like their name. Just like her name. Abby Peel. Ring any bells yet?"

"If you don't unlock these handcuffs immediately, you're going to be looking at the mother of all lawsuits."

"Speaking on Alison's behalf," interceded Orphie, "people fall down in showers all the time, and sometimes people die as a result. Accidents happen."

To which Grover couldn't refrain from adding, "According to the latest statistics, a quarter of a million bathroom accidents occur annually, although I can't quote the fatality rate."

"You're naturally assuming Ralph's death was an accident," countered Quinn. "The police department did too, until they realized the reason he fell was because the floor tiles in the shower stall were abnormally slick, and the reason they were slick was because someone had apparently coated them with wax. Ski wax."

"There's skiing in Kansas?" marveled Goldie. "I never would have guessed. I thought the primary recreational activity in Kansas was dodging tornadoes."

"Ski wax," repeated Quinn, his gaze fixed on Alison. "Colorless. Odorless. And extremely effective in expediting a fatal loss of balance."

"Why would I buy ski wax?" snapped Alison. "I don't ski."

"A clever crime," said Quinn. "So clever, in fact, that Ms. Peel apparently stole a page from someone else's playbook—an Amanda Pine from Naples, Florida, whose retirement-age husband died under similar circumstances. Ms. Pine expressed great remorse that her housekeeping idea might have caused her husband's death, but she explained that she thought waxing the shower tiles would prevent soap scum from building up. She was never charged in the incident. I guess her pretty face and copious tears were seen as signs of sincerity."

"Waxing the shower tiles," mused Orphie. "I wonder how she came up with that idea. You think it works? I get terrible scummy buildup in my shower."

Alison compressed her lips so tightly, her mouth disappeared. "I've never heard of Amanda Pine."

"How about Amy Price? Angie Post? They pulled off similar operations in Texas and Michigan. And the scam always started out on an over-fifty dating site and ended in a quickie marriage, followed by the husband's accidental death in the shower, a transfer of funds to the new bride, and the bride's immediate flight from the area. But in the case of Ralph Henry Carter, his new wife didn't even bother to stick around to explain about her brilliant idea to prevent soap scum. She cleaned him out and left before he even died. But she wasn't worried about the outcome. Her plan had always worked perfectly. She had three notches in her belt to prove it. But I guess what she hadn't taken into account was the accessibility of a nationwide database and the universal word search function. Funny how many hits you get when you type the words 'ski wax' and 'shower deaths.'"

"This is so bogus," sniped Alison.

"I imagine the former Mrs. Carter didn't realize she'd earned her own moniker from law enforcement: the Blue Butterfly Killer. She might have changed her name for each murder, but she couldn't change the tattoo on her neck."

Alison fisted her cuffed hands below her ear as if to hide the ink.

"Pretty much nailed it, didn't they?" asked Quinn. "You knock off your victim, then flutter off to another city to search for some other wealthy widower to fleece."

Grover gasped for air, making it sound as if his lungs had just collapsed. "Was *that* your scheme?" he accused in a wild-eyed rage. "Was that what you were planning for *me*?"

I fired a look in his direction. What?

Goldie followed suit. "What?"

"How could that be the plan?" Alison shouted back at him, dropping all pretense of innocence. "You're still married!"

"I told you I'd take care of that!"

"You lied on your website profile. How can I trust a man who doesn't tell the truth about his marital status?"

Killer scolds liar for purported dishonesty. Wow. That was rich.

"You lied more," bellowed Grover. "You're supposed to be a fifty-year-old widow!"

"I *am* a widow. And I thought you'd be happy that I'm younger than I said."

"I was! I was delirious. But you'll understand I'm a little unnerved to know you were planning to kill me!"

"I bet you're not even rich! Were you lying about that too?"

"HOLD IT," yelled Goldie, her voice ripping through the air with the force of a nuclear blast. "*You*"—she stabbed her finger at

264

Alison—"whatever your name is. I want some answers, and I want them now. What the hell kind of hanky panky is going on between you and my husband?"

"He started it!" cried Alison. "He was already profiled on the Frisky Seniors dating site, so I tickled him. He said he was widowed. He said he was searching for companionship with a woman who enjoyed the physical side of a relationship as much as he did. He said he had financial assets ranging in the eight figures."

"Eight figures?" Orphie gasped. "Wow. Not to be nosy, but how much is that?"

"More than a million," Florence calculated.

Orphie's jaw dropped. "Could it be close to a billion?"

"Less than a billion," said Ennis. "A billion would be ten figures, so eight figures would be anywhere between ten and ninety-nine mil—"

"*Quiet!*" screeched Goldie. Then, to Alison: "What else did my husband have to say on his profile?"

"We started having private chats. He knew where I lived, so he said maybe we could rendezvous here. He said he'd learned on the grapevine that a travel company in his town was planning a trip to Alaska, so he said he'd begin a covert campaign to encourage some of his book club friends to sign up, and he eventually convinced them all, so it was, like, full-speed ahead."

"Was it Grover who encouraged us?" puzzled Orphie. "I don't recall."

"I thought it was Grace and Helen," said Florence.

"Grace, Helen, and Lucille *told* us about the tour," corrected Ennis, "but if memory serves, it was Grover who was pushing the idea, even at the pricey fee that Emily was charging."

"You should have suspected something fishy right then," Florence advised Goldie. "Grover's usually such a skinflint."

"In this instance he wasn't thinking with his wallet," reasoned Ennis. "He was thinking with his—"

"Will you people zip it so the girl can talk?" Goldie darted a fiery look around the room, her gaze settling once more on Alison. "Where were the two of you planning to rendezvous?"

"It never got to that. Independent travel agencies usually like to hire local guides to shepherd them around, but Majestic cruises recruit most of the local talent for their optional land tours. So there's only a couple of us available for the independents to hire on a weekly basis, and in a well-calculated twist of fate, Emily's tour company hired me."

"The other local guide wasn't available in the time slot we needed," I objected.

"I know. I kinda made sure of that. I told him I'd accidentally double-booked, so he leaped at the chance to take over the gig I'd already accepted, which left me free if you came calling. Which you did."

"It was the perfect setup for you, wasn't it?" reflected Quinn. "Week in and week out, a brand-new cast of potential victims arriving in your orbit. A whole new batch of widowers to dupe."

Alison grew unnaturally still, but only for a moment. "I'll have you know that all my client reviews are five stars or higher. Sometimes the guests on my tours actually add stars to show their appreciation for the personal attention I've given them. So excuse me, but I do a lot more than prey on lonely old men. I'm an enthusiastic ambassador for Alaska tourism, and I do a damn fine job at it."

"Are you calling me a lonely old man?" challenged Grover.

Alison slatted her eyes. "How can you be lonely? You're married!" She threw a pleading look at the rest of us. "So get this: everything is arranged. I hook up with the tour in Seward. I ask everyone on the bus to introduce themselves. And guess who introduces herself right after Grover? Goldie Kristiansen. Grover's wife!"

"I kept telling you," insisted Grover. "She was only a minor glitch."

Goldie smacked her hand against Grover's chest. "What does *that* mean?"

"You couldn't even stick to the plan," Alison raged. "Stay away from me, I told you. Don't raise any eyebrows. Keep a low profile. But *noooo*. What do you do? You're on me like *boom* on an A-bomb. Putting moves on me when people are watching. Clinging to me like a hungry deer tick. Sneaking around after me in deserted hallways. Not real smart on that one, genius. Delpha Spillum saw us."

"She did not."

"Yes, she did! I know she did. That first night in Girdwood? When you put that slobbering lip lock on me in the vending machine nook near my room? She saw us. I caught a glimpse of her out of the corner of my eye before she disappeared. She saw us. So you gave us away before we even got out of the gate. You and your grubby little paws."

Uff-da! Is that why Delpha had looked so belligerent when I'd seen her in the lobby? Had she just caught Grover swapping spit with Alison? And if that were the case, then...then...

"Oh my god." I stared at Alison, horrified. "You killed Delpha."

"I did not."

"Yes, you did! You killed her to keep her quiet. You couldn't have her ratting you out to Goldie, so you *had* to kill her."

"Are you crazy? I'm not about to kill anyone over Grover Kristiansen. *Eww.* Have you heard the incessant stream of encyclopedic drivel that comes out of his mouth? He's the world's leading authority on *everything*. Doesn't matter what it is—he knows more than God, and he never shuts up! All the time talking, talking, talking." She slanted a look at Goldie. "How do you stand it?"

Goldie shook her head. "Earplugs come in handy, but deafness is my ultimate goal."

"But we love each other," Grover whined at Alison.

"Did you fail to hear the fate that was in store for you?" Orphie asked him. "Death by shower stall? I hate to put Al and me on a marital pedestal, but premeditated murder isn't one of the hallmarks of everlasting love."

"Well, *someone* killed Delpha," I sputtered as I glared suspiciously at Grover.

He blinked stupidly. "Why're you looking at me?"

"Because you're the only other person with a strong motivation and a clear opportunity."

"No, I'm not."

"Yes, you are."

"He's not," droned Alison. "He was with me after we left the museum."

Orphie gasped. "In the ladies' room?"

"In an isolated corner of the building. He was all hot to continue the physical activity stuff. *Bleah.*" She shivered. "Physical activity meaning his hands and lips were everywhere."

Grover slouched in his chair, head bent, looking like a turtle trying to retract his neck into his shell. Goldie thwacked his shoulder. "You are so busted."

"So you admit your original alibi was a lie?" Quinn asked Alison.

She nodded. "Yeah, I was lying. We were both lying."

Quinn raised an eyebrow. "So you're asking me to take your word—the word of an avowed killer—that you had nothing to do with Ms. Spillum's death?"

"Yes! I don't kill total strangers."

"That's right," said Quinn. "You only kill them after you marry them."

"So when were you and my husband planning to run off together?" Goldie asked, stone-cold anger flickering in her eyes. "After the tour? Halfway through? Or did you consider this a simple meet and greet to see if you were compatible?"

"They wouldn't have had to be too compatible if the only thing she wanted to do was kill him," Orphie pointed out. "And take his money."

"Hah!" Goldie laughed scornfully. "What money? He sold vacuum cleaners all his life. You don't find the names of vacuum cleaner salesmen at the top of the Fortune 500's list of wealthiest men."

Florence nodded in agreement. "You don't even find them at the bottom."

"You said you were a retired bank president!" Alison shouted at him. "I can't believe you! Did you tell me the truth about anything?"

"Everyone lies on the internet," defended Grover, sounding hurt and pouty. "So what if I embellished my profile? Does it matter? I still love you."

Goldie slugged his arm. "Were you planning to run off after the tour? Tell me!"

"How could he run off?" ranted Alison. "He's married! I'm not in the habit of running off with married men."

Killing them, yes. Running off with them, not so much.

Except...

My brain kicked into overdrive.

What if, by the end of the tour, Grover could no longer claim to be married? What if his marital status changed along the way?

What had he told Alison earlier when referring to his marriage with Goldie?

I told you I'd take care of that.

Oh. My. God. "You were planning to kill Goldie," I cried.

Alison shot me a startled glance. "Who, me?"

"No." I pointed a finger at Grover. "Him!"

"Me?" blubbered Grover.

"Mrs. Miceli." Quinn regarded me with indulgence. "Are you planning to accuse everyone in the room before the meeting ends?"

"He made a mistake," I burst out as the image of the zipline platform played back in my head. "He meant to unclip *Goldie's* carabiners from the hitching post, but they were so tangled, he unclipped the wrong ones. He unclipped Thor's instead."

Florence gasped. "Grover killed Thor?"

Grover looked desperately from Florence to Goldie to Quinn. "I didn't mean to kill him," he said in a small voice. "I—"

"No!" screamed Goldie. "You meant to kill *me!*" Springing to her feet, she whacked him over the head with her handbag and kept beating on him until Lieutenant Kitchen pulled her off. "Let me go!" she railed as she struggled to free herself from his grip. "Lemme at him. I'll save the system the expense of jailing him."

"Mrs. Miceli?" Kitchen called out as Grover hunched into a fetal position, fending off further attack by ducking beneath his forearms. "Some assistance please?"

Popping out of my chair, I answered his appeal by wrapping my arm around Goldie and ushering her across the floor. "He wanted me dead," she sobbed as Kitchen forced Grover to his feet, read him his Miranda rights, and cuffed him.

"I'm so sorry, Goldie," I soothed her as we watched Kitchen and Quinn herd their prisoners toward the door. "But we'll get you through this. All of us will."

"The fool. He's just thrown his whole life away. And for what?" She blinked away tears as she fought to regain her composure. "That girl wouldn't have been able to get rid of him fast enough if they'd ever gotten married. Imagine her disappointment when she discovered she couldn't kill him."

"Why wouldn't she be able to kill him?"

She laughed derisively. "Grover doesn't take showers. He takes baths."

"I have it all worked out," Etienne enthused as he rushed through the door. "Sorry I took so long, but I've cancelled our Anchorage accommodations for tomorrow night with no penalty and I negotiated luxury suites at the Majestic resort at 60 percent off the original rate. We're locked in with no option of cancellation, but with a deal like that…"

He stopped in his tracks as the rest of us stood still as statues, staring back at him.

"Have I missed something?"

TWENTY-TWO

"IT'S SPLASHED ALL OVER the Twittersphere," said Nana as she scanned the readout on her phone.

The "it" to which she referred was the "Death by Ziplining Murder" of Iowa tourist Thor Thorsen and the killer's almost immediate capture.

We were gathered in the guest lodge once more, taking time to commune with each other at the end of our harrowing day, which allowed me the opportunity to inform our regulars about the resolution of our most recent tragedy, even though most of them were already up to speed. It also gave the gang time to share ziplining photos, exchange views on the Grover and Alison affair, offer support to Florence and Goldie, and enjoy takeout pizza, which we all agreed tasted much better than the mystery meat at the Wilderness Cabins' diner.

I leaned toward Nana to check out her screen. "News sure got out fast."

"It's on account of Bernice. It's her new callin': cyberspace gossip. And she don't even gotta make no stuff up."

Our resident reporters had glommed onto the zipline death as soon as it appeared in their feeds and peppered us with questions as we'd made our way to the lodge.

"Do you think Bigfoot might deliberately disguise himself as a tree to avoid detection?"

"Could Bigfoot be indirectly responsible for this murder?"

"Is it safe to assume that Bigfoot is somehow linked to this killing?"

They'd seemed completely disinterested in the capture of the Blue Butterfly Murderer or the sensationalized May/December internet hookup between Alison and Grover or Grover's screw-up in accidentally killing the wrong person. I guess they didn't want to deviate away from the Bigfoot angle.

Creature stories were obviously their bread and butter.

The one piece of good news Etienne shared with the group, besides the securing of luxury suites at the much ballyhooed Majestic resort, was that the Majestic grounds would be off-limits to all reporters. Our current accommodations might welcome the press corps as a marketing tool, but the Majestic was famous worldwide and didn't need the publicity.

Unable to contain her exuberance, Mom had thrown out her arms and leaped to her feet at the news.

Dad had remained in his chair, eyes riveted on the floor as he regarded the shattered screen of the cell phone Mom had knocked out of his hands when she'd whacked him with her arm.

"What kind of pizza you got left?" asked Bernice as she crab-walked toward us. She flipped open the box on the table beside us and angled her mouth in disgust. "What is this? Pepperoni and cat food?"

I rolled my eyes. "Pepperoni and sausage. Have a slice."

"No, thanks. It looks like a petri dish for mad cow disease." She thrust her phone in my face. "I know you're dying to see my photographic masterpieces, so here's your chance. Knock yourself out."

Morphing into uber-attentive tour escort mode, I palmed Bernice's phone and began flipping through her photo gallery, starting with a selfie she'd taken against the backdrop of the *Kenai Adventurer's* lifebuoy.

"Next trip you take, I hope you'll leave those saps behind," Bernice suggested as she bobbed her head in the direction of the remaining book club guests. They'd circled their chairs in the middle of the room, where it looked as if they were offering solace to each other with kind words and soothing gestures.

"Come on, Bernice," I admonished as I flipped through images of a fountain of sea spray, a flapping whale's tail, and another selfie of Bernice in front of a wall of glacial ice. "Florence is mourning the death of her husband."

Bernice snorted. "She's the only one who's mourning him."

"Goldie is trying to reconcile the fact that her husband tried to kill her." More Bernice selfies: on the bus, in the lobby of the Grand Girdwood Hotel, against the backdrop of the aerial tram. "And poor Ennis. Lorraine is still missing, and he hasn't had any encouraging news from the police back home about where she is." Bernice's face set against a shelf of illuminated liquor bottles in the restaurant's bar. A couple of women in shimmery dresses. A parade of tourists wearing baseball caps with their all-American logos—the flag, the world champion Chicago Cubs, Kermit the Frog. The same people I'd seen while waiting in the foyer. "Orphie's the only one who's managed to avoid a major calamity." Trees. Mountains. Scrubby meadows with blond dots. Scrubby meadows with black dots. Gray squirrel with bushy tail.

I executed a surreptitious swipe on her screen that jettisoned me to the end of her photos. "Wonderful pictures, Bernice." I handed her phone back to her. "I'm sure I'll be seeing them again on social media."

"Already there. The only pics missing are the shots I'll take of my luxury suite at the Majestic resort tomorrow. And lemme tell you, if the hype about this place turns out to be inaccurate, *someone's* going to hear about it."

· · · · · · · · · ·

The hype wasn't accurate.

The resort was far better than advertised.

From its pristine grounds surrounded by a forest of fragrant balsams and pines, to the mountainous peaks on the horizon, to the flowers bordering the paved walkways, to its five specialty restaurants, movie theater, clothing boutiques, spa, saunas, indoor water park, and private lake, the Majestic resort was nothing short of spectacular. We were so awestruck, in fact, that it didn't even bother us that we couldn't check into our rooms until 3:00 p.m., which was a full four hours away. There was plenty to entertain us in the meantime.

"To avoid clutter in the lobby, we're going to leave your luggage on the bus until check-in," Etienne announced as we gathered around him near the front desk. "I hope that doesn't inconvenience anyone. And if you're interested, there are still spaces open for you to sign up for a whitewater rafting adventure this afternoon." He waved a brochure in the air.

"Is it dangerous?" questioned Dick Teig.

"Only if you drown," wisecracked Bernice.

Etienne scanned the brochure. "On a scale of one to ten, with ten being ranked as 'Don't even try it, stupid,' it comes in at a two."

"A two?" Dick Stolee guffawed. "Might as well take a bath. Probably just as exciting and a helluva lot cheaper."

"Do you have to know how to swim?" asked George.

Etienne shook his head. "It says here that life jackets and helmets will be provided."

"Well, that settles it." Dick Teig folded his arms across his chest. "I'm not putting on another one of those dorky helmets ever again. Forget it."

"If them raftin' folks don't got one big enough, maybe they'll let you go without one," suggested Nana.

"No." He massaged his crown. "My head still hurts from yesterday."

I grinned. "What happened with your helmet yesterday?"

"Them zipline fellas didn't have no helmet in an extra jumbo size," Nana explained, "so they had to Vaseline his head to get the thing on. Made an awful mess."

Jackie's ringtone sounded on my phone, prompting me to hurry away from the group to answer it. "Hi there." I spied an elegantly upholstered armchair in the sunken lobby area and sat down. "How are things in Iowa?"

"Thor Thorsen's death is plastered all over the news here," Jackie tittered. "I knew you couldn't make it through a whole tour without someone getting snuffed."

I groaned. "You don't know the half of it."

She sucked in her breath. "There's more than one death?"

"I can't tell you. Not until the police notify next of kin, which is proving rather difficult because the kin is in Mongolia."

"Inner or outer?"

"Does it matter?"

"Well, it might matter as far as all that broadband stuff is concerned."

"So which place has better access? Inner Mongolia or outer?"

"Beats me. I couldn't even point to Mongolia on a map."

I rolled my eyes. "So to what do I owe the pleasure of this phone call, Jack?"

"Just wanted to let you know that we're getting ready to leave this morning, and all systems are go. Mildred, Pearl, and Arvella are feeling well enough to take the bus back to Windsor City with us, so the only guests I'm leaving behind are the Toms. The docs want to give them a couple more days in the hospital just to make sure they remain stable. But their families are all here, so they don't seem to mind at all. The park's signature hotel was out of standard rooms so I had to book everyone into mini and luxury suites, but I figured you'd be appalled if I booked them into Big Bertha's Sleepover Inn, so I made an executive decision. The agency has a reputation to maintain, right?"

"Right," I agreed as I slid my hand into the outside pocket of my shoulder bag in search of a roll of antacids. "So you were treated to a quiet day yesterday, were you?" I popped a chewable tablet into my mouth.

"I deserved it, don't you think? To be honest, Emily, I think a group of three guests is just about perfect. They stick together. They don't run off in different directions. They enjoy taking pictures of me in my official tour escort clothes, which, I might add, I had to purchase on my own dime. Three people are so much easier to manage than a group of eight."

"Three isn't a tour, Jack. It's a music group."

"Nonetheless, I'm writing a report about my experiences and plan to include suggestions that'll improve the quality of future trips. It'll be on your desk when you get back. Meantime, I predict that this Green Acres venture is going to be the next Dollywood, so we should concentrate on booking as many tours as possible. Get in on the ground floor before prices skyrocket. So to that end I took the liberty of shooting video footage of the place last night that you can use as advertising. It still needs to be cut and edited, but with voiceovers and music, it could be the very thing to entice guests to sign up in droves. And if you'll agree to negotiate a modest clothing allowance, I'll volunteer to do the voiceover for free." I could almost see her preening on the other end. "As you know, that *is* my forte."

I leaned back in my chair, stunned. "Oh my god, Jack, that's brilliant. We can send the videos to our clients' social media platforms—Facebook, YouTube, Instagram. Email. We'll be able to save a ton of money on brochure production and mailings. We might even attract a broader client base!" Which might improve our bottom line once we paid for all the mini and luxury suites. "This could really work. It's genius! I wish you were standing in front of me right now. I'd kiss your face until all your foundation got rubbed off."

"I'll pass on the public display of affection, but…what about that clothing allowance?"

I heaved a sigh. "All right. I'm all for rewarding excellence. A modest clothing allowance. We'll discuss the details when I get back. Sound good?"

She let out a high-pitched squeal that nearly ruptured my eardrum. "I knew I'd wear you down eventually. Can we throw in a reasonably priced wig?"

"No wig."

"Okay. It was worth a try. So here's what I'll do. I'll send you the video right now so you can give it a look-see, and if you want additional input, you can share it with your group. I'm sure they'll be good for an opinion or two. They might even decide to sign up. Oops. Hate to cut this short but I've gotta run. Johnny's rounding up the troops, so that's my signal to vamoose. See you when you get home. Good luck with that Mongolia thing."

My phone pinged as her video hurtled through cyberspace to arrive in my inbox. Anxious to see the theme park for myself, I hit play and watched as Jackie introduced her audience to "the most exciting collection of agriculturally themed amusement rides west of the Mississippi."

Oh, wow. This didn't look half bad.

"Do you have a minute, bella?"

I looked up to find Etienne standing over me. Hitting pause, I smiled up at him. "What's up, sweetie?"

"The ladies are headed down to the lake. They've just learned that paddleboats are available for guest use, so in the spirit of safety, I'm thinking it might behoove me to accompany them."

"Good idea. What about the guys?"

"They've decided to try their hand at whitewater rafting. But when Dick Teig attempted to pay, he discovered he'd misplaced his wallet, so this is our current crisis."

"Have you called the Wilderness Cabins to see if he left it in his room?"

"I talked to the manager. He's sending someone to look for it."

"What about the bus? Could it have dropped out on the seat?"

"I called Steele. He said he'd run out and open up the bus if I wanted to send Dick out to look for it."

I could see where this was going. "But Dick is a guy, and as we both know, most men are incapable of finding things even when the item in question is staring them in the face."

Etienne flashed a disarming grin. "So my wife tells me."

I grinned back. "Your wife is right." I boosted myself to my feet. "Okay, I'll go. But I want to send you something you might get a kick out of." I tapped and swiped my screen a couple of times, sharing not only with Etienne, but with the entire group. "It's from Jackie—a video of the Green Acres theme park. We may have inadvertently hired ourselves a marketing genius." I dropped my phone back into the pocket of my shoulder bag. "So...where's the bus parked?"

· · · · · · · · · ·

The resort had relegated oversized vehicle parking to the farthest corner of the compound, on a tidy stretch of asphalt where the smell of gasoline and diesel fumes wouldn't befoul the fragrance of balsam and pine in the more elegant sections of the resort. I wandered around the lot for a while, searching amid the multitude of busses for a white one with an aurora borealis painted on the front and sides, and finally found it tucked neatly between two Majestic coaches, in what my dad would call the back forty.

"This was some precision parking," I called to Steele through the open door of the bus, noting how close the vehicle was to its immediate neighbor.

"I can't take credit," he said as I climbed the stairs of the step-well. "That space was empty when I parked." He was sitting behind the driver's seat, a logbook open on his lap.

"Allow me to be impressed anyway."

"Sure." He canted his head toward the rear of the bus. "I took a quick look around, but I didn't see anything that looks like a wallet. You're welcome to bat cleanup though. I can't guarantee I was thorough."

"If it's here, I'll find it." I nodded toward his logbook. "Bus business?"

"Yep. Fuel consumption. Mileage charts. Odometer readings. Driving hours. If not for all the interminable record keeping, I'd have the perfect job."

"You don't drive bus in the winter, do you?"

"Not much need for tour busses around here in the winter, Mrs. Miceli. Everything shuts down."

"So what do you do?"

"I still drive bus, but I migrate to the lower forty-eight. Southern states still conduct tours in the winter—Texas, Arizona, Louisiana—so they're always in the market for experienced drivers."

A kernel of an idea bloomed in my head. "Do you ever make it as far north as Iowa?"

"Never been to Iowa."

"Well, what if I could offer you a full-time position driving bus for our travel agency in the months when you're not in Alaska? We want to expand our domestic tour packages, offering trips in and around Iowa, like to casinos, historic sites, dinner theaters, a new theme park that's just opened south of my hometown, and hiring a permanent driver would eliminate our having to scout around for one all the time."

He arched his eyebrows in what I hoped was a sign of acute interest. "I dunno. I—"

"We recently hired a dynamite escort for our in-state tours, and if we paired the two of you, I think we'd create the most engaging team in the entire tour industry. Seriously. The two of you working together could set the world on fire. You'd be the most sought-after duo in travel history."

He crooked his mouth in a lazy grin. "You have a tendency toward hyperbole, Mrs. Miceli."

"Maybe a little. But it could work; I know it could. Plus we could offer you full health benefits, including dental."

He closed his logbook, looking pensive. "So tell me about this tour escort you hired."

"You'd love her. She's enthusiastic and funny and…runway model tall…and a fashion icon…and, due to a recent divorce, unattached. Oh yeah, and she's drop-dead gorgeous. You'd make the perfect couple." I'd save the part about her being my former husband until later.

"Any dead husbands in her past?"

"Not a one." I winced. "About Alison, Steele, I can't tell you how sorry I am. The whole sordid story was so unbelievable. She had us all fooled."

"One of us in particular. Talk about feeling like an idiot." He gave his head a woeful shake. "Why don't you look for that wallet, Mrs. Miceli? The owner is probably freaking out."

"Right."

I couldn't picture where Dick and Helen had been sitting on the drive over, so I began my search at the front of the bus and worked my way back, checking out the seats, the floor, and the magazine and map pockets attached to the seat-backs. Halfway to the rear, I noticed a dark bulge in the seat-back pocket of a window seat, and—with a shout-out of thanks to Saint Anthony—fished Dick's wallet out of the netting. "Found it!"

Steele laughed. "Told you I couldn't be trusted."

After finding a driver's license that assured me this was Dick's wallet, I dropped it into my shoulder bag and headed back toward the front of the bus, where Steele was wrestling with a small duffle bag in the overhead compartment directly behind the driver's seat.

"Bus manufacturers keep shrinking the overheads, and it's really annoying," he complained while tugging on the bag. "Man, this thing is really wedged in."

"I hope there's nothing breakable inside."

"Nah. Just my dopp kit and some extra socks and tee shirts." He wrenched it back and forth with both hands before gliding his fingers beneath the metal framework. "I think the zipper's snagged on something." Grunting his frustration, he torqued the bag violently, ripping it out of the enclosure in the same way a demented dentist might extract a tooth.

The zipper tore open, disgorging the contents of the bag into the center aisle like a ruptured piñata. "Oh dear."

I scooched down, frantically plucking his clean underwear off the dirty floor before the grit and grime from our shoes had a chance to—

I stilled my hand as it hovered over the rumpled tee shirt that was cushioning his cell phone—only it wasn't Steele's cell phone.

The case was a laminated sheet of black-and-white newspaper print.

It was Delpha's cell phone.

I snatched my hand away and stared up at Steele.

"Damn. I wish you hadn't seen that. I really liked you, Mrs. Miceli."

Liked?

I eased myself to my feet, mouth dry, heart pounding. I took a step backward. "Why do you have Delpha's phone?"

"I thought that might be fairly obvious." His features shifted as if they were carved from melted wax. The lovely curves of his face disappeared...to be replaced by the sharp angles of a ruthless predator. "I took it."

I said nothing. I didn't have to. The evidence spoke for itself.

He'd killed Delpha.

I shook my head in utter bewilderment. "Why?"

He gave his shoulder a casual roll. "No reason. It's what I do."

He'd killed Delpha.

And now he was going to kill me.

I turned on my heel and ran toward the back of the bus.

The rear exit door was closed.

Damn!

His footsteps pounded close behind me. His breath singed my neck. He lunged for my arm.

I spun around and bashed him with my shoulder bag.

He threw me onto the bench cushion of the back seat and snaked his hands around my throat, his thumbs pressing against my windpipe.

I kicked. I flailed.

His thumbs pressed deeper into my throat.

A haze crept over his face. Spots danced before my eyes. His features seemed to pixelate as I gasped for air.

I flung my hand over my shoulder bag, my fingers grappling with the opening as I groped for something…anything…

I felt something hard. And slick. I clawed at it, my thumb looping through some kind of hole.

I clutched it desperately, locking my fingers around it, remembering what it was. Remembering—

I…couldn't…breeeeeeeath…

I wrenched it out of my bag and with a final rush of adrenaline, aimed it at Steele's face and depressed the nozzle.

PSSSSSSSSSSST!

"*Aaaaaaaargh!*"

Slapping his hands over his eyes, he staggered away from me, crashing into chair backs and arms as he ran blindly down the aisle, falling out of sight when he stumbled into the rear stepwell with a thunderous crack of skull against steel.

I heard him cry out in pain, and then I heard nothing at all.

Coughing and wheezing to catch my breath, my eyes stinging with tears, my throat burning in agony, I squinted against the spray and dug out my cell phone. "Help," I rasped as the message turned itself into text and winged its way to Etienne.

Ten minutes later he found me curled up in the back corner of the bus, Nana's canister of bear spray still cradled against my chest.

TWENTY-THREE

"HE COLLECTED HIS VICTIMS' phones as trophies."

Lieutenant Kitchen relaxed in an armchair in our suite the following morning, filling Etienne and me in on the details of Steele's arrest.

"Pretty standard fare for serial killers. They take personal items to remind themselves of each kill. A search of his Anchorage apartment last night turned up a whole drawerful of cell phones. I suspect this might be the evidence we need to close a slew of unsolved murder cases."

I shivered as I cupped my hand around my throat.

I'd been transported by ambulance to a medical clinic in Healy after yesterday's incident. X-rays showed no internal damage to my throat, although my voice was still raspy and it hurt to swallow. After treating my eyes for exposure to bear spray, they'd released me, and the management at the Majestic had been kind enough to send a shuttle to transport Etienne and me back to the resort.

Steele had been taken by separate ambulance to a different facility, which I appreciated. I didn't want to run the risk of seeing him again.

Ever.

"I'm sorry for what you've been through, Mrs. Miceli, but if you hadn't discovered Ms. Spillum's phone, he'd still be running around loose, targeting his next victim. You're a hero."

I forced a smile. I didn't feel like a hero. I felt like an emotional wreck.

"Has he admitted to killing Delpha?" asked Etienne.

"He's not talking. Thinks he's smarter than everyone else, so he's clammed up. But it doesn't matter if he talks. We've got him anyway. Odd thing is, we don't think he killed Ms. Spillum."

"What?" I croaked.

"His MO, Mrs. Miceli. He strangled his victims with his bare hands. The pathology showed bruises on Ms. Spillum's throat from choking, but she didn't die from strangulation. She died from a fractured skull. Our theory is that she fought him off and was successful in breaking away, but in trying to escape, she tripped on a tree root and died instantly when her head hit a rock. But you were right about the cell phone messages. Even though he didn't kill her, he took her phone, so he was the one who was responding to your texts."

Which caused me to shiver again.

"And I hope you'll accept my apologies for refusing to divulge any of the circumstances surrounding Ms. Spillum's death early in our investigation. We suspected it was our serial killer for two reasons—the bruising around her throat and the fact that she wasn't carrying a cell phone, which in this day and age is nothing short of an anomaly. None of the other victims were carrying cell phones either, despite the fact that we discovered they all had accounts, so we decided to keep the information under wraps. We didn't want to release any details to the public that might inspire copycats. You really helped us out when you verified that Ms. Spillum did indeed have her phone with her, Mrs. Miceli. That was invaluable. So once again, we're in your debt."

Swallowing painfully, I regarded Kitchen in confusion. "But how was Steele able to be on that mountaintop…without any of us seeing him?" My voice was a hoarse whisper.

"You probably saw him. You just didn't realize it. He was toting an ample supply of stage make-up around with him. Fake beards and mustaches. Horn-rimmed glasses. Sunglasses. Baseball caps to cover his hair—the most unique of which was a cap with Kermit the Frog drinking a mug of beer. I didn't even know Kermit was old enough to drink."

"Oh my god," I rasped, waving my hand as if to flag him down. "I saw that hat. It was on a man who…wandered through the foyer of the restaurant. And he wandered into the bar area too…because Bernice Zwerg snapped a picture of him. It's…in the photo gallery on her phone. Etienne can give you her room number."

"This just keeps getting better, Mrs. Miceli." He jotted Bernice's name down in his notebook. "I don't believe I'm premature in saying we've nailed the bastard."

He stood up abruptly. "I'll be leaving now so you two good people can resume your holiday." He snugged his hat on his head. "I'll leave it up to you whether you want to press charges against Mr. Steele for assault with intent to kill. We can add it to the list.

We've already begun contacting bus companies in the lower forty-eight about his employment history with them. I expect to find a direct link between cold case strangulation deaths and the areas where Mr. Steele traveled. And of course, we have the corroborating evidence of the cell phones." He nodded in my direction. "Hope you recover real quick, Mrs. Miceli. Are you folks planning to head out this afternoon?"

Etienne chuckled as we escorted Kitchen to the door. "We're minus a bus driver, Lieutenant, so we'll be here until a substitute can make his way up to Denali. I'm told it could be another day or two, which isn't unwelcome news. I think everyone could use some time to decompress."

"You could be stuck in worse places." Kitchen stepped into the hallway. "By the way, we've finally gotten through to the sister in Mongolia, so we're cleared to release Ms. Spillum's name to the public. The sister plans to make a stopover in Anchorage on her way back to Iowa to coordinate arrangements for Ms. Spillum's body, so I thought you'd be happy to hear that."

Etienne nodded. "Mrs. Thorsen needs to make similar arrangements for her husband's remains, so perhaps they can coordinate their efforts." He clasped Kitchen's hand in a farewell shake. "Thank you, Lieutenant."

"I'm the one who's thankful," Kitchen said in a humble tone. "Your wife has literally saved the lives of countless women. Pretty invaluable stuff."

He offered us a brisk salute before heading down the corridor. Etienne circled his arm around my shoulders and hugged me against him, leaning down to kiss my forehead. "Did you hear the lieutenant, bella? You're a hero."

A knot vibrated in my throat, choking off words I wanted to speak but couldn't—words of terror and relief and gratitude. But all I could do was nod feebly while clinging to this man who meant more to me than life itself.

"You got a minute?" Ennis Iversen called to us from halfway down the hall.

"What can we do for you?" asked Etienne, inviting him into the room as he approached.

Fighting to regain my composure, I sucked in a calming breath and stiffened my spine as we sat down in the small living area.

"Lorraine's been found," he said without emotion.

I stared at him in silence, fearing the worst. "Is she…?"

"She's fine. Boy, is she."

Etienne paused. "I'm not sure I know what that means."

Ennis tapped his cell phone screen. "Have you watched the video you sent us yesterday, Emily?"

Jackie's Green Acres video. "Only about a minute's worth," I rasped. "Then I got called away"—Etienne squeezed my hand—"to look for Dick's wallet."

"Well, no one else has apparently watched it all either. Except me. I stuck with it all the way to the end." He leaned forward in his chair to hand the phone to Etienne. "I've paused it at the fifteen-minute mark, which is basically the penultimate Kodak moment, but you can press play if you want."

We studied the still image on the screen—an attractive middle-aged woman feeding cotton candy into the mouth of a balding man—her sultry smile hinting at how much she enjoyed their playful teasing, his arm curled possessively around her waist, suggesting that he couldn't get enough of her. They looked as deliriously happy as newlyweds, except—

"Omigod." I did a quick double-take. "Is that Lorraine?" She'd accompanied Ennis to all our pre-tour meetings, so I'd seen her on several occasions.

"She looks good on video, doesn't she? Yup, that's Lorraine. Not lying in an isolated cornfield in Iowa. Not holed up in an exotic hut in Tahiti. But hiding in plain sight." He tossed his hand out in anger. "What better place to hide, right? In a freaking agricultural theme park a hundred and fifty miles from home." His voice grew louder. "With freaking Al Arnesen!"

"Al Arnesen?" I squeaked. "Orphie's husband?"

"Yes, Orphie's husband. The little weasel. You don't recognize him? I guess you don't watch the local access channel that broadcasts the city council meetings."

"But...Al's in North Carolina. On a business trip."

"No, he's not. He's standing outside a cotton candy concession in Iowa waiting for my wife to stuff a hunk of spun sugar into his mouth."

"But...he called her from North Carolina."

"And Orphie stuck to that story too, until I played the video for her. There was no business trip. The meeting with the would-be real estate developer? All lies. Al instigated the lie, and Orphie continued to perpetuate it when he stopped calling her. Provided good cover. I guess she was trying to avoid the indignity of being utterly humiliated in front of all her friends."

I regarded the image again in disbelief. "Al Arnesen and Lorraine?"

"Go ahead," said Ennis as he nodded toward his phone. "Press play."

Etienne tapped the screen, giving life to the figures in the image. So we watched as Al sucked the sticky wad of cotton candy into his mouth, his eyes lighting up when Lorraine stuffed the opposite end into her own mouth and began eating her way toward him, their mouths eventually smacking together in a loud, unapologetic kiss. With unmistakable tongue action.

Eww.

My heart went out to Ennis and Orphie, but on a brighter note, at least I'd be spared the task of having to explain the concept of eminent domain to my dad.

"Have you notified Chief Burns?" asked Etienne as he pressed stop.

"You bet. He's notified the local authorities, and they're sending an officer to pick her up and hold her until he arrives. It's not a crime to run away with someone else's spouse, but when it entails cleaning out bank accounts without authorization, you're walking on thin ice."

Etienne handed him back his cell phone, which he held in his palm for a long moment, studying it with hollow eyes.

"Are you going to be all right, Ennis?" I asked in a quiet voice.

He laughed ruefully. "Eventually. Right now I feel like crap, but don't worry. I won't do anything foolish. And I've decided not to fly home prematurely. I want to be here for Florence in case she needs me. Florence and I...we'll see each other through the worst of this catastrophe."

He boosted himself to his feet. "Orphie's a mess, though, so she might need some TLC. Sorry to drop the burning embers of this dumpster fire in your lap right now, but I figured you'd want to know." He threw a sympathetic look my way. "Hope those bruises aren't as sore as they look, Emily. Hell of a business the two of you are in. Have you ever thought of switching careers to something less hazardous…like, say, skydiving?"

While Etienne ushered him out, I unlocked our sliding glass door and stepped out on the balcony, where the sun could warm my chilled bones. A broad swath of manicured lawn swept toward a copse of fir trees on the perimeter of the resort. Beyond that rose the craggy peaks of the mountain ranges that formed Alaska's backbone—razor-sharp and haloed by formations of puffy clouds.

Etienne came up close behind me, his hands capping my shoulders. "Hopefully this is the end of it."

"I wish that once, just once…we could enjoy a tour without losing anyone. Do you think that'll ever happen?"

"Maybe next time?"

I watched as a flock of birds soared above the woodland, squawking at the trees below. "At least my scheme to hire Steele as a permanent bus driver in Iowa didn't pan out. Please don't tell Jackie, but I almost fixed her up with a serial killer."

With the birds still squawking, I lowered my gaze to the forest floor, noticing a shadow amid the trees—a tall linear-shaped shadow. And it wasn't stationary.

It was moving. Very slowly. Prowling. Skulking.

"Do you see that?" I pointed in the approximate direction. "A shadowy thing in the trees. It's moving to the left."

"Your eyes may be better than mine, bella."

"Do you have your phone?"

He placed it in my hand. I focused on the shape and captured it in frame, then expanded the image to a magnification we could both see.

"*Merda*," swore Etienne.

"What does this look like to you?"

"*Merda*," he repeated.

"I can see how it might be mistaken for a tree…but trees aren't usually ambulatory, except in Tolkien movies."

"The press would love to see this."

"They'd have a field day, wouldn't they? All the time they spent hounding Dad would not have been in vain."

"Should we alert your father?"

"Nah. His phone's broken."

We watched the shadow lumber to the edge of the tree line, then pause, almost as if it was staring back at us.

"So what are you going to do?" asked Etienne.

I looked from the readout screen to the woods, then back to the screen. "Only one thing to do."

I hit the little trash icon on his phone and watched the screen fade to black.

I could hear the relief in Etienne's voice as he whispered against the curve of my ear, "Exactly what I was hoping you'd do."

THE END

ABOUT THE AUTHOR

After experiencing disastrous vacations on three continents, Maddy Hunter decided to combine her love of humor, travel, and storytelling to fictionalize her misadventures. Inspired by her feisty aunt and by memories of her Irish grandmother, she created the nationally bestselling, Agatha Award–nominated Passport to Peril mystery series, where quirky seniors from Iowa get to relive everything that went wrong on Maddy's holiday. *Catch Me If Yukon* is the twelfth book in the series. Maddy lives in Madison, Wisconsin, with her husband and a head full of imaginary characters who keep asking, "Are we there yet?"

Please visit her website at www.maddyhuntermysteries.com or become a follower on her MaddyHunter@AuthorMaddyHunter Facebook page.

Say No Moor

A PASSPORT TO PERIL MYSTERY

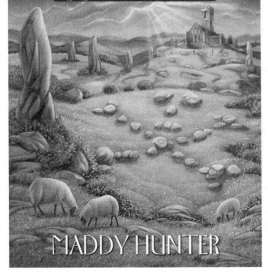

MADDY HUNTER

Say No Moor
Maddy Hunter

Tour escort Emily Andrew-Miceli's plan to boost her business with social media threatens to backfire in merry old England

Hoping to reach an expanded clientele of senior travelers, Emily Andrew-Miceli invites a handful of bloggers to join her group's tour of England's Cornwall region. But when the quarrelsome host of a historic inn dies under suspicious circumstances, Emily worries that the bloggers' online reviews will torpedo her travel agency.

To make matters worse, Emily is roped into running the inn, and not even a team effort from her friends can prevent impending disaster. As one guest goes missing and another turns up dead, Emily discovers that well-kept secrets can provide more than enough motive for murder.

978-0-7387-4961-7 $15.99

From Bad to Wurst

A PASSPORT TO PERIL MYSTERY

maddy
HUNTER